A Gold-Mended Life

CAROLYN STEGMAN

To contact author, e-mail
goldmendedlife@comcast.net

Cover Art by Phyllis Gillie Jaffe
Design by Rose MacGregor

ISBN-13: 978-0615709079
ISBN-10: 0615709079

Acknowledgements

To Gloria Steinem: I will never forget our road trip and our talk (at 2AM!) about never being too late for any woman to start over. You were so right: "The truth will set you free, but first it will piss you off."

To Hillary Rodham Clinton: Thanks for inviting me to the White House to share my work during Women's History Month, and my everlasting appreciation to Betty Freidan for her encouragement at that time. And yes Betty, for older women, it was the disease with no name.

To clinical psychologists and certified sex therapists, Lewis and Adrianne, for their guidance in the human sexuality parts of this book.

For all of my college students over the years in Human Sexuality, Gender Communications, Psychology of Death, Dying and Bereavement, Psychology of Women, and Psychology of Aging, who showed me that learning truly is a two-way-street.

To Peggy, whose dedication to older adults continues to inspire me.

To Charlotte Dison, the visionary former Director of Nursing at Baptist Hospital of Miami, and my mentor.

To Dr. Malcolm Knowles, the guru of Adult Education, who taught me the value of experiential learning.

To cancer patients of the Wellness Community, who came to my classes and shared their heartfelt stories of survivorship, and, for some, their impending death. No textbook could have provided a greater impact, and no student was the same after they left.

To the seniors at various retirement communities, whose life stories are the libraries of the 'Greatest Generation.'

To the *Women of Achievement in Maryland History* non-profit committee: Thanks for opportunity to research and author the history of so many remarkable women, most of whom were over sixty. And to my colleagues on the Board of Directors at the Maryland Women's Heritage Center, the first of its kind in the nation.

To Myra, who told me that dying is worse than death and who didn't live to see this book published.

To Dr. John Brantner of the Association for Death Education and Counseling, who inspired me with his work in death education; to Dr. Ellen Zimmer, grief counselor and former president of the Association for Death Education and Counseling, who team-taught with me and brought remarkable knowledge to our classroom; and finally to Edi

Stark, who first introduced me to the importance of death education.

To Sister Noreen Marie, the former Director of St. Claire's Hospital School of Nursing in NYC, who many years ago allowed two Hunter graduate students (one of which was me) to teach Human Sexuality to nursing students, and then when it was over, she said, "Let's do this again next semester!"

To Dr. Gilbert Shimmel, Dean, and Dr. Michael Carrera, of Hunter College School of Community Health Education, whose wise counsel taught me that *old people having sex* is <u>not</u> a nonsequitur.

To Michael Neff, Director Algonkian Writer's Workshops, and Julie Doughty, who helped me take my first steps, and special love to authors Connie Rinehold and Linda Windsor for helping me complete those final steps.

A very heartfelt thanks to Robin, Becky, Vonie, Marilyn, Kara Laine, Joni, and Adeline for their encouragement and critical reads. These colleagues and avid readers gave honest critiques and helped me surpass many hurdles.

In loving memory of the women who first inspired me; my mom Norma, and grandmoms, Maria and Katherine.

To my wonderful son, Neil.

Finally, for over 36 years of love, support, and endless manuscript reads, this is for you Charlie.

There is an ancient Japanese art called Kintsugi that mends broken objects with a special lacquer from the Urushi tree and then paints the cracks with gold, thus making them stronger and more beautiful than before they were broken.

Prologue

"Claire, what do you like?"

That's what he asked me as my sixty-year-old body lay naked next to his. Scott, five years older and light-years wiser, was my first new lover in forty years. I felt like a virgin.

"Uh…anything," was all I could nervously muster.

Actually, back in the 1960s, no one had ever asked me that question. Sex had always been spontaneous, not talked about. You just did it. I knew what I liked but had never told anybody else. Over the last few years, and especially since my separation, it had been so much easier to have a love affair with my vibrator.

But "What do you like?" is certainly an improvement over the most prevailing male question, "Did you come?"

Decades ago, I wasn't even sure what that question meant. "Come?" I determined that "yes" was the generic answer, even though, as I later found, if you don't know if you are having a big 'O,' then you are most likely not. In college, sex was performance-based, equivalent to an athletic event, measured by steam and sweating. Besides, if women acted as if they were having a grand mal seizure, even faked ones, men didn't feel compelled to ask the question. They were convinced (perhaps relieved) on hearing the multiple, increasingly dramatic AHHHHHs build to a loud crescendo. No man ventured to say, "Are you sure?" They didn't know or, in some cases, even care.

Men were certainly as naïve as I. Screwing was easy. Young penises attached to hormonally chaotic bodies were programmed to get hard in milliseconds. Male twenty-somethings need only think about sex and up 'it' popped. 'Coming' was their goal; a body's personal fireworks. Besides, no young woman was going to slam a sensitive post-ejaculatory ego with statements like, "I haven't come yet, let's do it longer," or "touch me this way," or "not so hard." How scary would those be if spoken to a supposed high-octane stud? Besides, by the time you thought of it, he had already turned over and gone to sleep!

I am wiser now...well, at least older. And I know there is a huge difference between screwing and making love. Anybody can screw, even in marriage, but lovemaking is an art. So when Scott asked me what I like, and I wasn't sure how to answer, I felt, at the ripe old age of sixty, sexually inadequate. He knew I was nervous, so we talked about that. Yes, t-a-l-k-e-d!

Then he touched, ever so gently. Until then I had been suffering from skin hunger—the lack of being touched and caressed.

Our respective orgasms were almost 'anti-climactic' and ever so peaceful. But it was the fore- and after-play that I cherished. Making love with him was erotic, from the heart, steamy without the sweat.

We were two older, imperfect bodies, but on that night, we put the young, beautiful ones to shame.

***

No, I will not be joining the first wives club, even though my life reads like those of millions of older women, the pathos of desperate 50-plus housewives over generations---that is, the same basic story told with a thousand different variations. My starter marriage to Ross lasted forty years and united our gene-pool with three children raised with semi-effective parenting. We played the part well— outwardly smiling, inwardly churning, lying to ourselves, pretending happily-ever-after, romance weakening with each storm, perpetuating the myth of divorce as personal failure.

Enter an alluring third party; younger, promising, stimulating a wave of excitement, reinvigorating forgotten passions in a stoic husband. Surprisingly, my anger was not displaced by a need for revenge. Actually, it was the jolt I needed to unhinge my pathetic complacency.

I was to blame as much as him. To be sure, I hate endings of secretive dishonesty and he pissed me off with his omissions. Forty years deserves a dignified finale, even if painful. A "let's not fool ourselves any longer" is quite different from "I'm having an affair." But something needed to happen, anything to get me out of my prolonged rut.

Trips out of ruts are exhausting and exhilarating. And getting over "bitter" is a full-time job that starts, as I would learn, with a mirror.

1

"A new life" was way too vague a dream, so with alimony check in hand, I gave it walls and a roof...and incidentally a new mirror, all of which were in a condo in the next town. In the middle of a frigid January, I left my central New Jersey Leave-It-To-Beaver home--and life--along with the albums containing thousands of photo memories. I was "separated," a predictable end step in an emotionally frozen marriage, but with an unpredictably abrupt, maddening finale.

Within one week, I knew I needed therapy, lots of it. Someone once told me that seeing a shrink is a sign of strength and courage, not weakness. Someday maybe I'll understand that after I tackle being scared, angry, lonely, and feeling old---all definitely needing more than what Dr. Phil can offer between twenty-two commercial breaks.

***

The first night in my apartment, I rummaged through boxes to find towels and took a long shower, then went to retrieve some clothes from the empty hollows of my new closet, passing through the dressing area with its full length mirrors. My towel dropped to the floor as I carefully surveyed my body, something I hadn't done in a while.

I was sixty but had been spared varicose veins or stretch marks on my 5' 6" frame. My breasts drooped down, and my stomach--which had ceased being flat a few years ago--hung out slightly above the scar of my hysterectomy. I was every bit a semi-full-figured size 14. In the last years, I had clothed myself so my waist didn't show as much. A small amount of skin sagged from under my partially raised arms and few skin tags presented themselves in various places. I liked my face and brown eyes, even my crow's feet, but could definitely do without the increasingly noticeable hanging skin under my chin, a genetic trait from my paternal side. I had thought about plastic surgery but rejected it. I would be what I would be.

Exercise had kept my body in shape but lately I had fed my loved starved, empty life with food. I would have to watch that I didn't continue this trend. I was attractive but on that day, looking particularly tired, I could see only what was wrong with my body. Age spots had begun showing. My layered auburn hair exhibited gray. Rolling my left thumb across my ring finger, I felt for my missing wedding band, which I had rather ritualistically left on the dresser of my old bedroom for Ross to discover, hoping he would feel guilty as hell and terribly hurt. Oh, the psychological games we had played and I still was.

Also, in the mirror, I began to see more than just my exterior—there was the tightness of anger around my mouth, the defensive stiffness of my posture, the deer-in-the-headlights look in my eyes. I was a mess.

I put on my jeans, a turtleneck and a sweatshirt to begin unpacking. My first order of business was to find the coffee pot with the French roast I had remembered to bring and then to call a therapist.

***

Dr. Shirley Hendricks had a calming grandmotherly voice. I vividly remember her statement, "The truth will set you free, but first it will piss you off." It was a scary statement. I was already monumentally pissed off at myself, my ex, and life in general. I wondered how long it would take to get 'free.' As our first hour ended, she suggested I keep a journal.

Journal? I bought a nice leather-bound one and a fountain pen. Three days later, I had already bought a second and was using any writing utensil I could find. Journaling would be a big part of my ticket back to vitality.

After a couple sessions with Dr. Hendricks, she had invited me to call her Shirley. I liked that…it made the atmosphere more comfortable. She didn't take notes while we talked, but I presumed she did immediately after I left. At first I had wondered what she wrote:

Anxiety disorder?

Immature personality due to late-adolescent pregnancy?

Latent neurotic needs?

Depression?

Total re-evaluation of life needed.

Underachiever---Very late senior bloomer.

Guilt? Thinks she's a victim?

Crippling stress initiated by ding-dong ex-husband who finally let his zipper down?

Angry? Very angry?

On our very first session she had said, "You seem angry."

"Duh? You think?" I blurted back, after which I suppose she had added 'sarcastic' to her list.

I thought I might have to spend the rest of my life in therapy getting to the bottom of this. Thankfully I liked Shirley. Her questions always came at the optimal time. I would be talking, and in a flash, as if she were on to some revelation, she might say, "Have you thought about how your anger is a reaction to loss? Or considered that you may find a gift in this loss?"

"Gift?" I inquired. I couldn't imagine.

Once, after telling her about my journal writing catharses, she asked me to read from it. Startled, I stared at her for a moment, then gazed down at my journal tucked into an outside pocket of my purse, a lump growing in my throat. Had I thought, when she'd told me to bring it, that she just wanted to admire the cover?

There were secrets in there. My barest soul. Pity sessions. I couldn't share all that.

Yet there Shirley sat, calm and relaxed in her chair, as if she had all the time in the world, and knew that I would read from my journal with nary a misgiving. A quick reality check reminded me that I was here for only an hour at a time, and that I paid handsomely for the hour. This hour. She couldn't help me if I didn't cooperate...

With a sudden feeling of being there, yet not, I slipped the journal out of its pocket and opened it to a page that had consumed hours of my time; a page with scribbles, cross outs, and rewrites---symbolic of my labile feelings. My voice broke the silence, a hoarse croak flowing into something like a creaky normal:

Ross and I promised to love and cherish…in sickness and in health. We meant it then. In the beginning life was good and there was affection. Then came children, mortgages, obligations, and change. Somewhere along the way something happened. The once trivial spats eventually produced sustained bitterness. I was suffocating and didn't even know it. Post-mid-life was final-straw devastating.

I started crying. Shirley handed me a tissue but said nothing. I was rather hoping for some mothering at this point. I blew my nose and continued.

The affair unleashed years of pent-up anger in volcanic proportions, bringing our marital façade to a head. Ross, you are such a shit and stupid too! Instead of confronting the problem on the home front, dishonesty and quick-fixes pervaded. Impulsive, dreamy, romantic love is very alluring and, of course, cannot be sustained. Didn't you know that? You foolishly chased the illusive happily-ever-after, replacing a long-term committed relationship in dire need of a jump-start with a superficial new virginal friendship, high on libido. Didn't you know that all couples have to come back from their trysts and get down to the business of day-to-day living? 'Love Boat' romances ultimately have to come back to port.

I'm sobbing now.

"Take some deep breaths," Shirley said gently. I did.

Where are we and where are we going? Lovers? Not really. We loved more like siblings, even adding our own form of rivalry to the script.

Without noticing, sustaining embraces disappeared. Fleeting kisses seemed out of habit. Why did you never like Neil Diamond? Or romantic walks on the beach? Should we have held on to false security or try to capture the remains of whatever we have? Should I thank you for the time we spent?

Or hate you for the time we lost?

For a while, we were in limbo—neither here nor there— neither married or divorced. We were just living together---in purgatory. The worst! Okay, let's get this over with. Who's getting the leather chair? Do you remember when we bought this lamp together? Would you please make me a martini—in an iced tea glass!

Perhaps in time, mourning will subside. Maybe I'll even forgive. But today I hurt. "Till death do us part"—I feel like dying.

My hoarse voice was loud now, still wiping tears. Another tissue was passed, before finally giving me the whole box.

Certainly a part of me has died. How, if, when can I heal? I am loaded with questions. I even have questions about my questions. I can hardly answer the telephone much less answer my questions. Right now, my long-term goal is to make it through the day.

"Thanks for sharing. Took guts. Very insightful. Want to read more?"

"Noooo." I was exhausted.

***

Edith, one of my new neighbors, knocked on my door. She was a widow approaching her eightieth birthday, whose full life instantly attracted me to her. She stopped coloring her hair years ago and its natural gray soup bowl effect hung softly around her weathered face, giving her the look of a wise elder. She had stellar posture on a thin frame and was dressed in a warm sweater over an oxford shirt, collar up, Katherine Hepburn style, with corduroy slacks and glasses hanging by a pearl necklace. Her age showed but she moved with the vitality of someone much younger.

She had brought me homemade cookies still warm from the oven. It was like comfort food from my childhood. I poured each of us a cup of hot tea, hopefully enhancing the warm fuzzies Edith had brought, while she gave me a recap of her background. I was immediately fascinated by her rich history.

Born during the Great Depression, she was raised wearing hand-me-down clothes and reminisced about missed meals, almost nostalgically. Like my own deceased mother, she had learned to "save for a rainy day because you never know when you might need it."

I loved her description of her youth: *When Johnny Comes Marching Home Again* played to the soldiers coming back from WWII, including her soon-to-be-husband. At seventeen, she was immensely patriotic, and like her parents, respected authority to the point of not removing furniture tags that said, 'Under penalty of law DO NOT REMOVE.' Her parents believed that children should be seen and not heard, and if there were family problems you sucked it up, which included keeping all family 'skeletons' in the closet. Inconsistent with the usual 1940s dearth of professional opportunities for women, Edith felt privileged to attend a teacher's college on full scholarship.

Edith had experienced loneliness. One daughter, Barbara, lived an hour away, making impromptu visits rare. Another daughter, Charlotte, was a plane ride away in another state. Edith had suffered from late life depression after Rudy, her husband of fifty years, died from a slow, agonizing cancer. She had diligently nursed him for two years---holding him tightly in the hours before his last breath. Her eyes welled as she related that experience.

"For months afterward, I sat in my recliner chair watching C-span and reruns of Lawrence Welk," she told me. "All I cooked was TV dinners and my arthritis got worse from being such a couch potato. I felt as if I was dying by inches. My daughters were investigating assisted living facilities and asking where I kept the insurance papers and will. It seemed like my children were burying me before I died, and I had picked up a shovel to help."

"Obviously they didn't succeed," I observed. "So what happened?"

"Success is always the best revenge, and hurts no one." Edith paused to dunk a cookie into her tea with childlike concentration. "So, I got out of the recliner, went to my family doctor and for the first time in my life, told someone that mentally and physically I felt like shit. He prescribed an anti-depressant, new arthritis drugs, swimming pool therapy, and AARP. Within a few weeks I had a renewed reason to get up in the morning, and no plans to join Rudy in the adjacent grave anytime soon. I sold our home, which had become way too much work for me, and moved here to be near two of my closest friends."

Two years after Rudy died, Edith had a date. Then another where they held hands while walking, at which time Edith overheard a passer-by remark, "Aren't they cute?" She became incensed, raising her voice, "Can you imagine they called us cute! Can't two seniors hold hands without being relegated to the status of second graders?"

One Thanksgiving she went snorkeling in

Hawaii—with boyfriend Fred—instead of participating in the family festivities at home. Their respective relatives went nuts. Questions, or as Edith described, interrogations, dominated face-to-face conversations and frantic phone calls.

"To my face, they said I wasn't acting my age. Do they expect that I should be in some senior center stringing beads and making damned potholders? Behind my back, I am sure they were muttering 'dementia,' and wondering if I was buying stock in Yankee Stadium. To top it off, my daughter, Barbara, refused to accept that I could have sex at my age. In fact, she acted disgusted, as if I was some kind of moral degenerate. I was hurt and confused. But in the meantime, Fred discovered Viagra and I bought *Intimate* by K-Y Jelly. We were slow, but damn, it felt good! Sex is healthy, you know, like eating fruits and vegetables—good exercise also," she said with a wink and mischievous smile.

"We had so much fun together. Fred tripped off the alarms of every airport security check-point because he had artificial knees and a metal-plated hip. We laughed ourselves silly as he was taken to the side for frisking. 'What made you trip the alarm?' he asked other old people. Pacemakers dominated. We were one hell of a prosthetic group."

As Edith talked I recalled what Bette Davis once said, "Aging ain't for sissies." I believe she was right. Edith had endured many losses, which she aptly called her personal mini-deaths, including her husband, several dear friends, her once perfect physical condition and youthful looks, and perhaps soon her driver's license, but she was still a healthy, youthful-*old*. Yet her family wanted to think of her as a dependent, old, demented relic with one foot in the grave. Pathetic, isn't it? I need to talk with my kids about this. In a mere twenty years, I would be her age. By God, I wrote in my journal, I was going to emulate her adventurous spirit. She did NOT fit my senior-sitting-in-a-rocking-chair-with-an-afghan stereotype. A 20th century pioneer woman, Edith was a classic unsung heroine.

I flashed on my future during a lull in the conversation. "Penny for your thoughts," she inquired.

"Edith, I never finished college and I never got over it." I blurted the non sequitur, and wondered where it came from.

"So what's holding you back now?"

Finding no answer that wasn't wimpy, all I could do was frown as the question echoed accusingly in my own mind. I would take her words to heart on that day. She became my conduit to action.

***

Cedric is another new neighbor--six-foot, skinny, yet in superb physical shape, great looking, Polo clothes, 50ish, brown hair with blond highlights, blue eyes, an interior decorator, and judging by his bold feminine movements, gay. He came over to greet me and within five minutes said my bland sofa needed green and mauve pillows. "Here's some free advice," he said with his arms swung out in a glorious gesture like a preacher making a point, "This apartment needs color!"

On that night, only the third evening in my apartment, this particular advice caused me to roll my eyes. "Cedric, I can't fucking think about color right now. My forty-year marriage has ended. I am totally grieving. I don't know how long my alimony will pay for my shrink, and I am considering going back to college to sit with some twenty-year-olds with tight asses and spaghetti string tops." As soon as these words were out of my mouth, I couldn't believe I had revealed this much to a total stranger. Jesus, I told him I was in therapy.

"Well, listen to her bitch," he said in a loving enough way that prevented me from strangling him. "Today some redneck delivery man whispered 'faggot' under his breath after I kindly asked him to be careful unpacking an outrageously expensive sofa. Do you know how scary that hateful word is? My parents, who disowned me years ago, now want money, and a dear friend was just diagnosed with cancer."

"Cedric, I'm sorry. I was tastelessly abrupt. You came here to welcome me and instead became the brunt of my anger." My eyes were wet, "Can we start over? I promise I'm not a witch."

"Witches can be goddesses. There are plenty of good witches." I smiled and he continued, "I accept your apology. My ex-therapist once said to me that when you are feeling dejected, rejected, neglected, and subjected, talking about it helps."

"Ever had a long-term relationship?" I said.

"Yep, for twenty years. I buried him three years ago."

"Cedric, I am so sorry. I guess I don't have a monopoly on stress."

"Is there anything we can do to cheer up this conversation? Perhaps we can save our tragic stories for another night?"

"How about some wine and cheese? You can

relax on my boring beige sofa and I will tell you about my first trip to Hoboken, New Jersey." I had just realized that we were both still standing.

"Good start. I accept, but I'd rather discuss your first lover," he replied laughing.

Cedric was wonderful, and I might add, safe. A man I could trust...with no ulterior motives. He was animated, talking with his whole body, hands and arms, head, eyes, a bevy of non-verbal expression. In talking with him, I realized that I had lived a closeted heterosexual life, aware of only one gay friend, years ago, who came out in college and was cruelly rejected by many. She moved abroad and I lost touch with her, having never told her I disagreed with the way she was treated. My children now had gay friends in a world decades more progressive than mine had been.

Cedric and I talked into the wee hours of the morning, something I hadn't done in years. We ended up ordering gourmet pizza delivered from a yuppie deli while disclosing our lives. Cedric was different, variant, not deviant, and a breath of fresh air. Somehow I felt instantly relaxed with him. He was honest to a fault, as if wearing his heart on his sleeve, not afraid to hold back or divulge intimate details.

"So what about your intimate details?" he said.

"Forty years ago, I quit college to get married because I was pregnant."

"Let me see, that would have been the height of the 1960s sexual revolution, right? Dear God girl, you women were finally breaking free from sexual oppression and you didn't know about birth control? Perhaps a little like putting the cart before the horse?"

"And how. The condom had broken but he said

he could pull out in time. What did I know."

" Oh, yeah, the old pull-out routine---Worked about three percent of the time," he said eyes rolling.

"Anyway," I continued, "Like many of my friends, I had a quick wedding. I birthed a 7 ½ pounder, who my mother labeled a 'premature' baby for those doing the math, which was just about everybody. In that era, God forbid you 'had' to get married.

"My wedding to Ross Pennington had all the trappings of a proper sacrament. You know the scoop: white dress, three-tiered cake, a gold-band, something-borrowed, something-new, etc. At the altar, we united our two lit candles into one flame while the minister said, "Let this symbolize the merging of their identities; that these two people have become one."

"Dear God girl, you are making me claustrophobic. You merged your identities? Two people become one? I am having a testosterone hot flash!"

"That's what we did," I said. "I thought it was romantic—then. Truth was, Ross and I might have, at regular intervals, merged our bodies or our Spock-crammed parenting skills, but when we merged our identities, we essentially just locked together our neuroses. As Mrs. Ross Pennington, I became a willing enabler. Yeah, we became one, but he was three-fourths of that while I dutifully withered away. The old adage—one man away from welfare—became sadly true."

Cedric leaned forward, a crease between his brows, as if he were seriously concerned for a troubled friend. "Okay, you became a stereotype right on cue. What got you out of that rut?"

"Hey, we called ourselves *The Stereotypicals* and formed a club," I quipped, but it sounded pathetic rather than amusing. I sighed in resignation. "I quit college and went to work as some executive's gopher while our moms babysat and Ross finished his business degree. I compromised my professional ambition and married it instead, rationalizing that I was in love because if you were going to 'make' love before marriage, at least you had better be 'in' love. The marriage lasted through two more kids, Ross's successful career, my full-time mothering, and a monotonous routine of cooking, cleaning, laundry, children, chauffeuring, and sharing recipes for carrot cake.

"Having lost myself, I lived vicariously through my kids. Not wanting them to repeat my mistakes, I taught my daughter about masturbation at thirteen and birth control at sixteen. I lectured both my sons about sex and female orgasm when they were trapped in a car with me for a three-hour road trip."

"I would have liked to be a fly in the car for that conversation!"

"You would have been one majorly impressed fly. I was on a roll that day. I told them I would stop talking when they wanted me to, but that never happened until we pulled into our driveway."

"You know, Cedric, on the surface Ross and I were right out of a Norman Rockwell painting. We took our kids to Sunday school, were active in the community, and had an array of stalwart friends. We treated one another civilly, in public anyway. Ours was a protracted erosion, no screaming matches, no blatant overwhelming crises or confrontations…just

20

gradual distancing, drifting into apathy, as if we were two zombie Dr. Spocks living together."

"Apathy is worse than hate, you know." Cedric said. "Totally emotion-less! Hate at least has feeling."

"That's so true," I responded. "And like a heroin fix with a high on lust, Ross's affair started at the end of our third decade of mediocrity. I actually knew her from the company gatherings---stand-offish, socially challenged, passive-aggressive, all deceptively disguised as sweet. He could have done so much better. But then again, it was my ticket to freedom. The last kid had graduated from college and we didn't have to force this marriage any longer. Take her. I won't be around when you discover your mistake. Someday I might actually feel sorry for you."

"You're aware your voice just changed to angry mode?"

"It is just below the surface, lots of it. Anyway, throughout the years, there were times when I was motivated to work on the marriage, go to counseling, raise it up a few notches…somehow strive for a soul-mate communication. Ross half-heartedly agreed but it never happened. If real love was anything, it was work, but he was lazy about it, then I was, then simultaneously both of us."

"I bet you became the bitchy wife."

"She the gentle maiden."

"Only *she* could 'make' him happy again."

"And I was baggage. The end." It was 3 A.M. I was tired, yet strangely peaceful as I cupped my chin in my hand and grinned at Cedric. "You know, we have to be friends now. You know too much about me."

The next day, Cedric brought me two beautiful emerald green pillows. I hugged him tight.

2

Meeting Edith and Cedric over the span of one week into my 'new' life turned into an unexpected and wonderful surprise. It made me think of all the friendships I had had in my life. Most had never realized their full potential, starting and ending with small talk on the way to PTA meetings. Two of my dearest friends, Paulette and Zoe, had both moved away with their transferred husbands and then just fell into my life's unwritten history book. Now I was beginning to see that these had been tremendous losses for me.

I hadn't worked hard to keep in touch with college friends, who now seemed superficially homogenous anyway, and I was too busy to nurture new friendships or open the doors to diverse and varied relationships. I must have said, "Let's get together" a million times over the years but it rarely happened. "I'm so busy," was the usual mantra.

I remembered my best friend, Gloria, my college roommate. We did everything together; eat, sleep, go to classes, study, and of course, talk endlessly. It seems if you brush your teeth with someone, a closeness can follow. This woman was like the sister I never had. Even my parents loved her and her parents treated me like family.

Then 'he' came along. Ron was a nice enough guy and genuinely kind to Gloria. But as they spent more and more time together, I felt as if she was divorcing me. I saw this happening over and over with other friends. Female friendships were strong, until…one by one, they were abandoned for a man. Soon Gloria spent her time getting ready for dates with Ron, studied with him, and eventually brushed her teeth with him.

When Ross came into my life, I did the same thing. He was actually jealous of my time with friends. Our first spat was over us not spending enough time together. As for me, well, I marveled at being wanted so much. I thought, hell, he must really love me. With all our youthful insecurities, our relationship became fatality flawed well before we marched to the altar with fetus in tow.

***

A few weeks after moving, needing to do some errands and grocery shop, I asked Edith if she wanted to accompany me and maybe have some lunch together. Wanting to get out, she gladly accepted. On the way to the car, we ran into a busy-looking Cedric, who we spontaneously invited to join us for lunch.

"I have a very 'hot' date tonight and a ton of stuff to do, but you know what? Lunch with two beautiful women sounds just great!"

"Isn't he a bit queer?" Edith asked as we drove away.

"Well, he's homosexual, gay."

"My cousin, Dennis, acted just like him when we were growing up. When I asked my mother why he was different, she told me to hush up. It was like he was that big skeleton in the family closet. At eighteen, he left for New York City and a year later, he was dead. My aunt, his mother, said he was mugged and murdered in his apartment but I overheard my parents saying that police had found a gun by his head. Suicide doesn't happen in 'nice' families like ours was supposed to be, so even murder sounded better I suppose. People hugged my aunt and uncle and told them how tragic it was, that the world was going to hell in a hand basket. My uncle exclaimed that he would find whoever did this. I think they couldn't deal with him being queer—oh, I'm sorry, gay—and then killing himself. However flawed, believing it was murder held less shame. They couldn't and wouldn't go there. Too painful."

"I'm sorry, Edith. That must have been hard for you."

"Extremely. I cried for months. Dennis and I had done so much together. He was older and treated me like a kid sister. When I would put on plays with my miniature doll collection, he helped me write the script and build the sets. He always talked about the theater. But he became increasingly unhappy in high school. He never dated. His parents seemed ashamed of him. So many times, I wanted to talk with him, say something, but I never had the guts. It is one of those things I have never been able to forgive myself for. He needed a friend and I let him down."

"My shrink would tell me that you have to forgive yourself."

"Shrink?"

"You know, a psychologist, therapist."

"You go to one of those? But you're not crazy!"

I was relieved when we found a parking place and could postpone this part of the conversation. Therapists didn't exist in Edith's prime. When suffering came, one maintained a stiff upper lip, pent-up feelings silently inside, and oh, prayed. My grandmother used to say, "God never gives you more than you can handle." I now take issue with this overused cliché because it stifles expression of feelings.

Edith and Cedric knew each other casually but had never socialized. At lunch, she told Cedric about Dennis and how guilty she felt. Even though his death was over sixty years ago, Cedric could relate to what happened. "It could have been yesterday," he said softly. We were all silent for a while.

Then we started talking about clothes…and the giggling started. "My date's a college professor and dresses like a frump," Cedric informed us.

"So wear a vest and bow tie," quipped Edith, "and take a pipe."

"Ey, God, you guys."

I couldn't help notice the three of us, unimaginably diverse, yet somehow our lives had joined, marking the beginning of a friendship family. I also noticed that I was laughing for the first time in a long time. When Edith tried eating sushi with chopsticks, Cedric and I cried with bursts of laughter straight from the belly. Being the good sport that she was, she told us to shut the hell up and teach her to use these damn-fangled contraptions! As arthritis prevented her from mastering the sticks, she soon succumbed to a fork. "Give me an 'A' for effort!" she proclaimed. Later she put her hand on top of Cedric's, "I am really glad I got to know you better."

Cedric landed a big, fat kiss right on her lips. Edith didn't budge. Lunch was a hoot. Ah...if only her daughters could see this.

3

By the time tree buds sprouted and crocuses popped up through the last vestiges of snow, I found myself feeling more peaceful. I had five journals full of angry scribbling and to my surprise, was significantly happier without Ross around. I enrolled in a university to start a new episode of my life and saw a job posting on a bulletin board outside my advisor's office.

The Area Agency on Aging seeks a part-time intake assistant who is needed to help triage senior citizens and recommend appropriate community resources. Twenty hours per week. Must have excellent communication skills. Salary commensurate with experience.

I hadn't had a job in thirty-eight years. Besides realizing the depths of my depressing underachievement, I was plagued with boredom, and perhaps this job had my name on it. Dr. Hendricks had taught me that "failure is not trying." Even if I fell flat on my face, at least I would have the experience of an interview. While copying down the information, a professor approached the board to post another announcement.

"Do you know about this agency?" I asked.

"Absolutely, a wonderful environment to work in. The people are dedicated and kind. On a shoestring budget, this agency has done wonders for the elderly."

Later that afternoon, before I would talk myself out of doing this, I made the phone call, and, to my surprise, landed an interview for the next day.

***

Dressed in my most professional gray slack-suit, I arrived early to fill out an application. The outdated two-story brick building, a converted tuberculosis sanatorium, was older than most of its clients. My first impression was, "So this is how we treat the elderly. Our local humane society is much nicer than this." Seniors awaiting appointments were crowded in hallways with peeling paint, sitting in unmatched, plastic-cushioned chairs. The bathroom sinks could have sold in an antique store except for the prominent rust-color stains.

Within thirty seconds of being handed an application, I had written down two years of college and one job decades ago, but that was followed by blank spaces. (I skipped the part about being a camp counselor after my junior year of high school.) My yet-to-be-written resume would be equally unimpressive: Cub Scout leader, charity ball clean-up committee, little league refreshment stand volunteer, church deacon, oh, and I live in a clean house with organized closets. I wondered if my career capability had shriveled up like an atrophied muscle.

Imogene, the agency's director, came from behind her desk to shake my hand. The room was furnished with low-end, discount office furniture. The curtains looked home made. Her desk was piled high with papers and two dogs, black labs, came forward to greet me, instantly breaking the ice and calming my nerves. As I petted them, she explained that they were trained therapy dogs, who often visit the dementia daycare unit downstairs.

Pointing to a small round table with chairs, she invited me to sit with her. A plaque on the table quoted Mother Teresa, "It is immoral to be deterred by the magnitude of a problem. The good we can do we must do."

I was way overdressed compared to her. She wore a simple cotton top over slacks. Her dark hair, easy-care short, topped a make-up free face and a five-foot, small frame. She looked my age, with a warm smile and soft, welcoming face.

"Tell me about yourself."

"I'm single, starting college again in the fall after dropping out almost forty years ago, taking one course in psychology and another in social work, and very interested in the needs of the elderly. I haven't worked in a while but would be motivated and willing to learn." There, my life in two sentences.

"Do you have any experience with seniors?"

"Not professionally," knowing I had to be honest. "Truthfully, I am searching for what I want to do with the rest of my life, but I do have a special place in my heart for seniors. I watched my parents age and die. I saw them struggle to maintain their independence, sometimes to a fault. I fought with my father about continuing to drive after he inadvertently got the gas and brake pedals mixed-up, miraculously causing only a minor accident. I watched him be robbed of his brain through Alzheimer's. When I visited him in the nursing home, I was plagued with guilt. I wasn't actively looking for a job when I saw your job opening, but I immediately wanted to apply."

"Thank you for sharing that. Many of us have been there," she said sincerely before lapsing in a pause, long pause. "This job, however, needs someone who knows the network of senior services in this area."

"As I said before, I am willing to learn. Can you tell me about some of these agencies?" I wanted to get her talking. She obliged, and as she did, I realized I had a cursory knowledge of most of them, which kept our conversation going. Still, I could see doubts in her face, appropriately so. It would take much effort to train me.

"Look, I understand your reluctance to hire someone like me, without prior work experience. But I can promise you I will study the system and try my hardest to be of service to this agency," I said in a desperate last plea.

"Do you understand what the job entails?"

"I would meet with seniors to hear their problems, then point them in the right direction for services so they can get the help they need."

"You understand that you would not be counseling them, and in most cases only referring them to others. If they need a service like Meals on Wheels, you could initiate that process."

Our conversation continued and we even talked about personal experiences with our respective parents. She made me a cup of coffee and I began to realize that even more than wanting this job, I wanted to work with Imogene. She was salt-of-the-earth, never married, had worked all her adult life, and openly showed her compassion for the elderly.

Finally, after we'd been together almost an hour, she looked at me with another long, contemplative pause.

"I'll tell you what I'll do. The woman who is currently doing this job is moving to Florida to live with her children and grandchildren. She would like to be relieved in one month, but has consented to stay longer if I need her to. If she stays six weeks that should be ample time for you to be trained and ready to operate independently. There is another woman, a senior, who I've hired for this job and is very well qualified, but, like you, she wants to work part time. Between the two of you, I can fill this position full-time. You and she will have to coordinate your hours."

I couldn't believe what I was hearing. I was being offered a job! With responsibilities! How scary! "I will not disappoint you," I said. "Thank you so much!"

"We are a shoe-string budgeted agency. I cannot pay you much nor offer you benefits. Can you work full-time for the first two weeks and can you start on Monday at 8 A.M.?"

"Yes, I'll be here," then with a huge smile on my face, I said, "Thank you, really, thank you."

While starting at the low end of the ladder, not that far above minimum wage, I felt satisfied. I would have my own money for the first time in decades, not enough to cancel my alimony, but something.

***

Ann, the woman I was replacing, met me in the reception area. "Oh, don't be nervous. Imogene thinks you will do just fine. I am so excited to meet you." We toured, and she talked about each department...social work, nutrition, the fitness program, Medicare and insurance assistance. I met Jake who drove the Meals on Wheels truck and he arranged for me to accompany him the next day.

The Alzheimer's daycare facility was difficult for me, bringing back images of my dad. He had deteriorated quickly after my mom's death, from a man who could fix everything in his elaborate workshop to being unable to change the batteries in his TV's remote control. A fall broke his hip and he never recovered, slipping inexorably into his mind's darkness, slowly forgetting the names of his grandchildren, then mine, and finally his own. His last few months in a nursing home were marked with the undignified wearing of diapers, eating pureed food, and sometimes having Haldol administered to calm his aggression. Once he grabbed the breast of a nurse in an attempt to seduce her. In his cognizant life, my father would have been mortified.

In this locked unit, an eighty-plus-year-old woman held tightly to a baby doll as though it was her child of years past. A once successful surgeon painted a primitive face on a gourd. One woman sat catatonically, while another walked almost frantically around the room followed by one of Imogene's labs. All of them were there for the day, giving families a much needed respite from the 24/7 grueling demands of dementia care.

One woman cried for a husband, dead over seven years. "When's he coming to get me? He's late for lunch!"

"We used to tell her the truth; that he was dead," an aide informed me, "and she screamed in mourning as if it were the first time she heard that he had died. Then, fifteen minutes later, she asked again when he was coming to get her. If we repeated the truth, she screamed yet again as if being told for the first time. So now we just say he'll be here soon. We call this a 'fiblet,' necessary lying to prevent continued severe stress."

Ann told me that I would help families register their loved ones, families at their wits-end. For some, this dementia unit would be a godsend. Then she gave me information on Alzheimer's support groups and national associations with local chapters. I barraged her with questions. At one point, she explained the concept of 'granny-dumping,' where families, stressed to the breaking point, take their parent (most often a woman, since they commonly outlive men) to a hospital emergency room frequently on a Friday night, and then leave.

My heart sank. Oh my God! I had done this once when Ross and I were leaving town for his company's conference and dad was running a fever. Knowing he would not eat and drink properly while I was away, I took him to the hospital and, complete with tears, begged them to keep him. Our family physician admitted him for dehydration, but I knew that he had not needed hospitalization.

My tour ended with a visit to the senior activities center. A small room crowded with sixty or so seniors in scattered groups. They were playing cards, singing with a music therapist, working on crafts, or simply socializing. Most, having long ago given up driving, had been bused to the center. It was a welcome sanctuary from loneliness and boredom. One disheveled woman grabbed me as I approached, rubbing my arm while holding tightly to my other hand. I stroked her in return. Touch seemed such a simple gift to give, yet, in looking around, I wondered how many were deprived.

Emotionally exhausted when I got home, I put my feet up in my lounge chair, sipped hot tea, and studied the thick manual of the agency's vast referral system.

The next day, I was up early to deliver meals to almost seventy people. Jake knew every recipient; many had been on his route for years. We covered the whole gamut of socio-economic society---little old ladies in maid-kept condos overfilled with antiques from their previous stately homes; couples in unkempt trailer parks with torn screens being useless barriers to shortly hatching summer flies; old men in broken down, neglected houses with cranked up space heaters providing their only source of heat in the chilly morning. Two common threads united them all: old and alone. As surrogate companionship, televisions blared--Bachelor number One was chosen because he was most sexy; Drew Carey hosted *The Price is Right*.

Jake, a vigorous seventy-five-year-old, always gave me the honor of personally delivering to the front doors, many of which were already open in anticipation of our arrival. Some places were filthy and reeking. One woman in a run-down remnant of a formerly nice home had no less than fifteen cats roaming all over, many lying on kitchen counters. The place was filled with empty food containers. "I just take in the strays," she said. "People just dump them, you know." Another had a home in such disrepair that I feared for a frail man's safety, yet outside, three adults, perhaps his children and grandchildren, were hunched over an open-hooded car. Why weren't they helping him? Why couldn't they at least fix the floorboards and wobbly stair banister? I wondered if they would eat his food.

From the security and shelter of suburbia, I was introduced to a world I had never seen. One woman begged me to stay and visit, but Jake, himself a volunteer, reminded me that we were on a schedule that didn't allow lingering. "I will come back. I promise," I said, while holding her hand. She had been a World War II nurse.

***

My first two weeks were busy and emotionally trying. I spent time in each program and with the many people who ran them. I made trips to assisted living facilities and nursing homes with an ombudsman who investigated family complaints. One case involved inappropriate touching of a bedridden lady by an orderly, while in another I investigated a large bedsore that needed more aggressive treatment.

"How do you keep from getting stressed?" I asked Imogene.

"You do your best. Solve the problems you can. Don't take your work home with you, and *don't* take things personally!"

Within six weeks, I was confident I could handle ninety percent of the queries, with immediate access to assistance when I didn't know what to do. My partner, Marion, the other half of this full time position, was a retired nurse, African-American, seventy-four-years-old, widowed after a tragic car accident. She spoke on the phone to seniors with confidence and a take-charge attitude. "Of course we can help ma'am. Don't you fret. No need to cry. This can all be solved."

One night she invited me to her apartment, a senior complex within walking distance of the agency, for a dinner of greens and pork, her comfort food. Her apartment was crowded with colorful crocheted afghans and framed photos, including one of President Obama. I envied her vitality, in spite of her rather severe arthritis. "I love God," she said. "He will take me when He is ready. Until then, no sitting around and sulking...I do His service," which also included singing gospel for her church choir. When she sang, "Wading in the Water" accompanying herself on her old upright piano with its worn and chipped keys, I thought I would cry.

4

Her feet shuffled as she walked into my office. Her faded red and blue calico-print dress hung loosely, the uneven hem draping almost to her ankles. Its simple lines gave the impression of being home-made. Over her breasts was a hint of last night's dinner. Her Hush-Puppy shoes, almost too small around her edematous feet, were shabby and scuffed—the soles worn. She grasped her cane as if it were a lifeline between her and the floor. Arthritis had deformed her fingers and hands, which also bore the calluses of decades of labor-intensive work.

She sat down slowly with deliberate motions, making sure her butt was centered precisely over the chair's seat, then introduced herself.

"How can I help you, Mrs. Behnke?" I asked.

"I think my step-son is poisoning me and my husband."

I tried not to show my shock, though I'm sure my eyes widened. Holy shit, they didn't cover this in orientation! "Tell me more. Why do you think this?"

"I don't know where to start…"

"Start at the beginning."

She proceeded to tell me that she and her

husband of twenty-five years, Earl, age eighty-two, lived on a 140-acre family homestead, which they had farmed until two years ago, when he'd suffered a paralyzing stroke. His sporadically employed forty-seven-year-old son, the offspring of his first marriage, resided in a trailer on the property with his on-again, off-again girlfriend. He had been urging his dad to sell. The house and barns, while run down, were located close to sprawling sub-divisions, and developers had inquired about their interest in selling, some baiting them with alluringly high six-figure estimates.

Her husband was hesitant to be displaced from his boyhood home, which also contained the graves of many family members. In his will, Mrs. Behnke stood to inherit half of the worth, a major contention for this son, who believed since she was the second wife and not his mother, that he deserved most everything.

Since his stroke, Earl had been unable to negotiate the stairs to the second floor, so she had converted the living room into his bedroom, complete with a hospital bed. One night, after she put Earl to bed, she retired upstairs. She told me that the sheets reeked of a perfume-like smell. After a short time in bed, she felt dizzy, nauseous, and developed a headache. Over the course of the next few days, her symptoms persisted and she developed abdominal pain. Earl started having similar symptoms. In addition, she had recently noticed that the son was eagerly volunteering to do all of the grocery shopping and bending over backwards to cook meals for them, mostly casseroles, neither of which he had done previously without their imploring. She never saw any grocery receipts, but was paying hefty bills for the food.

I listened in amazement trying not to press my bottom lip too tightly between my teeth. Do I call the police now? 9-1-1? Or, is this a paranoid, demented little-old-lady? Feeling quite out of my league, I left her sitting in my office (with a cup of coffee) while I bee-lined to Imogene, who was thankfully available. She remained calm—elder abuse was not new to her, even though a poisoning allegation was.

Speedy phone calls followed to the agency's attorney and a public health doctor. Tests were ordered at a near-by laboratory, which would test Mrs. Behnke for many drugs, including arsenic. I was instructed to tell her to go there directly before she went back home.

"Home?" I blurted out. "Quite possibly her stepson is trying to kill her. How can we send her back to that environment? And what about Mr. Behnke, who is also at risk?"

"Without proof," said Imogene, "there is no immediate recourse. Tell her to eat only canned food that she personally opens, or freshly bought, thoroughly cleaned vegetables. If the tests are positive, we will immediately involve the police."

As it turned out, Mrs. Behnke had taken the bus to the center. She had no transportation to the lab and there was no bus that went there without scheduling. I only had one more client to see, so I offered to chauffeur her when I was done. In the car, she relayed how hard it had been caring for her husband. Money was tight and numerous monthly medications drained their already sparse finances.

Since he had been a farmer, there was no company pension, only social security and dwindling savings. It seemed so strange that they were living on a gold mine of mortgage-free acreage struggling to make ends meet. Her husband had briefly considered selling the property, at a somewhat reduced cost, to a non-profit such as the Nature Conservancy, but his son had been adamantly opposed.

Her veins were frail and several vials of blood had to be taken. She winced in pain but said nothing. She seemed distant as the blood was finally extracted, staring blankly into space, her thoughts seemingly focused on the magnitude of this situation. After the blood test, they took hair, fingernail, and urine samples.

The drive to her farm was spent mostly in silence, interrupted by her occasionally saying, "Oh, my God. I don't believe this." The old farmhouse, at the end of a long, potholed dirt road, badly needed painting. Weeds had consumed the surrounding, now dormant fields, as well as large sections of dry brown front-yard grass under century-old maple trees. Neglected overgrown bushes grew wild around the house. A broken gutter hung precariously over the dusty porch, where chairs, in various stages of disrepair, spoke of a time, long ago, when people gathered on this once inviting refuge to relax after a hard day's work or to socialize on Sundays.

I helped her out of my car and she invited me in after I asked to meet Mr. Behnke. A worn mat by the front door was covered in caked mud, almost obliterating the faded 'welcome' printed on it. Inside, the tightly pulled drapes added to the dingy appearance. Mildew and urine smells filled my nostrils. I wanted to instantly grab a broom and dust cloth, and open windows for a long-overdue airing.

A *Bonanza* rerun blared loudly from the television in the former living room where Earl sat in a recliner chair, sleeping, mouth wide open, with no denture support to prevent his lips from caving in. Although Mrs. Behnke touched him gently, softly speaking his name, he was still startled upon awakening.

"Earl, I brought a friend of mine to see you."

"Huh?"

"I said I brought a friend," she replied more loudly.

I took the liberty of turning the TV down. He frowned trying to determine if he should recognize me.

"Hello, Mr. Behnke, I am a friend of your wife's," I said figuring her spur-of-the-moment use of the word friend would suffice.

"Oh, hello," he said faintly. "Margaret, where have you been?"

"I had some errands to run, so I took a bus to town. Remember, I told you I would be gone a couple of hours. Sorry, it took a bit longer than expected." It then occurred to me that she had hiked that long driveway to the road to meet the bus. She would have had to call for a pickup the day before since public transportation was not regular on rural back roads.

She handed Earl his dentures and a urinal. "Need to go?" In spite of her carefulness, a few drops of urine managed to spill onto his already spotted pants. I was starting to feel sick.

"Do you have any help, Mrs. Behnke?"

"A nurse used to come twice a week, but our Medicare stopped paying for it."

Then I heard someone come in the back door, yelling, "Hello? Anybody home? I brought a tuna casserole. I'll leave it in the fridge."

"In here," Mrs. Behnke yelled, while simultaneously giving me a knowing look. My heart sank; a tuna casserole laced with arsenic?

Earl Jr. was visibly surprised to see me. "Hi, my name is Claire," holding out my hand.

With a limp shake he replied, "Hi. Haven't seen you before."

Not wanting to divulge too much, I fumbled for the right words. "I met your, ah, mom at the senior services center."

"Yeah, why were you there?" he asked rudely, looking directly at Mrs. Behnke.

Before she could answer, I nervously described how signing up for Medicare Part D could help pay for medications. The bus had been late and I was happy to drop her home. I felt my fib was quite unconvincing, but Earl Jr. must've liked the idea of extra money because he didn't ask further questions.

This guy was right out of a Stephen King horror movie. A flannel shirt hung over grubby blue jeans on his thin, middle-aged frame. Long dark hair was slicked back. His blotchy reddened face, prematurely wrinkled, sported an unkempt goatee. After he lit a cigarette, he let it dangle from his mouth.

"Do you want to stay for dinner?" Mrs. Behnke inquired, almost as if baiting me.

Dear God, what was she thinking?

Before I could tastefully excuse myself, he blurted, "Sorry ma, there is only enough for two."

Ah, Mrs. Behnke was smart—it had been a test.

"Thank you for offering, Mrs. Behnke, but I must be off soon. Can I help you serve it?" I said trying to keep my wits about me and thinking I could perhaps get a sample of the casserole for analysis.

"I'll do that!" his impatience was showing. "Here let me walk you to the car."

"I'll be leaving in a few minutes," I blurted back. This son-of-a-bitch wasn't going to throw me out. "Is there a bathroom I could use?" I fumbled in my purse to feel for my cell phone…just in case.

I went to the bathroom down the hall, but I would squat outside before I'd sit on the pee-stained toilet. I tried to get my composure by taking deep breaths.

"I'll be back later," I heard him say while shutting the door behind him. I quickly ran out of the bathroom to find the kitchen and hopefully the casserole. Mrs. Behnke was already looking in the refrigerator. It was gone.

In a hasty plot aimed at rejecting the casserole, I quickly opened the canned soup on the counter. Neither she nor Earl were hungry, so I poured it into soup bowls, then emptied much of the contents down the sink. "When he returns, tell him you couldn't find the casserole so you ate some soup." Knowing he would probably not come back until I left, I waited another thirty minutes so our impulsive alternate plan would seem authentic.

"This is a nightmare," she sighed. "How could this be happening?"

"We don't know anything solid yet," I said feebly

attempting to reassure her.

I thought about taking them with me, but with no proof, there were few choices and I had no jurisdiction. If the Behnke's left with me, Earl Jr. would surely suspect something and possibly intervene. I could easily get in over my head, if I wasn't already. Besides, the lab tests would be back soon.

When I walked to my car in the fading dusk light, I saw him from the corner of my eye, behind some bushes. Terrified, I immediately locked the car doors when he suddenly appeared, knocking at my driver's window. Fumbling with keys, hands shaking, I turned the car on and put it in drive before I opened the window slightly. "Nice meeting you. Your parents are such sweet people."

"Comin' back soon? What did you say your name was again?"

I looked to see if he had a weapon. "My name is Claire, and I hope to visit again soon."

"I'm taking good care of them, lady. Why would you want to come back?"

"As I said, I am helping your mom with Medicare Part D. But now I am late for a meeting. Have a good evening." I drove away before he could say anymore. My face was flushed, heart pounding. A hot flash, similar to the ones I had experienced during menopause, consumed me.

***

That night I had felt unsteady, ruminating about Earl Jr.'s threatening tone and posture. A knock at my door jolted me from the deep thought of journaling. "Claire?" said a faint voice, "Are you home?" It was Edith, crying.

"What's wrong?"

"I just received a call from my cousin. Maria, my best friend from childhood, is dead. We've known each other for seventy years. She was maid-of-honor in my"---(The crying turned to sobbing as she rushed to grab me.)---"in my wedding."

"Oh Edith, I am so sorry," I said as she buried her face on my chest just under my chin, and I held tightly to her shoulders and the back of her head.

"Oh, dear God. I can't believe she's gone! So many years. Oh, God. I can't take this dying shit!"

After a few minutes, when she regained some of her composure, I sat her on my sofa, found a box of tissues, and got her a cup of coffee. Her blood-shot eyes indicated she had already been grieving for hours.

"Too many losses," she said after a few minutes of silently sipping coffee. "I am bereavement overloaded."

"Tell me about her," I asked.

"Where do I start? She was always there. We met when I was ten years old."

She reminisced about many experiences with Maria. After a while she even managed to laugh as she recalled memories, some sixty-five years old. For over an hour, she described their relationship and what it had meant to her. "The funeral will be on Thursday afternoon."

"Do you need a ride?" I asked knowing I would be available.

"Oh, Claire, could you take me? Would it be too much trouble? What about your work schedule?"

"This Thursday, I am scheduled off by noon. It is not a problem," I responded, while giving her my most reassuring smile.

5

There was no answer when I phoned Mrs. Behnke the day after returning her to the potentially dangerous environment. Imogene had not yet received the laboratory results. On my second call to Mrs. Behnke, she answered.

"Hi Claire. Thanks for calling. Earl Jr. is here now helping us," she said nervously.

"Just answer me this," I inquired, knowing she couldn't talk. "Are you feeling any different from yesterday?"

"No, the same. Doing what you told me."

Just then, he apparently took the phone from her, "Hey, can I help you?"

"Hello, Earl, this is Claire. I was giving your mom some information that she requested."

"Well, why don't you give it to me instead?" he said impatiently.

"I will even do better. Why don't you give me your address and I will mail it to you so you can study it."

"Route 16, Box 381," he said curtly. "Anything else?"

"Yes, let me talk with your mother again."

"We're busy now."

"Tell her I will call again later."

"Look lady, what do you want?" his voice raised.

"Your mom and dad are wonderful people and the Area Agency on Aging can help them with certain tasks. She has requested this help and I want to make sure she gets it. As their son, I am sure you would not deny them this." I attempted to make my voice as authoritatively firm as possible.

"Okay, you do that," he snapped and hung up.

***

The next day, I called Mrs. Behnke again.

"Claire, he brought that tuna casserole back after you left, but I told him we had already eaten. Then to top it off, Earl shouted from his chair that he was hungry, so I told him he could eat after I gave him a bath. I think Earl Jr. suspects. He asked me a lot of questions about why you were there."

"Have you smelled any strange odors?"

"No."

"Did you tell him about the sheets smelling like perfume?"

"No. But I am so scared. He is very rough with Earl. Last night, I asked him to help me get Earl back in bed, and he basically just threw him. I think he was half drunk."

"I think what hurts the most," she added, "was we treated him nice. He was never whipped or bad-mouthed. But his mother's death hurt him so. He was only fifteen when she died in a tractor accident. He was supposed to help but had detention in school, so was late. The crops had to be harvested and Earl was on the combine attached to the big tractor Libby was driving. After they unhitched the combine, she was hurriedly driving back to the house to check a roast she had forgotten was in the oven. When she hit a ditch wrong the tractor turned over on her, crushing her chest. She died in Earl's arms. A great woman she was. I went to school with her. Earl never blamed Earl Jr. out loud, but their relationship was never the same after that. Junior started drinking and just sort of curled up into himself."

This phone call made me ache. Such a devastating past tragedy, now playing out in Earl Jr.'s own self-destruction as well as the abuse of his parents.

Shortly after talking with Mrs. Behnke, Imogene called me with the laboratory results. Although not imminently life threatening, abnormally high levels of arsenic were present. The physician, who ordered the tests, had called the police. Mr. and Mrs. Behnke needed to be immediately brought in for a complete physical.

***

Escorted by Imogene, Lieutenant Cyril Savage of the State Police arrived at my office a while later. He wanted a full report on Mrs. Behnke's appointment at the agency and my subsequent visit to the farm. I relayed my story, including my growing suspicions. Knowing it would be difficult to prove culpability, a game plan was devised.

"I bet arsenic is all over that farm," said Savage. "Unused insecticides and rodenticides have probably been in their barns for years. We also cannot rule out well water contamination. If any food contained intentional arsenic powder contamination, that food is probably long ingested."

"In other words, this is going to be very difficult

to prove," I said.

"Absolutely."

"How can we help?" asked Imogene.

"If this guy is putting arsenic gas on his stepmother's sheets or powder in their food or water, it is premeditated, attempted murder. But we have got to prove he is intentionally doing this. Claire, you have a relationship with this woman. If possible, we have got to get food samples and sheet analysis."

"Mrs. Behnke washed the sheets the next day after she got sick from them and it hasn't happened since. I tried to get a food sample but he took the casserole away. What do you suggest?"

"Are you taking Mrs. Behnke to the doctor?"

"I hadn't planned on it, but I can do that."

"Okay, you pick her up, and if there is any suspicious cooked food in the house, put it in this plastic bag. After her doctor's appointment, bring her to police headquarters for questioning. We have got to move on this quickly because once he suspects, all evidence is going to disappear. Since she could be living in a dangerous environment, we can't risk being slow. Her husband might be suffering worse than she. They will both need treatment."

I called Mrs. Behnke regarding the follow-up doctor's appointment but divulged nothing over the phone. Her voice was audibly shaking. She felt weak and started to cry, "Now, Earl is complaining of a nagging headache."

"Is Earl Jr. home?" I asked.

"I haven't seen him today. I think he's on a job."

Relieved that he was gone, I said, "If you do see him, tell him I am picking you up to show you the senior center for Earl. I will see you in one hour.

Please be ready."

Lieutenant Savage had given me his cell phone number and a pager. Two back-up police cars would be deployed down the road from the farm. "Keep this in your pocket and press this button if you need assistance. Do not hesitate. Your safety is paramount."

I drove down the isolated driveway thinking that this was a long way from my formerly sheltered suburban life. When I arrived, I looked around for any signs of Junior, and quickly headed for the front door. There was no sense dallying—I wanted to get out of here.

"Well, well, hello again," said Earl Jr. after he opened the door. My hand felt for the pager but I did not press it.

"Good to see you," I said while thinking that getting any food would now be very difficult. "I'm here to take your mom to check out the senior center. It might be just what your dad needs to perk him up."

"They ain't got no money for that kind of stuff."

"No problem, it is calculated on a sliding scale. Some seniors pay nothing. I'm sure you want your dad to have what's best for him," I said, hoping to appeal to whatever sense of caring remained.

"Fine, I'll take her then!" He barked.

"No, Earl Jr.," came a voice from the dining room. She came to the door with her coat already on. "This nice woman just drove all the way out here and I am going with her."

"Jesus Christ, mom," he shouted. "Why are you sneaking around like this? Haven't I been taking care of things?"

"This has nothing to do with you," I said as

kindly as I could so as not to exacerbate his anger. "Mr. Behnke needs to get out of that room and interact with people his own age. This will actually be a big help to you."

"And I suppose you'll want me to trek him back and forth? Well, I ain't got the time!"

"There is a bus that will pick him up and bring him home. Besides, it would only be twice a week."

"Earl Jr.," chimed in Mrs. Behnke. "Dad just ate breakfast and I'll be home to give him lunch. Let's go Claire," she said, walking briskly to my car. I was relieved to be pulling out of the driveway. "This will be resolved soon," I said to Mrs. Behnke.

"My tests are abnormal, aren't they?

"Yes." Then I added, "But it looks like we caught it in time."

Both the doctor and Mrs. Behnke wanted me present at the physical examination, where she revealed recently developed tingling in her fingers and feet. Her abdomen was tender, her skin dry and scaly, and she had complained of a chronic cough. Consistent with the lab finding, the doctor determined she was suffering from chronic arsenic intoxication. He prescribed two drugs, which he would monitor closely since one's side effect included hypertension, which she was already being treated for. He wanted to see Mr. Behnke immediately.

Later, at the police station, Lieutenant Savage asked Mrs. Behnke many specific questions, such as, "Have you had your well water tested?" To which Mrs. Behnke answered, "Yes, found normal a couple of years ago."

"Are there insecticides in the barn?"

"Lots, including rat poison, some of it years, even

decades old." I knew that could be key since arsenic was no longer used in current agricultural chemicals.

Then Savage paused for a while, tapping his pencil on the desk. Finally, after taking a deep breath, "I've decided not to fool around any longer. Treatment won't help if we can't remove the source. Your husband is already an invalid, so this may be even more serious for him. And putting you, Claire, in harm's way is not appropriate. In fact, as we speak, evidence may be disappearing.

Having said that, he picked up the phone to obtain a search warrant of the house, barns, well water, and, of course, the son's trailer. "The search warrant may take a couple of hours. Mrs. Behnke, you stay with Claire—and Claire, give me your cell number. I'll call you when we leave for the farm."

"What about my husband?" cried Mrs. Behnke. "This will really scare him."

"Ma'am, nothing will happen in the next couple of hours. You'll be home by then."

"Charlie," he said to his partner out of earshot of Mrs. Behnke. "Let's get forensics and the lab mobile ready to go. We might only have one shot with this."

I took Mrs. Behnke back to the agency and straight to Sylvia's office, the center's senior social worker. Imogene had already told her we'd be dropping by. By now, Mrs. Behnke was fatigued and looked highly anxious. One of the agency's volunteers was dispatched to the pharmacy to pick up her new medications.

She sat down in Sylvia's office and with quiet resignation put her elbow on the chair's armrest and laid her head in her hand, whispering, "I can't believe this is happening to Earl and me, by our own kin, no less."

Holding her hand, Sylvia wasted no time, "I can get you out of there today. We have funds for temporary emergency housing. It's an assisted living facility nearby. Once you are there, we can work on arranging something more permanent."

"I have no money unless we sell the farm."

"Mrs. Behnke, that might be your ticket to an independent life, where Earl is given the care he needs and you can get the help you need in caring for him. The money you make from the sale of the farm will give you the financial freedom you have worked so hard for."

"What if Earl Jr. is innocent?"

"We must consider him innocent until proven otherwise. But you, and probably Mr. Behnke, are sick from arsenic poisoning coming from someplace on your farm. Whatever the source, it is no longer safe for you to be there."

"Earl won't understand. He grew up there. Maybe I jumped to conclusions. The pipes might freeze this winter. Who will take care of the house? Earl will be mad that I did this." I could tell from Mrs. Behnke's voice and disjointed thinking that she was overwhelmed.

Sylvia was gentle, empathetic, yet didn't beat around the bush. I was impressed with the way she worked. "Tell Mr. Behnke it will only be temporary until the source is cleared up. Mrs. Behnke, this is serious. No one should be afraid to be in their own home. You and your husband are at risk. Arsenic could kill you both.

Just then my cell phone rang and Sylvia directed me to answer. It was Lieutenant Savage.

"It's okay to bring her home now. But her husband looks bad."

Dear, God, they were already there. "Will you stay until we get there?"

"Absolutely."

Sylvia accompanied us back so she could see for herself and do a full report. The farm's front lawn was filled with police cars and a crime scene investigation mobile unit. Savage was talking to Earl Jr. who was visibly shaken and kept balancing himself as if inebriated. "How can you accuse me of this? I didn't do nothing! I moved back to take care of them and this is how they repay me. Go ahead search…you ain't goin' to find nothing!"

Upon seeing his stepmom, Earl Jr. shouted, "Thanks a heap, stepmother dearest. Hope you are satisfied!" Mrs. Behnke almost ran to the front door, panting, tears streaming.

When we entered the house, Earl seemed confused and complained of headache and belly pain. Even though an officer was by his side, he still seemed unaware of what was happening. Sylvia wasted no time calling an ambulance to transport him to the hospital, then asked me to help Mrs. Behnke gather a few of her things. It was hard to know what to pack and the police told us to be quick. Upstairs, forensic personnel were already in her bedroom looking for evidence.

"Oh God!" Mrs. Behnke cried. I quickly helped her put some underwear, a couple of dresses and some toiletries into a bag. She grabbed a framed photo of their wedding day.

"Where are your important papers?" asked an officer as he followed us. Mrs. Behnke went directly to a shoebox in the closet. It contained the will, Medicare forms and the farm's bill of sale, dated 1897. "How about your checkbook, Mrs. Behnke?" I added as the police removed her sheets and pillowcases from the bed and bagged them, asking us to leave the area. "And your medications."

We could now hear the sirens of the ambulance making its way down the driveway, and she quickly retreated to Earl's side. "Honey, we are taking you to the hospital. Your blood pressure is up."

"Margaret, why are the police here?"

"They came to help get you to the hospital." He was too weak to comprehend how little sense this made.

When we left the farmhouse, Savage was still talking to Earl Jr. I put Mrs. Behnke in my car as I heard him shouting at me, "You bitch! You put her up to this!"

"She did no such thing," Savage replied. "Your parents are both sick from arsenic poisoning."

"Fuck you," Earl Jr. angrily retorted, then spit on the ground.

"Okay, we need to continue this questioning at the police station."

"I ain't going nowhere!"

With handcuffs out, Savage replied, "Yes, you are." Two other police officers rushed to assist Savage. "Don't fight this or it will be considered resisting arrest."

"Okay, okay, God-dammit!" Earl Jr. allowed himself to be handcuffed and put in the police car's back seat. The look of rage on his face was directed at me, a look that seared into my mind.

Mrs. Behnke wept as we left. I grabbed her hand

and she squeezed back tightly. No more words were spoken as we drove first to the assisted living facility, where she was warmly welcomed and shown her room, and then to the hospital, where I left her by Mr. Behnke's bedside. She gratefully accepted my ten dollar donation for cab fare back to her interim home.

So much for a safe desk job.

6

When I picked Edith up on the day of the funeral, she was dressed in a gray striped suit with a cameo pin on a high-collared white blouse. Her black pillbox hat had a small veil that extended just below her hairline. Before we left, she checked her make-up and found it already blotched from tears. She dabbed her crocheted-bordered handkerchief under her eyes. Her hands were shaking as our elbows interlocked for stability. I put my free hand on her hand, holding it tightly as we walked slowly to the car.

"I hate funerals and it seems I am going to a lot lately," she finally said. "This funeral is going to be as hard as any I've attended. You know, death does not get easier with practice."

"I never looked at it that way, Edith," thinking how profound that statement really was. We rode to the church in silence, as if any spoken word would have precipitated a deluge of tears. Upon arriving and taking our seats, I noticed how few people, maybe only fifteen, were in attendance in the large church sanctuary. A young minister, who I later found had only met the deceased once in the nursing home, started with the normal obligatory words. It seemed like he was filling in the blanks to a conventional funeral service. "We come today to mourn the death of," he looked down to make sure he had her name right, "Maria Dombroski."

He would need much more practice in personalizing. After ten minutes, he hadn't given me any indication of who Maria really was. He presented her life as if he was reading her obituary-style resume. He apparently felt much safer reading scripture, which he did for way too long. Dry and boring...just the sort of emotionless funeral I hated.

Next a nephew spoke, and it was immediately obvious he didn't know her well either. He recalled two occasions with his aunt, one when he was thirty-plus years younger, where she read to him on her lap while he visited on a family vacation. Edith's tears had entirely dried up. In fact, she was biting her lips and squeezing my hand with nails dug into my palm as if to control her anger. Finally in a burst of energy, she rose bravely from her seat. Knowing she had not been invited to speak, she now asked to say a few words. Before this follow-the-script minister, his mouth wide open, could even respond, she was up at the ornate podium, her head barely showing.

She spoke slowly. "If Maria's funeral had been held ten years ago, many more people would have been here. You see, Maria was active in the community after her retirement as the principal from an elementary school located about 100 miles from here. She volunteered for the Red Cross, knitted hats for newborns at the local hospital, coordinated the local library's literacy program, and taught numerous adults how to read for the first time in their lives. Even when her memory played cruel jokes on her and she couldn't recollect the day of the week, she could still help someone learn to read."

Edith took a deep breath and continued. "And, if her funeral would have been twenty years ago, there would have been hundreds of people here. She was an extraordinary principal, one who teachers loved. It didn't matter if they were brand-spanking new or experienced teachers like myself. Somebody once said she was like a radiator, because you wanted to warm yourself in her glow. If you did well, she praised. If you messed up, she picked you up, dusted you off, and gave you the encouragement to try again. She set high standards and motivated people to live up to them.

"And, if her funeral were twenty-five years ago, hundreds of children would have filled these pews to overflowing. As a teacher, she pushed with love. She went that extra mile. Her classroom was alive and exciting. Her kids looked forward to coming to school because of her. And she wasn't afraid to confront deadbeat parents who were quick to request some Ritalin for their kids' behavior problems. She once brought a doctor to speak to the PTA about the overuse of ADHD drugs and personally called every parent to make sure they came.

"Maria never had children of her own, but she was a mother to hundreds of children. She got more Mother's Day cards than most of us mothers ever did. Once, she even took into her home two siblings who had been abused. She gave them strength to face their future, in spite of its hurdles. Today, one of those kids is a teacher, the other a social worker. They visited her last year from California. Perhaps they don't yet know she is dead.

"Now, so many years later, she dies with only a few surrounding her coffin. Her husband died years ago, as did most of her friends. She is two hours away from the place she spent most of her life. Old age was not kind to her. Her mini-strokes induced dementia and she lay forgotten in a nursing home, save a few visitors, whose presence she gradually became unaware of. I know if she could have, she would have wished for an earlier demise. The last five of her eighty years on earth were sad to witness.

"I grew up with this wonderful human being. Our childhood was extra treasured because we had each other."

Edith cried as if a dam had broken. "I…I, loved her." Then, looking over to the closed coffin, "Thank you Maria for being such a wonderful part of my life. I will never forget you, and we *will* be together soon.

"Say hi to our men for me," she finally said, as her smile broadened from behind the stream of tears.

Edith was shaky descending the three steps towards the pews and I jumped out of my seat to help her. As I led her back, I didn't see a dry eye amongst the few congregants. The minister was the first to thank her, sincerely, for her words. Then the nephew confided that he did not know those things about his aunt. At the cemetery, there was more spontaneous sharing before Edith placed a rose on Maria's coffin and sat, eyes fixed, crying quietly, refusing to leave until the coffin was lowered in the ground.

On the way home, I told Edith that her tribute had touched me greatly. It had. She continued sharing Maria stories as I listened. After arriving home, she went straight to nap without even undressing or folding back the bedcovers. I found a throw blanket to drape over her, placed the flowers Cedric sent on her coffee table, and left. Grieving is hard work.

***

After Maria's funeral, I looked forward to being alone, time I now treasured as my apartment was quickly becoming a refuge. But one small problem prevented that; I had a date, arranged by Betty, a social acquaintance for many years. Our kids were similar ages, therefore we had often sat together on bleachers for little league and soccer games; then as years passed, we hobnobbed at various social functions, where this ex-homecoming queen sported her new Gucci's as she dripped with diamonds.

I found her a gossipmonger, so I was always careful how I talked to her. She was everything I loathed about the desperate housewife---with too much time on her hands, and a closet full of tennis and golf regalia. At times, she reminded me of myself. To be sure, I was less showy, but we were only separated by degrees of lifestyle.

Ross had cowardly given her my new unlisted number, so within a few weeks of our separation, she was opining on the phone about mid-life divorces. I figured I needed to be civil but her insensitive badgering was trying. "Tell me, Claire, was he having an affair?"---(She already knew the answer.)---"You know, men will be men. Listen, Claire, I know somebody at NASA (where her husband's firm did business) who is single and went to Harvard. It is not good to isolate now."

Oh my God, give me a break. This woman would love to add 'Cupid' to her resume! "No Betty, I am not ready to date yet," I said, hoping she wouldn't pursue the affair question again.

I told her about my busy work schedule and my soon-to-be college student status. "Thank you for your kind thoughts about my welfare. Have to run to help a neighbor. I'll call back soon." I hung up with thoughts of getting another new phone number. I knew I should have when she called back again a couple months later.

"Sorry, I haven't called sooner. I have been so busy." My now amateur psychological skills knew that 'so busy' was her mental one-upmanship game, entitled, *'I am busier than you, therefore I am extremely important.'*

Anyway, I just have a minute. Ralph, the guy I told you about months ago, you know, the rocket scientist from Harvard...well, I gave him your number."

"Betty!"

"Oh, come on Claire, he's nice, smart, successful, and single!" Besides, what could one evening hurt? I knew you would say no, which is why I went ahead and gave him your number."

I was livid, but wanted to resist a big showdown. It wasn't worth it. Later, if and when he called, I could simply turn him down by saying "I'm not ready."

Shortly after Betty hung up, the phone rang. It was him, Ralph. After a short conversation, I surmised that my kids would have classified him a major nerd. At fifty-five, he had never been married and I figured he had had about three dates in his life. I don't know why I said yes. Hendricks would say, "So why did you?" To which I would answer, "I didn't want to hurt him? I am lonely? Desperate? Horny? All of the above?" Sick, right?

He was picking me up tonight at six. Please, I thought, can we go to a restaurant in a different state? I would hate being *seen*. I told Cedric, who laughed wildly. "Take a condom," he joked.

"Cedric, go to hell," which just made him laugh more.

The doorbell rang. My first date with a man not my ex in forty years! At the door stood a gentleman in thick framed glasses, thin tie clashing with his sports jacket and avocado shirt. I almost blurted, "Do you want to eat here?" when he said, "I've made reservations."

I decided to curtail my major attitude problem and try to enjoy the evening. We were on different planets. His IQ was double mine, at least. He used words I'd never heard before, not to impress me, but that's, well, how he talked. He talked about his research in the gravitational collapse of black holes and nuclear isotopes in the cosmos. Harvard, to him, was okay for undergraduate study, but he preferred the higher intellectual stimulation of MIT for his doctorate.

He was sincere, excited about his work. I was impressed. After a while, the conversation dragged. I wanted to tell him about my experiences with Mrs. Behnke, but that was confidential. I did talk about the concept of, 'Death does not get easier with practice,' but that conversation was short…he did not appear to have an equally high Emotional IQ. Then, to break another period of silence, I asked, "Read any good books lately?"

"Yes, as a matter of fact, I am reading the *Oxford*

Dictionary."

"You're kidding." I was truly stunned. "You mean the one that's two volumes?"

"That's it. It even comes with a magnifying glass."

Words failed me. My debut date and I am with a guy who is reading the dictionary. "What letter are you on?" trying not to sound sarcastic.

"L"

"Wow, tell me more…"

"Well, it is not as monotonous as one might presume. The *Oxford*, unlike *Webster* and others, actually incorporates the derivation of each word. It is utterly mesmerizing where words come from. For instance, the first dirigible was known as an A-limp. Its faulty design and structure doomed its first test trials, causing it to crash almost immediately after being airborne. So they went back to the drawing board and designed a second limp known as the B-limp. It worked and the blimp was born.

He was right—this was more interesting than I had thought. I was hooked for another hour. I kept throwing out words, below the letter "L," of course, and with his photographic memory at maximum recall, we had a lively discussion. Somehow, however, we both knew there would not be another date. Certainly it would have been fun to proceed through the rest of the alphabet, but we needed more mutual chemistry to sustain us. I had always wondered where the word "mesmerize" had come from, but I could buy my own *Oxford* to figure that out.

At my front door, I told him I respected him a lot, that he was doing worthy work, and reading great books (Ha Ha). But good-bye really was good-bye. I smiled as I shut the door behind me. Eight months post-separation---I had done it!---gone on a date and, after the first five minutes in the restaurant, never again looked around to see if anybody I knew was watching.

***

Shortly after my forgettable date, I found myself thinking about the funeral and Edith. Her friendship was a catalyst for thoughts of my own mother, Alberta, who had died almost two decades ago of pancreatic cancer, a horrid disease. I pulled out my journal and began writing in a descriptive, biographical way, starting with a seemingly inconsequential memory and progressing into the depths of our relationship.

Like Edith, mom was a product of the Great Depression and that experience shaped the rest of her life. As an adult, she had shopped with a cooler, buying on-sale chicken from one store, two-for-one pork roasts at another. Save every penny. Once, when I was knee deep in diapers and crying toddlers, she phoned to announce that broccoli was fifty percent off at the Acme. When she sensed my I-could-care-less attitude, she inquired if she could buy some for me. "Sure, mom, knock yourself out," I thought.

Love/hate defined our 'normal' complicated mother-daughter relationship. I had always laughed at her when she described walking one mile to school in two feet of snow. How stupid I had thought. I wouldn't have done that in a million years. I just couldn't fathom it.

As an adult, she was dismayed once again when telling me a thirty-year-old story of a cousin ruining her new shoes by running in mud puddles after trying them on during an afternoon visit. She had cried for days. I hadn't a clue what new shoes meant to a young girl during the Depression.

Her father had rejected her desire to attend nursing school back in 1940 ("It's not for you."), after which she resigned herself and seemingly accepted her societal place. She appropriately married at twenty-two so as not to earn the title, 'Old Maid.' Later as a young mother, she wanted me to get the education she never attained, while still modeling my life after hers as if to validate her existence.

Once she revealed that as a new mother (perhaps still drugged in the delivery's recovery room), she wept when told her newborn (me) was a girl because she thought my dad would be disappointed. He, of course, along with countless other post WWII men, had coveted a 'junior' to become his baby boomer namesake. By not being the preferred gender, I threw a temporary wrench in their American dream. My mom's own self-esteem was so low that she decided to share this tidbit with me one day, as if to knock my confidence down a notch or two. Her pent-up hostility worked. Later that day, for no reason, I kicked the shit out of my younger brother after which I had to clean his room and iron my father's underwear. Another angry young woman, 'made-in-America.'

Sometime later, just before Tampax became part of my life, we had the obligatory sex talk. Visibly nervous, she proceeded to inform me that men put their 'thing' into a woman and, well, like, pee into you. I was grossed out. At 13, I would stay a virgin forever, I thought. So much for my sex education.

When I got pregnant and dropped out of college, she was horrified, demanding, "Don't tell anybody!" Again, skeletons in her closet were painstakingly kept there. Loose women didn't publicly exist in her friendship circle. Premarital sex was sin. Still, she would see to it that her knocked-up daughter (as well as her ability to raise a virtuous child) would not fall victim to the scandalous gossip circuit. She worked non-stop to produce a quick, albeit proper, wedding before my dress size changed.

Thankfully my mom lived long enough for me to mature, and I came to appreciate the good qualities she had. Before her death, we made strong attempts to understand our relationship. Cancer does give you the gift of time, limited but not wasted. She had been unsung, unrecognized, and unpraised. Yet over the years, I watched her volunteer at church and firehouse fundraisers and for my 4-H club. While I longed for the preppy clothes of rich kids, she made my dresses with love. When I cheerleaded my way to a varsity letter, she went to every game. To send me to college, she even took (secretly, of course) a second job cleaning the offices of her own father. I credit her with, for better or worse, giving me that same pride.

When I had walked away from the fresh grave containing her ashes, I focused on a memory of my eighth grade graduation, circa, 1961. The boys wore dark suits and the girls white dresses. The skies were dreary on the day that my mother and I were to shop for my special dress. We were both excited as she went to the bank and cashed her week's paycheck.

Going to virtually every store within a certain radius, we shopped until we almost dropped. I tried on what seemed like a hundred dresses. Some didn't fit, some were not to either of our taste; some were too expensive. We noted the contents of each store in our search, talking the whole time on this exciting day. Our final decision took us back to the store with the perfect dress.

I knew it was more than she had wanted to spend, but this was her daughter's graduation. The beautiful white dress was wrapped in tissue and boxed. I hugged her as we left the purchase counter. Then it came...thunder and lightning raging from a dark sky. A torrential downpour met us at the store's front door, forcing us to wait it out. Finally, after the storm had subsided a bit and impatience got to us both, we decided to make a run for the car, a 1958 black Ford sedan. We got soaked, but each of us protected the dress. By the time we were safely inside the car, we were laughing almost hysterically.

"Thanks, Mom," I said as we took turns surveying our dripping hair in the rear view mirror.

Oh, the stories I could tell...the snippets of time that become treasured memories. My mother was dead...my pain was unbelievable. As I tried to dissect my feelings by her graveside, this rather trivial story was foremost in my mind. It was what I had left. As the final shovel of dirt fell over her urn, I regretted not thanking her ever again for that white dress.

Her death and funeral were the toughest days of my life. I was numb (when I was not crying). Then, for weeks after, I tried to capture the vivid details of our lives together. I sought solace in my memories. My intense grief seemed almost my final gift to her; my last thank-you played out in thousands of painful, guilt-ridden tears. I pitied her lost potential, and the compromises she made for me, all at her expense. For her entire life, she frequented doctor's offices with vague complaints, amassing thick charts that most likely had 'depression' scribbled somewhere.

Later, after I was done sympathizing for her, I started pitying myself for the same reasons. Perhaps I carried my own inherited burden of neurosis. We were not the perfect family but it was not a tortuous upbringing either. My parents had done their best with the imperfect tools they had.

Oh Mom, I miss you.

Tomorrow, thankfully, I could process this further in therapy.

7

"Know what a significant emotional event is?" Shirley asked.

"Not really, but I bet it has something to do with divorce." I replied.

"Or death or illness or going back to school, maybe even reading a book. It is when something happens in your life that forces you to rethink or reevaluate former beliefs or values."

"Bet you are going to include the big word--- *change*."

"Yep, it is an opportunity to learn and that, my friend, changes you."

"Not all people take advantage of significant emotional events when they present themselves," Shirley continued. "And many more never seek them out."

"An example here would help," I said.

"For instance, a woman who finally leaves a long-term pathetic marriage, then finds herself suffering from anger, loneliness, and insecurity, and gets more focused on finding herself a replacement man than using the opportunity for self-evaluation. More than a few of those women get into another pathetic marriage."

"I am not looking for another man."

"I am not talking about you specifically. You just asked for an example. But this journaling that you have shared is significant and emotional and it is helping you reevaluate your whole being. It is hard work but worth it."

"Like the truth will set me free but first it will piss me off."

Shirley smiled.

***

Besides journaling, I usually left her office with an assignment. My book list was long: Alice Miller's *The Drama of the Gifted Child*, Rollo May's *Love and Will*, Karen Horney's *The Neurotic Personality of Our Time* among many others. When I would be at the bookstore, I also purchased less-weighty materials such as *How to Survive the Loss of a Love* (a book which took twenty minutes to read and hours to think about). Once I found a book on creative divorce (written by a man) that talked about the "rebound" phenomenon. Like Shirley said, seems too many people seek to replace the missing spouse too soon. I hadn't known the divorce rate for second marriages was even higher than it is for first ones. Once again, the ridiculous concept of two half-people seeking to become one by "merging" doesn't work. Some divorcees run around pursuing replacements like chickens with their heads cut off, doing all sorts of searching except of the soul, like rearranging the deck chairs on the Titanic. Not me, thank you…single is not a bad life. Right now I can handle alone….I think.

One time, Shirley gave me a quote from a letter

written by Rainer Maria Rilke (1903):

"Be patient toward all that is unsolved in your heart and try to love the questions themselves… Do not seek the answers that cannot be given you because you would not be able to live them. And the point is to live everything. Live the questions now. Perhaps you will gradually, without noticing it, live along some distant day into the answers."

***

Of course, Shirley had asked about the kids. "They have endured their share of growing pains," I said. "Rossy, a nickname after Ross Jr., was our love baby, with parents barely ready to start their own lives, let alone raise a helpless other. Our small family's surviving strength was, I suppose, our inherited sense of responsibility and the assistance of our parents. Ross and I were able to get an apartment that was midway between families, and with his parents footing the tuition, he commuted to the university three days per week while I got a job as some executive's gofer. Grandmothers served our infant son well, but were tired after the day and surely not enamored with such time-demands as they approached their own senior years."

I flashed again on the sacrifices my mother had made. She had even gone to flea markets for cheap kids' clothes.

"Thankfully Ross was older than I and finished college when Rossy was just one-year-old. With some luck and a fair amount of nepotism, he landed his first job as an assistant manager in a manufacturing firm. His salary was adequate, so I could quit work, much to the relief of grandmoms."

"And were you happy to do that?" Shirley had

asked.

"I spent my days scurrying around with a toddler thinking about my peers taking fifteen credits, going to football games, and preparing for *careers* not jobs. With a huge demarcation between the college single life and us, my reunions with Gloria were sporadic and many old friends just disappeared from my social radar screen. When Rossy was two, I was pregnant again.

"Our second son, Peter, was special in that Ross witnessed this birth after we took childbirth classes. There was an immediate bonding between father and son.

"Ross continued to get promotions and eventually an MBA. When the kids started school, he was recruited by another large firm as a mid-level manager with a commensurate salary that put us into our first rental home. We were on our way to the American dream. Within two years and more advancements, we moved again…up, of course, into our first purchased home.

"I was now living *Father Knows Best.* I mixed well with my suburban neighbors, became active in church, volunteered some, and even hosted a Tupperware party. Ross was a good father, outwardly a hard-working, blue-ribbon husband, who was home except for a weekly golf game with colleagues. On our tenth anniversary, he brought me that long overdue engagement ring that sparkled, making others envious. 'You are so lucky,' they told me. I felt fortunate."

"So you were happy?" Shirley injected.

"By mainstream definition, our 1970s life was good. By the time the boys were approaching middle school, we had bought property to build our dream home. I would spend two years doing such things as picking out the fixtures for bathrooms and planning color and curtains. We moved in, complete with house-warming party. I was also pregnant again.

"Our new daughter, Katherine (Kate), would be raised to become a doctor or a lawyer. The women's movement was in full swing, and with my prodding, she would ride the wave. Later I would both love her and envy her for the opportunities she had and I squandered."

"You didn't answer my question," Shirley persisted. "*Were* you happy?"

"I pretended to be. Shirley, I think that's when it hit me about what I had blown. Until then, I never consciously questioned my life. Sure, there were pangs, but I mostly brushed them aside. One episode of acutely feeling in the dumps, which I described as 'blue' to my doctor, landed me a prescription for Valium, complete with its lethargic side effects. I hated it. A talk with my minister made me realize what a terrific life I had, after which I threw the remains of the bottle down my new garbage disposal.

"So, was I happy? No, Shirley, I was not."

***

On a lovely March Friday, I drove away for the weekend to the Jersey shore all by my blooming existential self. Bundled up, I took a sailing lesson on Barnegat Bay. I was historically prone to seasickness but on this windy day I didn't feel nauseous as *I* controlled the boat. With the guidance of my experienced instructor, who I might add informed me that his mother was my age, I steered that forty-foot catamaran like a seasoned sailor. Twenty-five knot winds caused us to heel considerably but I white-knuckled the helm and repeatedly came-about with precision.

"Coming back?" he inquired at the mooring.

"Maybe," although I had begun feeling a bit queasy and had my doubts.

I chalked it up as another significant emotional event, albeit not earth shattering. Later that Saturday night, I ate by myself in a restaurant and the calamari was delicious.

The very next weekend, on Shirley's recommendation, I attended an assertion for personal effectiveness workshop. At first hesitant to participate in some sophomoric how-do-you-feel group, I eventually became stimulated and realized I had wasted a lot of time being passive.

That night Edith had cooked a delicious stew for us. "Okay what did you learn today? I am all ears."

"Do you know that giving someone the silent treatment is passive-aggressive behavior?"

"Like if your husband forgets your birthday and you don't speak to him for a week?"

"Yes, something like that….especially without telling him why. Or giving a poor waitress a penny tip because you didn't like the way your steak was cooked?"

"Ouch! So what else did you learn?" Edith inquired. "I know us old-fashioned dames were never taught to be assertive. Remember, *obey* was in our marriage vows."

"True for me also. In fact at this workshop I got a new version of the fairy tales we all grew up reading. Do you know that Cinderella is classic child abuse?"

"Not surprised."

"The step-mother and daughters were ever so uggg-ly. Of course Cinderella is drop-dead gorgeous. Cinderella was a slave in her own household, even though she happily cleaned while singing merrily with birds and mice. And, after the prince announced he wanted to check out the *meat* market of available women, otherwise known as a ball, these same creatures find cast-off remnants to make a gown, which is cruelly ripped off her body by the jealous step-sisters."

"Cute! Ripping off clothes, jealousy—all dysfunctional." chimed Edith.

"Cinderella, of course, cries instead of proclaiming, 'Screw this shit…I am getting out of this oppressive household.' Where is social services when you need it?" I hollered.

"But, Edith! Alas! Enter fairy godmother. Don't you wish you had one? Pumpkins get an extreme makeover and turn into carriages. Mice become horses, and a magic wand produces a magnificent gown that surrounds her eighteen inch waist. We are pleased that her small feet get glass slippers."

Edith laughed. "Remember the Fats Waller song…*Can't love you if your 'feets' too big.* Okay, okay, I know what's coming next…Be home by midnight!"

I was on a roll now. "Upon entering the castle, the prince is immediately enamored with her beauty. They dance the night away, unfortunately failing to exchange names and addresses. Beauty trumps the two brain cells in her head. The clock strikes. She runs. He follows and searches until, Viola! The shoe fits and they get a 'happily-ever-after,' where we can only assume she has a maid and is an ageless, perfect mother. Can you imagine a future decided solely by the size of your foot?"

Edith stared intently, "Dear girl, I never looked at it that way. With all the conditioning us women have been tricked into believing, it almost seems like heresy to trash this age-old fairy-tale. Kind of like condemning apple pie."

"Wait till you hear about Snow White! It's another story of competition and prejudice among women, a sort of horizontal hostility."

"Wait a minute. What's that? Horizontal what?"

"Horizontal hostility; basically prejudice against one's own kind. Like black-on-black or women-on-women. And women can sure have hostilities towards one another. Not that we need to be some cozy bunch banded together solely because of our gender or our shared societal suppression. Like, here's an example--many stay-at-home moms are looking for ways to fault the working mother. The best way to do this? Find the ways that their kids are screwed up. As for working mothers, well, some may look at full-time moms as pathetic creatures chained to an allowance, slave to a man, and living in a ghetto of professional deprivation while climbing the suburbia ladder instead of the career one."

"Wow! 'Ghetto of professional deprivation?' You go girl."

"You know though," Edith continued, "I *have* seen women be more catty and backstabbing towards each other. When I was teaching and the kids were still young, a woman from our church told others how sorry she felt for me because I had to work—implying her status, and that we must have been too poor for me to stay at home. What a crock. Anyway get back to Snow White…"

"Well, the evil queen is obviously menopausal and plastic surgery hasn't been invented yet."

Edith almost fell off her chair laughing, then snorted, "Mirror, mirror, on the wall, who's the fairest of them all?"

"Then, one day the vain queen, who I suspect was more than a bit egocentric and expecting the same daily pretentious kudos, becomes enraged when the mirror takes an about-face, proclaiming, "Sorry queen, but you've got younger competition."

"After the initial temper tantrum, the queen, now in a totally bitchy, hubristic mood, composes herself enough to think through a solution. 'Kill her!' she demands of a spineless huntsman. 'And bring me back her heart as proof of her demise.' Thank God the huntsman's wimp-like qualities spare her. Instead he brings back the heart of a deer and sends a trembling Snow White into the dark forest to be rescued by seven dwarfs, metaphorically representing children. The dwarfs, it turns out, are in dire need of a good woman. The house is a mess and they have most likely been eating Spam for months."

Edith howled and reached for the Chardonnay, "I need another glass of wine for this!"

"Before long, Snow White has a broom in her hand and is making pies. She implores Grumpy, to his chagrin, to wash his hands before dinner. Afterwards, she entertains them with dance, and tucks them into bed with a kiss on the forehead.

"'Don't open the door,' they tell her before hi-hoeing off to work. But can a passive Snow White turn down a poor, aged lady, who also happens to be very uggg-ly? She eats the apple and goes catatonic.

After seeking revenge and killing the queen, the dwarfs, in a final act of sociopathy, seal her in a glass coffin. Enter prince, who has heretofore been on the periphery. One kiss, apple falls out, and off she goes to the castle with a man she just met."

Edith added, "You know, even in the 1950s, I refused to read this story to my third graders. Even then, I thought it too violent—but come Halloween, many of my girl students were dressed like Snow White…or Cinderella."

"And Edith, there are modern day versions. In the movie, *Pretty Woman,* a beautiful prostitute, Julia Roberts, rescues Richard Gere, who in turn rescues her, or maybe he rescues her first…whatever. Both Cinderella and Snow White have their 20th and 21th century updates. They still don't have it right, although they are better. But beauty still towers, still wins, as does getting a prince, preferably a rich one."

"What's changed?" I continued. "Same story, different venue."

"But, can watching *Cinderella* and *Snow White* really screw you up that badly?"

"I guess one has to ask how often these stories played out in schools or in the work place? In my life, I can think back on many incidences—like in eighth grade, circa early 1960s, a veterinarian telling me *his* profession is no place for a woman. And, we still have not made Cinderella, let's say *average* looking. Sure we have now given her some brains, sometimes even a Ph.D. For a time, she might even 'bitch' or repel her rescuer. She hasn't forgotten her lessons in how to play hard-to-get."

Edith started laughing again, "You mean, No, No, No! Yes! She melts into his arms. The shrew is tamed. Let's drink to that!"

"You know, I remember going to my childhood bedroom after hearing Bert Parks sing, 'Here she is, Miss America.' I even reenacted the questioning part...with perfect answers. There I was, in my ten by thirteen foot room with a catalog-ordered Sears & Roebuck bedspread dreaming of the 1950s ultimate goal for women, Miss America."

I continued. "Women's liberation, of course, really stomped those little fairy tales. Many women I suppose became very angry, like I am now, as they became protagonists in their own stories of subjugation and dreams that did not include being president of the United States."

"I am sixty and grew up in the 1950s and 60s. That is what it was...before those radically labeled bra-burning feminists tried changing the way it was, just like Martin Luther King was trying to get people into a multiple-step racist recovery process. The women's and black liberation movements were, I suppose, significant emotional events for a whole society. My mother couldn't do it and I could have but didn't. I rooted for them but didn't join or take advantage of this. My baby's diaper needed changing. I am a very late-bloomer."

"My girl," said Edith, "you are changing, right before my eyes."

"Gosh Edith, I am doing all of the talking."

"I am loving it. This is mentally orgasmic! You know, once I had a girl student, maybe nine-years-old, who wanted to be a doctor. I remember telling her, 'That's nice.' That's all I said. I didn't really advocate for her, or push.

"Claire," Edith continued in a soft, introspective

voice, "you know something--you don't have the monopoly on regrets. And, as much as I am laughing, there is sadness right below the surface."

***

Now thirty-nine, Rossy, who had grown to detest that name, came over for brunch on Sunday, with Jennifer, his significant other of two years. Nervous about him seeing my apartment for the first time since all the boxes had been eliminated, and in an effort to make it look especially cozy, I sprinkled fresh bouquets of flowers around.

Our separation had been painful for him, despite his being older and independent. He had kept asking both Ross and I, "Why can't you work it out? You've had forty years together!" It was hard to answer that question because I did not want to put him in the position of having to take sides.

I didn't want our children hating their father. Tough as it was to behave rationally, Ross and I promised not to talk vindictively about each other to the children.

Even so, Rossy knew about the 'other woman' and had angrily expressed his disappointment to his father. He had actually told his father to leave her out of his life; he had no intentions of 'double-dating' at this point. This had been a blow to Ross, Sr. who rather loved showing off his new woman. He hadn't anticipated this rejection from Rossy, and for that matter, all of his children.

I would be lying if I pretended not to be pleased about this. I rather enjoyed envisioning Ross's awkwardness. He loved his kids, but the kids felt sorry for me, and it was tempting to milk their pity.

After a short first marriage and three years of

bachelorhood, Rossy, now an attorney for a private law firm, met Jennifer, an ICU nurse in the area's largest hospital. Even before the separation, Jennifer and I had had a nice relationship and, when she was off-duty, we had spent a fair amount of personal time together shopping or going to lunch.

"Well, um, want a tour my new apartment?" I said to them with a nervous giggle.

"Sure Mom." The short, but enthusiastic tour began. By now I loved my apartment in a mid-sized adults-only complex, its dark wood nestled in the woods and within sight of the meandering Delaware River. I had two bedrooms, a den, living-dining area, a kitchen with granite countertops, and a two-hundred-year-old oak tree whose leaves gently touched my long balcony.

Small talk followed. Then, as if waiting for just the right moment, Rossy looked at me and announced that he and Jennifer were getting married. I was ecstatic and continued with a multitude of questions. When? Where? How big? It was Jennifer's first marriage and she wanted the full deal. But I had learned that, as the mother of the groom, you don't push with wedding advice. "Ask the bride what she wants you to wear, including the exact color, then just show up," one of my girlfriends had told me. "It's the bride's (and her mother's) day. Ask how you can help, then do *only* what you are told." I would follow that wise counsel.

Rossy hugged me tight when he left. He made me feel proud…that I had mothered him right. "I love you, Mom." That was music to my ears. Afterwards, the pangs of sadness started…Ross and I would not share this day as a couple. I had a strong urge to call him and share my feelings about this wonderful event. Instead, I pulled out my journal and started with the words, *"Ross, you son-of-a-bitch…"*

***

My other son, Peter, is working in China for a large computer firm. When he had heard about the separation, he offered to fly home, but seemed relieved when I told him it wasn't necessary. Besides, he was scheduled to come back to the states permanently in a few months. At thirty-seven, he was married to Linda and childless, but thinking seriously about adopting a Chinese girl (boys don't often go up for adoption in China).

Three months before the separation, Ross and I had visited them in China. I e-mailed him or Linda almost every day. He was a nice kid and a hard and affable worker.

***

My beautiful daughter, Kate, now twenty-eight, attends graduate school in Boston, getting her master's in public health administration. She is independent, ambitious, self-disciplined, maintains a part-time job, and is confident as a single woman. She visited during her spring break, and was my first overnight guest. We could talk about many things but I honored my word about not trashing her father. Kate prodded some but backed off when I set the boundaries, even saying she admired me for taking the high road, thus sparing her and her brothers from getting in the 'middle.' And, like Rossy, she was angry at her father's indiscretions. I did finally level with her that it had been for the best, and I meant it.

We talked about my plans to start college in the fall and finish my degree, in what I wasn't sure. Kate was encouraging, minimizing my nervousness by relating how many older, non-traditional students attended classes with her. "Mom, a lady in one of my classes is seventy-four-years-old, and will soon be celebrating her fiftieth wedding anniversary."

All in all I felt the kids adjusted healthily to our separation. Certainly they grieved. It was a big loss for them. But, they had their own lives now, and the stability of a tenuously united home was no longer necessary. Besides, I had my own life also, including a fulfilling job, except for the Earl, Jr. part, which played in my mind frequently.

8

Imogene stuck her head in my office to relay that Officer Savage could not yet press charges on Earl, Jr. due to insufficient evidence. As anticipated, arsenic had been found in numerous places throughout the barns, namely in decades-old insecticides and pesticides. The well water was negative, adding to the unproved hypothesis of purposeful food pollution.

I had already done my personal investigation on arsenic. *Wikipedia* said it was once called the "inheritance" poison because of the difficulty in detecting it once ingested, and included several famous case studies. All I had remembered about it was from my senior high school play, *Arsenic and Old Lace*.

While most of the containers of powder on the farm seemed untouched, having crusted outside layers, one appeared recently disturbed, causing the contents to settle differently, like some utensil had pierced through the crust and scooped out the middle powdery part. Still no incriminating finger prints could be uncovered and no traces were found anywhere else, save a small amount mixed with oatmeal on the floor under a cabinet in Earl Jr.'s trailer, which he said was used for rat poisoning. Of course that was plausible.

The news was disappointing. The opportunity to obtain food samples had passed. Earl Jr. would likely go free. While I hadn't heard from him, I still worried about his words, "I'll get you for this." I was thinking about the Behnkes when Marion came to relieve me.

"Child, don't let that man intimidate you," she said after I told her my thoughts. "And don't let this man ruin your day. You're starting college again this afternoon. Kick butt! This is an exciting time. You've been waiting for this for forty years!"

***

Having already been to campus to purchase books, I knew to dress down so as not to call more attention to myself. My uniform of jeans and a tee was actually easy for me. Walking into that classroom would be the hard part. I was well-prepared, complete with pencil case, a brand-new notebook with neatly labeled dividers, and the unused eighty-nine dollar Seventh Edition of *Developmental Psychology*. My palms were seriously sweating.

As I veered my way through the morass of adolescents, who were either talking on cell phones or screaming joyfully at reuniting with friends they hadn't seen all summer, I wondered if I was crazy. Besides the professors, where was somebody my age?

My first class was instantly disappointing. The professor, Dr. Hal Stevens, seemed hardly older than Kate, and had probably spent the last ten years progressing from undergraduate school to grad school, then directly to his Ph.D. Except for internships, this was his first teaching position. He was a straight-from-the-book theorist, all business. From my corner seat in the back, I considered dropping the course. He was an arrogant elitist academic, who read from his state-of-the-art power point presentation. Since the class was large, I knew he would give multiple-choice tests, which I hated. I was out of my element, the oldest student in the classroom. What the hell was I doing here?

After class, I spoke with him. "Dr. Stevens, I haven't been in a college classroom in forty years, ah…"

He gave me a look of "So, what am I supposed to do about that?" He was not going to be warm and fuzzy. Now stuttering, I said, "If I, ah, need more help, would you, ah, be available?"

"My office hours are listed in the syllabus," he said while busily packing his things. "I can answer your questions then, but you must keep up with the work."

"Asshole," I thought. Actually he was probably as nervous as I was, lording his power and status because he was insecure. My shrink has nothing over me. I can diagnose a repulsively pompous, phony know-it-all in a heartbeat.

The one saving grace to the whole disastrous class was when Linda, a twenty-one-ish co-ed with flawless skin, leaned over her desk chair and introduced herself, "What's your major?"

"Psychology, I think."

"I love seeing older students like you. You have so much to add to classes like this. You bring all of your life experience. My mother has thought about going back to college. I'm going to tell her about you."

"Thank you. You have made my day," I replied with a relieved smile.

My second class, a social work introductory course, was immeasurably different. Dr. Marilyn Short was hugging familiar students as I walked in. "So good to see you again. Did you have a nice summer? Ready for another semester?"

"Did you go for that job?" she directed at me. How nice she had remembered talking to me that day at the bulletin board.

"Yes, I am working as their information assistance person."

"Like it?"

"Yes, but it's challenging. Just like you said, there are a lot of seniors with problems."

"Lots of work to do. A very worthy organization. You will learn a lot. Met Imogene yet?"

"Oh yes. She is great, knowledgeable, and patient with me."

She placed the chairs in a circle and told people to make nametags on folded five by seven inch index cards. Nametags? No professor had ever done that before. She had a motherly look: short hair, done in a simple short cut, with a purple blouse draped over her long, flowered skirt. Her sandals with matching socks told me that comfort was of the upmost importance, and her body said, 'I stopped dieting years ago and I am content without a waist.' As she gently called the class to attention, her smile spread from ear to ear. "I hope this is an exciting semester for all of us. Please call me Marilyn."

What? She can't be for real!

I was taking this class because social work intrigued me. Forty years ago I was a psychology major, with dean's list grades, but I wasn't sure what I would do in this field now. Given my age, advanced degrees were unlikely and taking a social work introductory course might move me closer to a more immediately usable major. So far, based only on professors, social work was more appealing.

The class was actually relaxing without being dull. The students participated. Marilyn would lecture but her main objective was experiential learning, where students actually went into the field and learned first-hand. We would have choices; some students, like me, were interested in senior citizens, others in cancer care, or troubled teenagers and drug addictions.

There would be no tests or exams, just writing; journals (Oh boy, more journaling!) and book analyses. By the end of the semester, Marilyn assured us, we would have a good idea about the social work profession, enough to decide if we wanted to pursue it further. Fair enough, I was game. Mostly, I just loved this teacher. When we went around the room and introduced ourselves, she welcomed me and two others as non-traditional students, saying we could bring much to the classroom. I was honored, even though I was nervous about how much I could really bring.

After class, students milled around as if not wanting to leave just yet. Most wanted to talk with Marilyn about field experience ideas. She was positive when I asked her about doing mine at the Agency on Aging. "Check with Sylvia, their chief social worker; a great teacher." The thought of a student experience with Sylvia captivated me. I already admired and respected her greatly for the work I had seen her do, not the least of which with Mrs. Behnke. Plus she worked practically next door to my office. I could put in my work hours and then assist her, certainly learning a great deal in the process. I hoped she would be open to accepting me for the few hours this introductory course required.

9

By mid-October spectacular multi-colored leaves dotted trees on hillsides luring me into taking long walks. I loved fall, along with the fact that I had made it to mid-semester and settled into student life. Most importantly, I hadn't needed to see Professor Stevens for extra help, and I was learning quickly at my job, which was proving satisfying beyond my expectations. While I referred a lot of seniors to appropriate resources, I had the opportunity to work personally with many. I initiated Meals on Wheels for those who, being too frail to cook, had reduced their diets to bologna and Wonder Bread. I had also helped several families register their loved ones for the dementia day care unit. The Behnkes were recovering slowly and after Mr. Behnke's discharge from the hospital, they were living together again in a sunlit room at the assisted living facility.

On one very beautiful day, I was walking briskly from Stevens' class to Short's. Stevens had been particularly boring, reading to us from his sophomoric power point, which also corresponded exactly to our hand-outs—the proverbial triple whammy---read it on the screen in front of the classroom, while the professor also reads it to you, then read the very same thing in your hand-outs, after which he turns and gives some lame example that he most assuredly read from some book. With each frame, I could anticipate the multiple choice question for the next test. Rote memorization was the core of this class. The main game was to handle the 'trick' questions. I began thinking that this course was costing me, with books, over $1500. Thankfully I had alimony because at the agency, it would take me weeks to earn that.

I would probably say an 'A' when someone like Cedric asked, "What'd you get?" I would have more difficulty if he asked, "What did you learn?"

Stevens had already picked out his most favored students, all female co-eds with long hair and daunting looks. He called on them more, made jokes and snickered while they begrudgingly smiled, careful not to insult him and jeopardize their grade. One of the 'chosen' was my friendly seatmate, Linda. "Be careful," I warned her with motherly wisdom.

On the other hand, Marilyn's class was stimulating, learning at its best. I couldn't wait to get there and see what she had in store for us. The provocative discussions were lively. No questions were regarded as stupid. She talked without notes and rarely read more than a couple of sentences to us. She told stories from her extensive experience that helped us grasp relevant theories. While her classroom seemed casual, she was masterfully prepared and pumped up with contagious enthusiasm.

At the end of class that afternoon, Marilyn mentioned that a special guest speaker was coming to a nearby auditorium. His topic, non-profit organizations, would be a great potential for learning.

"It is rather early in your social work studies for this, but when opportunity knocks, we go. I realize many of you have other obligations but come if you can."

I was tired and thinking of going home to put my feet up, but decided I could learn something. After all, it was only an hour.

When he walked into the auditorium, I was instantly captivated. "*What a dignified-looking man*," I thought. Tieless shirt, sports jacket, tall, athletic looking with only a hint of a bulging stomach, thinning salt and pepper hair with a natural curl, and a smile to die for. He had crow's feet around his kind, clear blue eyes. He was not quite Robert Redford or Paul Newman, but his smile made him just as striking.

He seemed comfortable in the classroom, having hugged Marilyn upon entering. I watched him talking to her, hand in one pocket, appearing so professional, confident. Who was he? I quickly flipped to the hand-out given at the door—Scott Dison, MBA, MPH, retired director of the Community Foundation.

Scott Dison gave the impression of being a CEO of some major corporation, which he later verified was true. But corporate life had proved too cutthroat, too compromising, and too hypocritical. He took his money and went back to school for a Masters in Public Health and later launched the area's first foundation dedicated to helping non-profits.

By the time he retired as president of the foundation, he had garnered millions of dollars for numerous local charities. His efforts had won national recognition, and his ongoing consultant and volunteer efforts had assisted communities across the country in modeling their foundations on his remarkable work. Yes, now I remembered reading about him in the newspapers.

His talk was on the plight of non-profits in this faltering economy. I listened intently to his words and philosophy, and I couldn't keep my eyes off of him. Then it happened…he mentioned that his wife had died two years ago. Instantly, I felt like a school girl, only I'm sixty and he's sixty-five…or so.

Does he date? How could I approach him? I couldn't believe how my post-menopausal brain rushed from one thought to another. At what age does hormonal attraction stop? Or does it ever? Well, shit, I guess not at sixty.

I raised my hand to ask the most intellectual question I could muster, only half-heartedly caring what the answer was. "I work for an agency that has to have bake sales to support Meals on Wheels for the frail, vulnerable elderly, and we still have a waiting list. What other options would you suggest?"

"Good question," he began launching into a detailed answer.

Then I caught myself—I had played these fucking games in high school and college. Is sixty a *carte blanche* for a repeat performance of the same age-old trickery? Was I going to expect him to make the first move after I cunningly put out feelers? Was this a quest to have another man by my side? Was I really attracted to him or was I just having yet another attack of anxiety and loneliness after ten months of being separated? "Grow up Claire," I said to myself. Thankfully I had an appointment with Dr. Hendrix the next day.

After the lecture, I quickly packed up my notes, and having talked myself out of any further pursuit of this fantasy, proceeded to exit. Besides, I was one week overdue to get my hair highlighted, dressed like an aging hippie, and sported a senior citizen white-headed pimple.

"Oh, ma'am," he shouted as I was almost out the door. A 'ma'am' must be me, since almost everybody else would be an 'Oh, miss'. I stopped and took a deep breath before turning around. He was looking straight at me.

"I forgot to add one more thought when I answered your question," he said as I approached him.

Question, I thought? What was my question?

He explained and I listened, looking straight into his eyes.

"Thank-you, Mr. Dison, for your input. I really enjoyed your talk." Then looking around to make sure nobody else was in earshot, "By the way, do you date?"

"Er..ah…" then he paused, eyes squinting. "Well I don't keep a little black book, if that's what you mean." Finally chuckling, "Actually, a couple of months ago, I had my first date since my wife died. It was, shall we say, a one-time only."

"On my first date after my separation, I went out with a guy who was reading the dictionary."

"You're kidding."

"*Oxford*, unabridged, complete with a magnifying glass."

Come on assertiveness training, I thought---this might be my lone shot. Only in the movies would I ever run into this guy again. "Would you like to go for a cup of coffee sometime?" Jesus, for the first time in my life, I just asked a guy out!

Just then Marilyn approached, after having been

talking with another student. "Hi, Claire. Nice talk by Scott, huh?"

"Yes, I learned a lot."

Then, turning to Scott, Marilyn said, "I want you to meet our dean."

"Sure," he said.

She started to lead him away, but he stopped, came back and handed me his business card. With a slight twinkle in his eye he said, "Claire, call me."

***

On the way back from class, via the grocery store, I was still beaming with pride over my courageous move with Scott. All relationships begin as strangers, I had been told. An ambulance's flashing lights caught my eye as I pulled into my condo's parking lot. Seeing the medics at Edith's apartment, I sprinted to her door. "May I help you?" asked the rescue worker blocking my entrance.

"I'm a neighbor and good friend. What happened?"

"Seems she has fallen and possibly broken her hip. She's in a lot of pain and can't move."

When I tried to rush past him, he stopped me again. "Edith!" I shouted.

"Oh, Claire, help me, help me!"

With that, he let me pass. Still lying on the floor in her bedroom, the other medics were preparing to transfer her to a stretcher. Edith grimaced in pain.

"I'm here, Edith."

"Oh, Claire, I was so stupid. I left a damned box on the floor and then tripped over it. Now I have really gotten myself in trouble."

"I'll call your daughters. Where are their phone numbers?"

100

"In my address book by the phone. Oh, I don't want to worry them. Claire, these medics said I might have broken my hip. Shit! Shit!"

As she was being wheeled out on the stretcher, I grabbed her hand. "They can repair hips readily these days, don't worry. Only problem is you'll trip off the security machines in airports."

She laughed. "Dammit!"

I called Barbara on my cell as I followed the ambulance to the hospital, and stayed with Edith in the emergency room. After pain medication she continued ruminating about being mad at herself. In one split second, life as you know it can change. The pain was lessening with nominal groggy effects by the time a young orthopedic surgeon entered. "We will do X-rays, but according to preliminary assessments by the ER doctor, it appears you have broken your hip. If that is the case, you'll need surgery." He was nice and gentle as he examined her and took her medical history. I offered to leave but she pleaded that I be allowed to stay.

Later I accompanied her to X-ray and we talked while waiting. "Will I have to go to a nursing home? My daughters have wanted me to live with them and now I might have to. Oh, I don't want to be a burden. I love my apartment."

"Edith, stop with projecting worse-case scenarios. Let's just take this one step at a time. Lots of people have hip repairs and go back to a normal life."

Just then Barbara, her oldest, entered. "Hi, Mom. What happened?" she said with a concerned but skeptical look on her face. After Edith explained, Barbara pounced, "Mom, didn't I tell you not to leave stuff lying around?" What a bitchy remark. Somehow Edith's gene pool of gentleness had ignored this child. It was time for me to exit before I said something that might make it worse for Edith.

In the hospital parking lot, I found my forgotten groceries and carton of melted ice cream. *"Don't sweat the small stuff,"* I thought. This morning Edith had cheerfully greeted me as I left my apartment, and now, only several hours later, she faced an uncertain future.

The surgery was uneventful. The hip was repaired with no surgical complications. But when I saw Edith the next day, she was confused and irritated. "Where am I? Claire, is that you? Claire, I need to go home and water my plants. Why am I here? I have got to get out of here!"

No doubt, the elderly meet their match in a hospital. Strange environment, anesthesia, pain, immobilization—a downward trajectory can be triggered by a simple fall over a damned box. I had already learned at the agency that elderly falls can often mark the beginning of the end.

Both of Edith's daughters, Barbara and Charlotte, were there now, both unjustifiably treating her like a child. Their 'we'll-take-over' tone made me cringe. I began to fear them more than the broken hip. After bickering within earshot of Edith's room, they informed me that their mom was doing fine and would be transferred to a rehabilitation center after her discharge, perhaps in a couple of days. She would stay there a couple of weeks and then, they decided, be transferred to an assisted living facility. They would clean out her apartment while she was in rehab. What paternalistic bullshit!

"What does your mom think of that?"

"Oh, we haven't told her yet, but this is for the best. We have worried about her living alone for a long time. This proves she isn't able to any longer. She needs to be closer to family," Barbara replied with a matter-of-fact tone.

I imagined Edith would resent those daughters if they rolled in and attempted to seize her life against her will. Perhaps Edith's health would deteriorate and destine her for a more dependent living situation, but to take that step prematurely, without her consent, repulsed me, so much so that I left them in the hall and returned to Edith's bedside. Interestingly, they both followed me as if they suspected I might inform Edith of their dreadful plan.

Both daughters were utterly stunned when Cedric pranced in, carrying a dozen helium-filled balloons, and enthusiastically said, "So how is my favorite little old lady?"

Edith's cognition immediately perked up. "Cedric, dear, where have you been all of my life?" Cedric and I laughed while her daughters remained stoically clueless. In the meantime, he landed his usual prolonged big kiss on her lips. "Ummm, you taste so good. I miss you. You have got to get better soon…Hear me?" By now the balloons were spread across the ceiling and ribbons were draping down over everybody. Barbara was noticeably upset over the compromised aseptic environment and circus-like atmosphere.

"Mom needs to rest now," Barbara blurted, at which time Edith, again regressing, shouted, "I think I left the coffee pot on. Cedric, I have got to get out of here."

Cedric and I each said, "See you tomorrow," and left. "What's with the bitches?" he remarked as we headed toward the elevator.

"Edith has more trouble than her hip. *Their* best interests are trumping Edith's. Cedric, they are talking about moving her out of her apartment...without even consulting Edith. God, I would kill my kids if they ever did that!"

"I detect major *pissy*. How about we talk more over dinner?"

"Sounds good. I'm starving."

***

With my schedule, Cedric and I had spent most of the last weeks catching up in short chats as we passed in the parking lot. I was perfectly comfortable around him now. Sure, I admit to enjoying his persona, played to the hilt as the outlandish stereotypical gay man, *Will and Grace* style. But one-on-one he could quickly forego that façade, becoming stimulating and soothing company.

He was a *cum laude* graduate in English literature and read incessantly. His impeccably decorated apartment was cluttered with books of all genres. His life had not been easy. Coming out in the 1980s, during the height of the AIDS epidemic, he had endured the wrath of his Mid-Western parents, complete with their God-will-condemn-you-to-Hell verdicts. Over the years he had developed a surplus of defense mechanisms.

His first, and only, long-term partner, a civil rights attorney, had died of leukemia. The song, *Philadelphia*, by Bruce Springsteen, could bring him to tears. He coped with the loss by becoming a workaholic at a prestigious Princeton, New Jersey design firm, where he kissed wealthy women, and with his extroverted personality, easily made them delight in the brag-able status of having a *gay* friend. He knew it was phony but it made him rich and much of that money he gave to AIDS and cancer research in memory of his partner.

His humor masked his pain remarkably well, and probably saved his sanity. "I'm unique to most of my clients… their 'gay' decorator. Many treat me like I am some kind of trophy signifying their supposed tolerant personality. To prove their superficial acceptance of homos, they use clichés like, 'Some of my best friends are gay.' He actually detested many of his clients, especially the ones who hurtfully waved a limp wrist while saying, "That's sooo gay," as if that was really funny.

It saddened him to watch reruns of the TV show *Queer Eye for the Straight Guy*, because of the blatant contradictions; five gays helping a pathetic straight guy redo his apartment and self-image so he can romantically, over his home-cooked gourmet dinner, ask his girlfriend to marry him. Ironically, marriage is something they themselves are NOT allowed to do in most of our society.

"I have to laugh at the absurdity of it all. Too bad that too often we are not laughing for the same reasons. Yes, I admit it…I have played into, even encouraged it. Before I came out of the closet, I led a double-life. Now I am doing it again, only in a different way."

"What do you mean?"

"I am gay and it is written all over me. I will always be gay in every inch of my being. I can play the part so well. Not doing this would reveal my depression, depression at my family's rejection, my partner's death, my own insecurities. You know Claire what my biggest addiction is?"

"What?"

"My biggest addiction is the approval of others, and they certainly approve this act." He paused almost in tears. "You know, I had a woman hand me a thousand dollar bill the other day because I kissed her frantic ass and helped her arrange her dinner table to seat some self-centered B-minus movie star. A table of narcissists. How repugnant."

"Please," he continued. "Let's move on. How are classes going?" Cedric had been extremely supportive of my going back to school and always asked about my work. He knew about the Behnke mess. "Details please," he demanded when I told him about meeting Scott in class.

"Hardly any details yet, but Scott sure caught my attention. I wasn't expecting those feelings."

"You're sixty, not dead. Claire, you are a beautiful woman but we must work on that prudishness left over from your former life."

We both giggled. "I relish how you can get me laughing more than I have in years."

"And I appreciate how I can be myself with you. I mean that. It has been a long time since I shared some of the sadder parts of my life with a friend. Notice how I said *friend* and not mother-figure."

"Thank you, Cedric, for sparing me reminders about my senior status."

As we dined and chatted in his favorite Italian restaurant, Betty, the Cupid who brought Mr. Dictionary into my life, approached our table. Of course, she already knew him. "Cedric, my love, how are you? I just adore my new family room. You were so right in forcing me to consider those striped drapes. Claire, are you decorating your apartment? You look tired. You seem stressed." Passive-aggressive bitch, I thought. I have always hated when somebody feebly diagnoses me—mind-raping, Shirley called it.

"She certainly is in full-tilt decorating," Cedric said spontaneously. "And we've been busy shopping for pillows and some fresco. But you can't shop hungry, now can you?"

"Oh Cedric dear, I must call you. Now that my daughter is off to law school, I need to redo her room. Ta ta," she said as she blew him a kiss while walking away.

I told him how I knew Betty. As for his connection, she had, over the years, contributed thousands of dollars to his income. Interestingly, neither of us said anymore about her. Somehow, we were both too tired to waste time judging Betty. She just wasn't worth it.

Journal: *Oh, what a day! Edith's girls are going to complicate her recovery—I can see it coming. Barbara has 'hidden agenda' written all over her face. Emotional baggage comes to center stage. Nothing like a crisis to arouse hibernating dysfunction. What will be my part in this drama?*

Thank you Cedric for your friendship. Your unsurprised attitude about me meeting Scott has helped me with my confidence. I am sorry you have clients like Betty and I am sorry for the cruelties in your life. Do you know how important you have become to me?

And Scott? I still can't believe I asked, 'Do you date?' Even as I blushed, I hoped I behaved like a sophisticated, liberated woman rather than—what's the term?—a man-

hungry cougar.

10

I called Scott and on our first date, in a quiet restaurant, we comfortably exchanged synopses of our lives. Being old(er), we had lifetimes of territory to cover, talking our autobiographies, skimming over some parts, testing our values on each other.

"So what are your biggest regrets?" he asked casually. I had a long list, embarrassingly knocking over my full glass of wine mid-way through, having to call the waiter for dish towels. Let's face it—a downright personal question. But I was getting used to giving my stock answers:

"Got pregnant, quit college, let go of my dreams of being a psychologist."

"How about you?" His list was rather short. "I wasted way too many years playing the capitalism game and dreaded going to work."

"Accomplishments?" he added. My list was short.

"Yours?" Very long list.

Family? Friendships? Religion? Marriages? We checked over it all. Sometime during the evening, I felt we both anticipated subsequent dates to elevate the level of detail.

"You don't give yourself enough credit," he said,

finally adding some judgment.

I later wrote: *This was definitely different than 'dictionary' date. I talked myself silly and felt comfortable exposing my warts, at least some of them. Funny how much of my conversation centered around my recent experiences at the agency and my return to college. It is much more thought-provoking than talking about a day rearranging kitchen drawers.*

Our conversational intimacy resonated into a second rendezvous three days later. By the third date, we gave ourselves a dialog breather and went to a movie. On the way out he briefly grabbed my hand as we strolled to a coffee shop, but I gently pulled away by pointing out something in a store's window. *Don't rush*, I thought. Two more dates followed.

So far, meeting on neutral territory seemed safe enough, as if visiting the other's residence would surely take us to the next level. Finally he did it.

"I make a killer lasagna. How about Friday?" There it was, the implied question: My place or yours? Oddly enough I had no problem forming a reply, as if I actually knew what I was doing.

"Can I bring a salad?"

Anxiety slammed against my ribs as I drove down the tree-lined street to his home. What was I thinking? I had no business going to a man's "place" for dinner and quite possibly breakfast the next morning. My only thought was that I wanted to do this and did I need more reason than that? The question lingered until the light I was stopped at turned green then faded into nothing. I drove on and calmed down enough to admire the neighborhood.

He lived about twenty minutes from me in a small town on the banks of the Delaware River. The well-kept grand Victorian houses, all facing an unobstructed view of the river directly across the street, had sizeable windows and inviting porches. Parked Volvos were common in driveways. A stately old brick church stood next to a cemetery, abundant with smoothed-out tombstones, some tilting after a century standing guard over the deceased. The sidewalk was old and worn from when grandparents skipped over them as young children and bulging oak tree roots had caused decades-old cracking and elevations. On the river side of the street floating wooden-planked docks were tethered to the high banks by long cables. Pontoon boats waited for the next picnic day, all facing the same way due to the southerly current of the peaceful Delaware.

Scott's home fitted in perfectly with this picturesque setting. He had lived there many years, raised his family, and actively participated in the community's affairs. His wife had also died there. Inside, it was warm and inviting, not fancy, not *Better Homes and Gardens* stylish, but cozy. The rooms were filled with homemade Afghans draped over earth-toned furniture and numerous framed photographs of his wife and family, still-lifes of another time.

"Tell me about this photo," I asked after he took my coat and offered a glass of wine. I held up one of the two of them obviously hiking a mountain trail. He did not hesitate to tell me about that particular trip. "Kate loved to hike, but she was tiring easily, troubling both of us." He reminisced about the trip in a tender, loving way, their last one before Multiple Sclerosis seized her physical stamina.

"There were bumps in our marriage, to be sure, periods of doubt and struggle, but we weathered the storms and rekindled our love more than a couple of times. The year before she died, we did a lot of talking. Our bond was strongest, perhaps out of fear, dreading the outcome."

I couldn't help thinking that I most probably wouldn't be there if she were still alive. I didn't mind him talking about Kate—in fact, I was all questions. I admired how he answered every one, so obviously comfortable with his memories—no regrets, no hesitations.

"Kate's battle with MS must have been hard to watch?"

"A huge battle it was; arduous and painful. It consumed her energy and she got addicted to pain killers. That was the worst time in my life. Neither of us knew what to do. Trying to get off of them was horrible. Yet, she didn't want to spend her last days in agony, and we both knew she was dying." Scott made no attempt to stifle his emotions. With tears in his eyes, he added, "Oh, and to watch my children suffer so. They were really being cheated---heartbreaking."

We had a wonderful dinner on the sun porch, complete with fresh white lilies and linen napkins. I told him about my extensive reading over the years but how I had not translated that self-directed learning into measurable life experience. He said he admired my intellect, a compliment I valued.

Deciding not to proceed to any expanded intimacy that night, I rather cowardly left at ten P.M. almost hoarse from talking. He kissed me at the door and told me to call him when I made it home safely. That phone call lasted another hour, ending with my extending a dinner invitation to my apartment next. I was relieved he hadn't asked me to the bedroom. As old as we were, there was time.

***

New love is not just for the young. I kept focusing on this cliché as I ran my errands.

My grocery list was rather routine, except when I added lubricant. I had decided I was ready to have sex with Scott---*if* the decision was mutual, and we could manage the thing without being acutely self-conscious. Was I being too presumptuous? Dear God...even sex after sixty can't be spontaneous. While birth control is not a factor, one has got to think about annoying friction. The lotion I used with my dildo would not suffice for intercourse.

I went to the drug store first, thinking they would have more to choose from. Upon finding the section, I looked around to see if anybody was watching, feeling again like I was in high school. I also wondered if I should buy condoms—STD's, you know.

Dinner was tender pork roast in a yummy citrus sauce and crisp broccoli. While I finished tidying the kitchen, he came behind me and kissed my cheek. Oh yeah, I was definitely ready for sex!

After dinner, with coffee and a bowl of fresh fruit in hand, we retired to the living room. I continued telling him about my neighbors, Edith and Cedric, while a Laura McKenna CD played in the background. The phone rang but I let voice mail pick it up.

Scott brought it up. "You know, I would like to kick our relationship up a few notches. I am ready to make love with you. Really ready. Do you feel the same way?"

113

"Yes." Jesus, I had hoped to sputter out some more romantic words.

"I haven't done this since before Kate died," he revealed. "It's been forty years since I was with another woman."

His honesty continued to impress me.

"Me too," I blurted. "Oh, er, well, it's been about a year for me, the same man for forty years also."

"So, how are you feeling right now?"

My mind flashed with thoughts--what a great psychology 101 question. How did I feel? Well, like ripping his clothes off and suspending any more talk. I had a let's-just-do-it attitude. I mean that's how Ross and I did it. No talk, just action. Was I really any wiser? I was nervous as Hell.

"I am nervous as Hell," I admitted. "I feel like a virgin." I wondered if he would care for a little fellatio? What will he say when he sees my sixty-year-old body?

His arm wrapped around my back. He gently touched my chin, turned it toward him and kissed me. My hand automatically rose to his cheek. Oh yes, I was thoroughly turned on and getting less apprehensive.

"*You're nervous?*" he finally said. "I'm worried about getting it up, premature ejaculation, and satisfying you. I was raised to perform, you know."

"Shut-up—kiss me again."

The next kiss lasted a long time. He touched me all over my face. I wanted to plant my hand right between his legs but nervously hesitated. His hand touched my legs but seemed in no hurry to progress to center stage. Let's face it….this was scary for both

114

of us. Trusting each other was also somehow new. I think he was relieved when he could see and feel his penis hardening.

"I just added sex with a new lover to my list of insecurities. I'm worried what you will think of my body."

"Your body is beautiful."

"Liar…You haven't even seen it yet!" I said smiling. Then, recapturing my confidence, I figured my body is what it is. If a man flipped out over my skin tags or the fact that I had stopped shaving between my legs long ago, then he could get his own drooping ass out the door.

His hand came gently down my neck to my chest and rubbed directly over my breasts. I was beginning to wonder if I really needed lubricant after all.

"Let's go to bed?" he said quietly.

I got up from the sofa and extended my hands to his, helping him to his feet. Then he hugged me tightly…a strong, firm, prolonged hug. He stroked my hair. In the bedroom, I lit four candles. Of course, I had remembered to strategically place them that afternoon after I put freshly cleaned linens on the bed.

Finally more words, "I'm no Tom Cruise."

"And I'm old enough to be Julia Robert's mother," I added.

"Still scared?"

"No, just horny."

Unbuttoning his shirt, I found that his chest, like his sideburns, was filled with dignified gray hairs and even some long ones. I had never seen a sexier chest in my life. I slipped off my blouse, then he unhooked and removed my bra. My nipples were already erect.

We hugged again. Fewer and fewer words, more and more caressing. My slacks drifted to the floor. We were down to underpants, touching each other with hands and lips. Gently, over his erect penis, I lowered his boxers to the floor. He sat on the bed, legs spread, and pulled me close to kiss my breasts, then sucked my nipples, a marvelous feeling. Then he pulled my hip-hugger black lace underwear down.

Naked, vulnerable, finally relaxing, I realized I would trust and make love again.

"Claire, what do you like?"

"Uh, anything." The only answer I could think of.

The touching was sensational. Mutual back rubs with lotion. Foot massages. The lubricant came center front. We nixed the condoms once we relayed that neither of us were STD positive. For a while his penis became flaccid, then hardened again as I kissed it. I gently rubbed my tongue in his urethra. "Does that feel good?" I asked.

"And how…more."

I had never experienced as much erotic foreplay. Sometimes we stopped and talked. Covers were down—full body exposure. I finally got it—sex was as much an act between the ears as between the legs, just like I had told my kids. I wasn't even thinking about the big "O" goal. I was enjoying the process, savoring each sensation.

"Where did you get that scar?"

"Hysterectomy. Fibroid uterus. How about yours?"

"Hip replacement. The end result of a skiing accident years ago."

After I told him about my vibrator, he playfully

said, "Let's get it out."

The lubricant bottle opened. His finger slid into my vagina. Then he started rubbing my clitoris gently. "How's this?"

"More. Harder." My head curled back. His tongue replaced his finger. He pulled back my labia. My legs stretched out and my muscles tightened. This was not Ross. Not what I was used to. Already, this was the longest sex in my life. No rushing. Slow, tender, verbal, meaningful.

He turned on the vibrator, and with lots of lubrication, labia still pulled back, its pulsations riveted around my now very engorged clitoris. Within a minute, I could feel the nerve sensations in my back. Just as I was about to climax, I put my hand on his in a way to stop the vibrator. He interpreted my gesture perfectly. He put his finger in my vagina just as it began to thrust and contract several times. No screaming. I wasn't sweating. I took several deep breaths, the contractions stopped, and I relaxed.

After a few minutes of savoring, I opened my eyes, "Dear God, that was nice."

He turned on his back and I laid my head on his shoulder, my hand clutching his penis, repeatedly pumping the foreskin up and down in gentle motions. When it became hard, I poured lubricant over it and continued, then I straddled him, placed his penis in my vagina and slowly moved up and down. We turned over without losing contact. Now on top, he thrust hard into me a few times, then along with some quiet, pleasurable groans, he ejaculated.

We laid motionless for a few minutes, until he finally said, "I'm sorry."

"About what?" I really did not know what he was

apologizing for.

"That I came so fast."

"I'm lying here, completely satisfied, having enjoyed sex for the first time in years, and *you are apologizing?*"

He chuckled, and smiled broadly, as if laughing at himself. "You know we men have this performance issue. I was raised to be John Wayne—never mince words, don't shun an unnecessary fight, and for God's sake, be sexually potent."

Now I was laughing. "What a crock of shit! And I thought women were the only victims of a sexually repressive society."

"*Ah contraire*, my lovely maiden; we men were supposed to know everything. You just had to fall into our arms, and after an appropriate hard-to-get ritual, follow our direction. Trouble was, we didn't know anything either. Every once in a while, like right now, an issue that I thought was tucked away in the file of stupid youthful woes comes to the forefront. Actually, however, premature ejaculation is quite new for me. Time was when I could hold back at will."

I draped my body next to his, our legs intermingled. His arms wrapped around me. My fingers stroked his balding head. "Jesus, I can't believe you're not sleeping already." Our laughter filled the room.

"I'm wide awake—but if you think I am going to do a repeat performance, please give me another hour to recuperate."

"Were you a virgin when you married?" I asked.

"No, but I am not proud of my pre-marital history. During my two years in the Navy, I did some pretty stupid things, like getting drunk, passing out, and waking up with a strange woman next to me. Back then, my buddies and I all strove for sexual prowess. Once, I got gonorrhea."

"Bet that was a significant event," I chimed in.

"Let's just say, it wasn't my proudest moment."

"Well, I gave Ross the responsibility of pleasing me, as all well-trained Cinderella's do. When he fell short, through no great fault of his own, I still pretended he was the greatest of lovers. I learned it was important to boost his ego. Sexual dishonesty permeated our marriage."

Scott whispered in my ear, "Not right this minute, but do you want to do this again sometime, maybe sooner than later?"

"Very much." I said with a kiss to his forehead.

"Why?"

Ah, oh...was this a loaded question? Were we going overboard with the dialog? Was psychology supplanting passion? This was such new territory for me. We were now forty-five-minutes post coitus.

"Er...." I started to answer but he interrupted immediately.

"Sorry that question came out wrong. Let me start over. I want to do this again and sure hope you do. You are an amazingly loving person, mentally and physically. What a special night."

What a romantic! We talked more, then cuddled. He finally drifted off to sleep. I was feeling, well, marvelous---relaxed, sexy, alive!

***

The phone's voice mail blinking light distracted me as I turned over in bed some hours later, so I decided to retrieve the message, if only to stop the

119

flashing. It was Ross, "I need to talk to you. I have been diagnosed with cancer. Please call as soon as you get this." The clock read four A.M.

I laid awake, next to this gorgeous new lover, contemplating what the morning would bring. What kind of cancer did Ross have? Had he told the kids? What would my role be? At times in the darkness, I loathed Ross for dampening my near perfect evening. I should be thinking about sex, not this! At six A.M., I perked a pot of coffee.

"What a wonderful morning smell," Scott said as he strolled in the kitchen wearing only a shirt and his underwear. We hugged. For a few seconds, I felt ready for a repeat performance but instead told him about the phone call.

He grabbed me again and kissed me, finally whispering in my ear, "I'm sorry. Cancer does suck."

"I guess we both know firsthand." Both his parents had died of cancer.

"What are you going to do?" He said, still holding me.

"I don't know. Call him back I guess, then call the kids." We stared intently at each other. Both of us realized there would be no sex this morning.

"Do you want to be alone?"

"I'd much rather be making love to you than calling my ex. But I do need to make this phone call."

"Can't make love if we can't concentrate. Why don't I go home and do some chores. Let's talk later. Remember, tonight I have a hot date with my almost fourteen-year-old granddaughter to celebrate her birthday. Maybe we can make plans for tomorrow, Sunday?"

I hated to let him go but my mind was swamped. This would have to do. We had coffee together, but he took a rain check on breakfast. I offered the use of my shower but he politely said he would do it at home where he could put on fresh clothes. "Thanks for last night," he repeated at the door with a kiss. "Call me when you know more and have collected your thoughts. I'll be waiting."

After Scott left, I took my coffee to the sofa, took a deep breath and dialed my decades-old home phone number.

"Hello?" Ross's voice muttered.

"Ross, it's me."

"Claire," he started sobbing into the phone. "Fuck this shit!"

He proceeded to talk about the bloody stools and abdominal pain, and how he put off going to the doctor (which he had always done). A colonoscopy confirmed colon cancer and an immediate operation was necessary.

"How soon?"

"Probably next week. The doctor has been brutally honest. He won't say it hasn't spread. He makes no promises he can remove it all."

"Have you told the kids?"

"No, can you come over?"

I figured that request would come. "Sure," I said with conviction. A part of me wanted to be by his side. All of a sudden, I was unwilling to make forty-years of history go away.

The drive to his (formerly our) home was tense. It would be the first visit since I moved out. I still hadn't built up the steam to plow through the numerous photo albums, not to mention the boxes of stuff crowding the attic as if waiting for me to get a bigger place. My old street seemed welcoming. After I parked in the driveway, I focused on the stately front-yard maple, whose branches had held laughing children from the ropes of many swings. I could imagine the countless times I walked the sidewalk to the front door. But it seemed strange when, without my keys anymore, I rang the doorbell.

Ross answered with his Saturday morning sweats on, his curly gray hair disheveled and his handsome face wretched with pain. He nervously grabbed me and we embraced as he started crying again. After ten months of absenteeism, our dog, Zep, barked as if I were a stranger.

"I am so sorry, Ross, that this is happening to you. You don't deserve this." As these words came out, I started to cry also.

With gallows humor, he said, "You always nagged me to get my annual check-up. See how I have screwed up since we split?" Our forced laughter and sniffling noses broke the ice.

"Let me take your jacket," he said, as if knowing I would stay for a while. He hung it in the hall closet, something I had done for him a million times.

His phone rang. From caller ID, he knew it was Kate. "Would you tell her?" he asked handing me the phone. "I can't talk right now."

To say the least, she was surprised when I answered. "Mom? What are you doing there?"

"I just got here. Honey, where are you calling from? You're not in your car, are you?" She wasn't. I took a deep breath, "Dad has colon cancer and needs an operation."

Since I had only cursory details, our conversation

was mostly consoling after hearing her anguished, "Oh, God, no!" She was rightly upset. Hearing the big "C" is always jolting news.

"Should I come home?"

"Probably, but don't rush to the airport this second. Why don't we call you back after Dad and I have talked, when we know more…in a couple of hours." I was acutely aware of my use of the word "we."

"Ross," I whispered with my hand over the phone's speaker, "Do you want to say something to her?" He shook his head no, tearing eyes closed. "I'll call you back, Kate."

Then, like so many times before, we sat on each end of the sofa, legs crossed, bodies turned towards each other, backs resting on the pillows by the thick arms, dog, who was now licking me, between us.

"Ross, this is not a death sentence, you know."

"I have had pain for a while now. It could be a death sentence."

I wanted to wring his neck and scream. What was he thinking by waiting? I didn't say it.

Instead I said, "This waiting period is going to be the worst part. Not knowing. Ruminating about what ifs, if only, what now, whatever……."

"I know. I am just so fucking mad at myself. This last year, since you left, has been a nightmare. I could hardly deal with my emotional health, let alone my physical. I hope you are okay that I called you?"

"I am. Truly I am." Besides, I already knew that his affair had lasted a mere few weeks after our separation, and had already been over for many months. I remembered journaling about it when I found out. That entry had been a bit smug, self-righteous; I had felt somehow vindicated. Today that entry would be world's different. It took cancer for him to ask anything of me. How sad.

We talked a while longer, his frozen emotions unleashed with the magnitude of this diagnosis. The phone rang again, and this time it was Rossy, obviously fresh off the phone with Kate. "I think you need to talk with the kids." He agreed. "Can I make some coffee while you talk?" It felt strange asking.

In the kitchen, everything was in the same place as when I left. As I retrieved the French roast from the freezer I could overhear the conversation. Ross had regained his composure, and now, with familiar paternalistic stoicism, he calmed Rossy and told him he was hopeful…adding that "Mom is here."

After another couple hours passed, we were left with nothing more to say or do. This was not my home anymore, and I certainly didn't feel compelled to put away the laundry or stretch into a cozy chair with a good book. I had already begun thinking of Scott again. Ross walked me to my car, the one he had bought two years ago for my birthday.

"Do you want me to take you to the hospital next week?"

"Would you?"

"Sure, are you going to call Kate back and Peter, or do you want me to?"

"I will. Claire? Thank you…" He seemed to want to say more, but I prevented that by hastily getting into the car. Could he possibly be thinking reconciliation? As I drove home, I felt pity and fear.

Later Scott and I talked by phone. He had been shopping for birthday presents for Elisa, his granddaughter, and was puttering around the house.

"I feel so numb right now." As soon as the words were out of my mouth, I started crying, just what I did not want to do. I mean, what a way to complicate a budding relationship! This was stuff that casts up red flags.

He didn't say a word as I regained my composure.

"Sorry, I don't know where that came from."

"Don't be sorry," he said. "It's a huge bombshell, and your kids are going to need you. Trust me, I have been there."

Yeah, I thought, but you were still married. For fear of scaring him away, I hesitated to share all of my feelings, which were all over the place, confusing even me. Ross and I had just spent the afternoon together, for the first time in eight months.

Until this moment, I had been completely honest with Scott. Oh God, how quickly things can change!

11

Ross was restless and a pile of nerves waiting for surgery, constantly ruminating about the 'what ifs.' Not knowing is always the worst—another type of excruciating limbo. Kate had already flown home from college, and Peter would be flying in from China the day before surgery. Both wanted to be with their dad, even though Ross had half-heartedly told them it wasn't necessary. The excitement of Rossy's engagement and wedding plans took a back seat to the cancer, now a priority for the whole family.

I also became ensconced in this drama. The kids wanted to talk about their dad, and now felt renewed permission to discuss feelings with me. After all, they knew I had become involved.

With surgery still days away, Scott and I managed to pick up where we left off. Our love making was truly artful. On one occasion, after having put on a recording of ocean sounds, I gave him a full body massage with lotion. I started with his arms, one at a time, massaging every inch, including his hands and each finger. Next I attended to his legs, first the backs, then fronts, then each toe. I spent a long time rubbing his back and neck, then his chest. Each stroke was slow, no rush. Eventually I got to his face.

My body was now above his head, my legs stretched out around his face and shoulders. I rubbed my fingers on each eyebrow, then massaged his forehead. I made a circular motion on his temples and did the same on his cheeks.

"This is so delightful, I can hardly describe it," he whispered.

I saved his genitals for last, first rubbing his testicles, ever so gently with lotion. Finally I lubricated his penis and masturbated him to orgasm. When I was done, he was smiling.

"Did I miss any spots?" I inquired.

"Not a one. We are going to have to do this more often. This could be addicting."

Within a few minutes, he turned over and said, "Okay, your turn." He repeated almost exactly what I had done with the same non-rushed feeling and a new CD playing soft, classical guitar. The sound of my vibrator pleasantly interrupted the serene atmosphere.

When we were done, totally relaxed, we napped. That afternoon, we went for a long walk by the river, wondering if our children made love as passionately.

"I bought Rossy several videos on lovemaking when he was seventeen," I said. "It was not pornography, rather erotica by monogamous couples. They were actually educational videos used for college level sex education classes."

"Now that is what I call progressive."

"He was, needless to say, embarrassed that *his* mother would be so brazenly straightforward. Sons are not used to moms getting involved in sex education. But considering the ignorance of both his parents, I felt obligated to introduce him to this valuable information. Naturally I watched it first, and

I must say, learned a lot myself. It showed the enormous difference between having sex and making love."

"Did he watch them?"

"'Don't ask, don't tell' applied there, but I noticed lots of his buddies going into his room. I became nervous that one of his friends would report us for showing 'dirty' movies but that never happened. Guess the kids appreciated getting such information. I felt good because none of the videos were in any way denigrating to women, instead showed a wonderful, mutual respectfulness. I was proud I could heighten my son's understanding of that. I think the one on female orgasm was especially popular."

"They also made a huge point about the importance of using your head and talking."

"I agree with that," Scott interjected.

"Me too. One even specifically focused on the question about the appropriate age to start having sex. Naturally, they didn't specify a particular age except to say this: 'If you can't talk about sex with your potential partner before you do it, you are too young.' That, of course made many forty-plus-year-olds too young also."

"By the way," I added. "One of the videos was on massaging each other."

"Oh, so that's where that came from. Sometime soon will you show me what else you learned?" he added. I was impressed by the frankness of our talks about sex. Not lost was the fact that while I had talked openly with my children, Ross and I had rarely veered from our non-verbal routine.

"Stay tuned!" I finally said. "Actually they also

have a series for older couples like us, but I never ordered them."

"Well, what are we waiting for? I love being reinvigorated."

***

I related the events with Ross and Scott during my next session with Shirley, and she looked at me smiling. "You made me think of Kintsugi," she said.

"Kin—what?" I asked, clueless.

"Kintsugi is the Japanese art of repairing porcelain, ceramic vases or other objects with gold," said Shirley. "They are fused with lacquer from the Urushi tree after which the crack is painted with liquid gold. It stems from the belief that a damaged object repaired this way can be stronger and more beautiful than before it was broken. Unexpected magnificence can result from trauma, now mended with gold. I once saw an exhibit of Kintsugi works and I marveled at the beauty of the imperfections. Instead of trying to camouflage or disguise the repair, the thin gold line of the crack celebrates the painstaking restoration."

"So are you saying that the vases serve as a metaphor for the fragility of life, and the possibility of recuperating to a higher level of emotional health?"

"That sounds like a good beginning for a metaphor."

"It's cute. But is it better than merely using crazy glue?"

"Crazy glue works, I suppose, but it'll never make your vase superior to the original."

"Okay, I like it—my inner self can be one big heap of gold-filled scars," I said, not kidding.

"Don't forget the work it takes to repair the

cracks. Some people never mend them, they just live with them broken or try to hide them. Some only do superficial fixing, neglecting the considerable time and energy needed to mend the imperfection meticulously. Sadly, some actually throw their broken selves away in the form of suicide."

"And just maybe, I am stronger and even more beautiful after the suffering?

"Maybe. I give you this metaphor to do with as you please."

Ah, Shirley, I thought. A wise sage never jams answers down one's throat. On the way home, I imagined my body and soul as a vase, broken and ugly. However, I didn't want to get too carried away with metaphor. Just like clichés, you can overdo them, spit them out at inappropriate times, as if they are the supreme truth, only they don't always apply and are often bullshit, usually spewed forth by either a quite gullible person or a well-seasoned bullshitter.

One casual friend once blurted out after my separation, "Misery is optional," and I almost wrung her neck. Am I supposed to be happy at one of the saddest intervals in my life because 'misery' is optional? How fuckin garish! Guess she never heard that grieving is actually healthy. This reminded me of yet another one, often used by want-to-be wise people pretending to be therapists: "No one can ever *make* you miserable, sad, mad, glad, (fill in the blank), you *chose* to be miserable, etc." Too cute; too simple; analogous to 'don't feel.' Please excuse me while I scream! But I liked Shirley's metaphor of meticulous, long, patient work on a scar to make it strong…and even beautiful.

I shared with Shirley the words used by the

clinical psychologist who had taught my assertion classes. "All, all, all relationships begin as strangers, and it's nice to know there is a goodly supply of strangers."

"Perhaps," she had continued, "you have not even met the person or persons who could become your most intimate friends, so be open to strangers." (I remembered feeling a "BUT" was coming.) "*But*, all significant relationships end in sorrow and separation and suffering."

"Here's the real kicker," the psychologist finally said. "The more you give, the more you get...but, and a big but, the more you will suffer when that relationship is over by death or separation. Healthy relationships take great risk, causing many of us to hesitate, hold back in fear, afraid to take the chance of being hurt--maybe again. Hence, sometimes we hold back our giving, ultimately getting less, and of course, suffering less, if at all.

"If you don't want to grieve," she concluded, "then don't love. It's that easy." I was blown away by her words. So was Shirley.

***

That night I took a rather inexpensive Oriental vase and purposely dropped it on the floor. It broke rather cleanly into four sections with only a couple of small chips. I couldn't find Urushi lacquer at the craft store, so I settled for another glue. But I did find gold paint. The next day, I painstakingly repaired it, then added water and fresh flowers to demonstrate its leak-proof renovation. Sure enough, it was beautiful. I showed Cedric, who likewise thought it was a meaningful metaphor---before telling me that I should open a Kintsugi store.

Later, the thought hit me like a ton of bricks: Did I even know the extent of my brokenness? Plus it is one thing to fix myself, but I don't exist in a vacuum. What about my relationships? Surely my separation from Ross represented one huge break, but did I want to fix that? How far did I want to carry this metaphor? Later, I wrote in my journal:

Honestly, I am surprised by my level of emotional involvement with Ross's illness. But even more so, disturbingly comfortable with that, and, with him at this time. What do I want to mend? How do I want that to look? It's jagged and in numerous pieces. Surely I will need a magnifying glass to fit some of those pieces back together and that's worse than a mirror!

***

"I want to talk to you about my trip to Arizona," Scott said one night.

He had already invited me to join him. A son lived in the Tucson area, and he (and Kate) had been going out there yearly to stay for an extended time. In fact, last year he had purchased a time-share south of Tuscan in the Madera Valley. He loved the area with its beautiful forested mountain hiking trails, contrasting with the desert below. He described one path as starting at 5000 feet and winding down past towering oak trees, babbling brooks, waterfalls careening over enormous boulders spewed from primeval volcanoes, and ending in the flat desert sands among twenty-foot high saguaro cacti. The trek took him all day. With wooden stick-poles found trailside and a backpack, he took his lunch and often napped during the all-day hike. To augment his solitary hiking, he had also joined a hiking club, which introduced him to abundant trails in this amazing pristine wilderness park.

When he wasn't hiking, he played actively with two grandchildren, ages six and eight. I imagined him as the typical doting grandpa, loving children on his lap, creating memories they would cherish.

"Yeah," I sighed with a smile, "Arizona. Can we go tomorrow?" After a pause, "Actually, I have been thinking about you being away for three months."

"Well, if you didn't have school and a job and an ex with cancer, I would seriously want to whisk you away with me for the whole time."

"Right now, that sounds mighty tempting."

"But…if I can't have you the whole time, how about a week or two? Or three?"

"Yes, I gladly accept. And I really welcome your offer. Will your son be okay with another woman in your life?"

"He already knows all about you and is excited to meet you." What an amazing family, I thought to myself. "How nice. Speaking of kids, you have yet to meet any of mine."

"It might be a bit early with Ross's surgery approaching. Introducing me into the mix might be premature. There's no rush."

He knew I was tired so we turned in early. In bed we hugged and massaged, and essentially made love with our clothes on. It was just as nice as having intercourse. In the morning, we both awoke early and stayed in bed sipping freshly perked coffee.

"Do we have time for a quickie?" he said.

"You mean you don't have an hour and a half?"

"I do, but do you?"

"Well I guess not. But I bet we can be creative for fifteen minutes. What position haven't we tried?"

Part of the fun was talking about it, something still incredibly new to me. I already knew that boredom was the bane of many couples. Routine was the enemy.

Scott and I started throwing pillows around us until we settled into a sideways position, however, after a few minutes, our legs couldn't tangle right and one of his fell asleep. In addition his penis was level with my belly button, making it way off target. Laughing, we readjusted until it was perfectly comfortable.

He was only inside of me for a few seconds when his penis went flaccid. We changed positions but it didn't respond. We changed positions again. He became tense, frustratingly masturbating himself so he could reestablish an erection, but it wasn't working.

"Stop with pressuring yourself," I said.

"I am on this new blood pressure medication. It might be affecting me. Please know that it is not you."

"I know that. Come on Scott, give yourself a break. Hypertension medications can cause erectile dysfunction. But these medical problems can be solved. It has nothing to do with you, me, or us."

"Thanks for being so understanding. This is really embarrassing. And the more I try, the worse it gets."

"I can still love you without your penis inside my vagina. Here let me show you." With that I pulled him close to me for one very long, sustained, tight, full body hug, but he remained tense.

When I got out of the shower, he was already on the phone to his doctor's answering service trying to make an appointment for that afternoon.

"Stop with the long face. This is not a crisis. It's a bump in the road. I'm not going anywhere."

"My body is certainly not what it used to be."

"Oh, but mine is. I have been waiting all of my life for my boobs to drop south and it has been delightful having to rely on K-Y Jelly because my natural lubricant dried up when the last kid went to college. So Scott, you are not a stud anymore. Thank God. I did my stud dating back in college. With age comes old penises and you know Scott, old penises have a life of their own...they don't always listen." Jesus, I could not believe I was talking about my new lover's flaccid penis over breakfast with no sense of awkwardness or embarrassment. "But if you think for one minute that I am going to trade you in for someone with a hard dick, think again!" And if you think this will get you out of taking me to Arizona, well..."

Sensing my desperation in trying to make him feel better, he put his index finger over my mouth, saying with a smile, "I get your point. Thanks. I am going to take my old dick to the doctor's office and see if I can get it to perk up again...perhaps an enhancement drug. And no matter what the outcome for me, I will make sure that you are satisfied."

I removed his finger from my lips. "While you are there, can you see if enhancement drugs have come out for women yet?" We both burst out laughing. Humor took the edge off.

"We can 'viagrafy' each other," he said with a loud chuckle.

Then lifting my boobs up, one in each hand, "Do you think these will respond to drugs? Breast feeding three mouths, plus sixty years has made them so tired looking."

"Truthfully, I like the casual, let-your-boobs-down look."

"Yeah, but when I am on top of you, you have to hold them to keep them from swinging out of control."

"I have been waiting for years to steady the swinging boobs of a mature woman. Besides, it gives me something to do with my hands."

We laughed until tears ran down our faces. In the car on the way to work, I thought about it more. Being older, with its inherent complications, would not dim the romance that Scott and I were nurturing. I was feeling love for this man.

12

"I work at the Area Agency on Aging," I said to Barbara, as we watched Edith in physical therapy at the rehabilitation center. "There are a lot of services there that can help your mother when she returns home. For instance, a bus can pick her up at her doorstep and bring her to and from physical therapy. I can get Meals on Wheels delivered to assure she is eating properly."

"You saw how she acted after surgery. Do you really think she can live alone?"

"Anesthesia can cause confusion in the elderly. Doesn't she seem better to you now?"

"I am an hour away and cannot come to respond to her every need, take her to the grocery store, doctor's appointments, and to see her friends. And I am sure you don't want to be burdened with that responsibility! She shouldn't be driving anymore either."

"But if she continues to progress, she should be able to drive herself again, especially short distances to the local stores and her doctor. Some of her friends live in the condo complex, which is why she moved there in the first place."

"Look, I know you are friends with my mom, but I am her daughter. I have known her for just a bit more time than you! And now I have got to figure out finances and pay her bills while she is here. Look, I am not trying to be this cruel ogre. I am only thinking of her best interests. Let's face it, she fell over a box. In time, this will probably happen again."

Okay, I succeeded in pissing her off. My proactive approach on Edith's behalf was not working. This daughter's defensiveness was preventing her from listening to alternatives. Did she have Edith's best interests at heart? I doubted it. She lived an hour away and that was inconvenient. Truth be known—she wanted Edith closer even before she broke her hip.

"I'm sorry. I wanted to offer what was available."

"Well, I already know this." Then quickly changing the subject, "God, the care in this place stinks. The nurses are a lazy bunch of do-nothings. Every time I come here, they are sitting on their asses."

Barbara's chronic complaining irritated me, especially since Edith had told me how good the care was—and the fact that the center had an outstanding reputation in the community. We stood a few minutes in silence until Edith wheeled her chair toward us.

"Did you see me walking? Tomorrow I will start training for the marathon," she said laughing.

"There's a 5K walk in two months to benefit the American Cancer Society," I said joking back.

"Stop it, you two!" shouted Barbara. "For God's sake, Mom just had major surgery!"

Edith's frowning face shook sideways, "Come on

Barbara, lighten up."

"Neither of you are being realistic here, but isn't it so nice to paint me as the bad guy? Come on mom, let's *you* and *I* get back to your room for lunch." I was unequivocally not invited.

That night Edith and I talked on the phone. Unless Barbara tried to declare her mentally incompetent, Edith retained the right to make her own decisions. But dealing with Barbara was going to be a royal pain-in-the-ass. She had already reverted to using guilt tactics; "Why don't you want to be closer to your grandchildren? Don't you love them? You say you don't want to be a burden—well, making me drive two hours round trip is sure burdening me!"

Burden is the supreme cuss word for seniors, and Edith was starting to feel paranoid about this. "Let's face it…I will probably only be able to live on my own a couple more years before I will need assisted living. God, I wish Fred was still around." (Fred, her snorkeling boyfriend, fell victim to a stroke and was now living with his son in another state. Last time she phoned him, he didn't remember her.)

"Claire, what should I do?"

I figured my role should be helping her dissect her choices and come to a decision that was in her own best interest. I went through all of her options, most of which were dependent on her successful progress in rehab: "You can go back to your own apartment, or get another apartment closer to Barbara, or move to a senior complex with assisted living upgrades for when that time comes, or move to that studio Barbara said she'd build next to her garage." With each option, we outlined the pros and cons.

"Living with Barbara is not an option," insisted Edith. "I'd be crazy in a week. There wouldn't be enough Prozac. I wouldn't be able to fart without her worrying if I need a laxative." I have loved her well with some distance between us; change that, and I go down the tubes."

"What about your other daughter, Charlotte?"

"Any move closer to Charlotte would prompt major friction with Barbara. Besides, she lives far away from all my friends. Claire, I hate to bring you into all of this family turmoil. You have got enough on your plate."

"I'm okay. I want you to make the best decision for you."

Edith promised she would think carefully about her options. Before we hung up, Edith said, "Tomorrow is the fifth anniversary of Rudy's death."

I wondered if Barbara wasn't engaged in her own form of elder abuse. After all, abuse can be gauged in degrees, from mild to severe. While there was no arsenic involved here, her controlling attitude was inflicting much anguish on Edith, and might prematurely rob her of her dignity and independence.

***

I channeled my frustration into a presentation on elder abuse in Marilyn's class. Like children, elders can be at the mercy of others because of advanced age, dependency, disability and frailty. And like child abuse, most cases, excepting the extreme, go unreported. Of the two plus million cases reported yearly, many more exist, perhaps five times as many. Physical abuse is a real attention-getter, but equally as serious are sexual abuse, emotional abuse, blatant neglect, financial mismanagement, and abandonment. Ninety percent of abusers are family members.

I was unnerved by these statistics. I couldn't imagine living a full life and then, in my senior years, being at the mercy of an uncaring family, who would just as soon dump you to get their inheritance early. To be fair and unbiased, I also showed the difficulty of caring for a frail senior in today's society, especially one with Alzheimer's, a known 24/7 challenge. Some families 'crack' under the demands and need all of the support available.

On the other end of the continuum are the senior parents who were dysfunctional throughout their entire lives. Not every mother develops into a cute, sweet, little old lady with neatly coiffed blue hair serving tea and knitting Afghans for the grandchildren. Some are downright nasty and always have been. Others regrettably abused their own children yet now expect to be taken care of by the emotionally scarred adult child.

My presentation stimulated a lot of discussion and I felt especially satisfied after Marilyn gave me an enthusiastic thumb up. By now, I loved the challenge of being a student. I started fantasizing about my sixty-plus-year-old-self donning a cap and gown and marching to "Pomp and Circumstance." This time around, nothing would deter me from a college diploma. I decided to major in social work.

***

Even before breaking her hip, Edith had mentioned the upcoming fifth anniversary of Rudy's death, a significant milestone for her. I had made a conscious effort to remember the date, marking it on my calendar. I went to the rehab center after class with a single rose in hand. She seemed comforted to see me, as if anxiously anticipating the prospect of a compassionate ear.

Since his death, she had refused to mourn in silence, to tuck him away as if he hadn't existed. Even two years later when she started dating, Rudy was not eliminated from conversations. She told me that she did not gush endlessly about Rudy this or Rudy that, but his life with her would not become a black hole either. Barbara was predictably absent on this day.

"On what we realized would be his last day," she began, "the children and grandchildren came early. Everyone knew death was in the air. I could just feel it. Rudy's respirations were more labored as he drifted in and out of coherence. Morphine doses and their frequency had been increased."

She continued, "Barbara had wanted to shelter her children (then ten and twelve) and hesitated from having them participate in final good-byes. I begged her not to be over-protective—that Grandpop needed to be surrounded by voices of a new generation."

"Christ, if a kid is old enough to love, they are old enough to grieve!" she said raising her voice. "Rudy loved his grandchildren—spent endless hours doting over them. He took them fishing, bought them their first bicycles, and gave them wonderful afternoons of horseback riding lessons on gentle ponies. Barbara would deny them the tears of 'thank-you's" and 'I-will-never-forget tales.' Mercifully she relented."

Edith's voice calmed. "In fact, at one point, the hospice nurse got us all seated comfortably around a blazing living room fire. With much assistance by two visibly nervous sons-in-law, Rudy's emaciated body was snuggled into a La-Z-Boy borrowed from the den. The children sat cross-legged on the floor."

"Then, with a slight probing by the nurse, there began a catharsis of 'Do-you-remember-when' stories:"

"Dad," said Barbara. "Do you remember when we built those doll houses?"

"Rudy smiled. Of course he remembered. When Barbara was twelve, she chose to build a doll house for a Girl Scout project. Intent on an I'll-do-it-myself attitude coupled with the impatience for a speedy completion, she silently faltered with major measurement mistakes and sloppy work. Rudy, the ultimate perfectionist, who could create, build, or fix anything, chomped at the bit to help, or rather, I should say, take over."

I sat back and listened intently, feeling as if I was getting to know Rudy for the first time. I could picture him watching from the sidelines and anxious to help. My father would have been the same way.

"Finally, after Barbara screamed in pain as a hammer hit her thumb and the whole doll house teetered and threatened to implode, utter frustration drove her to call her father. It turned out to be one of Rudy's finest moments. Ditching his normal take-charge attitude, he dried her eyes and helped her devise a workable, age-appropriate plan."

"Within a week, the completed doll house stood testament to this pre-adolescent's know-how and stamina. Rudy's eyes sparkled. Later, they would complete many more doll houses, from Victorian to the post-war Levittown, Pennsylvania suburban starter homes. They even did a split level just for fun. Of course, birthdays and Christmases were filled with miniature presents to furnish these budding works of art."

Edith looked at me, "Claire, smiles filled the room as Barbara and Rudy exchanged memories from this golden-age of togetherness." I was smiling too as I thought about how simple, day-to-day experiences can create the most notable memories.

"Charlotte, on the other hand, still had some unfinished business with her Dad. At eighteen, she had come home drunk—puking drunk. It seems that the spiked punch at a college fraternity party, which tasted so innocent, was gulped rather than sipped.

"A worried Rudy was relieved at seeing the car's headlights pull into the driveway; a relief quickly converted to anger when his sloppy-speaking daughter, who thankfully wasn't driving, fell out of the car. After he dragged her into the kitchen, her arm forcefully held around his supporting shoulders, projectile vomit was all over the kitchen. Rudy administered a hefty dose of Alka Seltzer and fluids, and then put her to bed before returning to the kitchen to fetch a mop.

"Charlotte recalled that, the next day, after a couple of more doses of headache remedies and several bouts of dry heaves at the toilet, Dad calmly, but firmly, talked to her about drinking. Now, twenty years later, Charlotte turned to her now dying dad and thanked him for his understanding. She told him she had learned a remarkable lesson on that day, the last time she ever got drunk." Edith started chuckling, "Rudy barely remembered the incident and certainly hadn't been aware of his impact. So much for a belated thank-you."

"I guess better than never extending that thank-you and living with the regret," I added.

"You can say that again!"

"As the afternoon progressed," Edith continued, "the family shared stories in abundance. 'Grandpa! Remember when I caught that bass with your favorite lure?' recalled nine-year-old Danny. 'Grandpop! Do you remember when that old pony decided to lay down and take a nap...while I was still riding her?' asked Alice giggling." Edith's face was aglow in sharing these tidbits of time about grandchildren.

"Sometimes there were tears, even sobbing. At other times, spontaneous belly laughs produced a different kind of tears. Up and down we went on our emotional roller coaster. I can feel those emotions now just like it was yesterday." Edith took some deep breaths and looked away for a while. "Anyway, Claire, finally Rudy was exhausted and the nurse put him back to bed where he slept soundly and peacefully.

"At two A.M., Rudy woke up. He started calling in the grandchildren one-by-one. He wanted to be alone with each of them. At first Barbara protested waking them but he persisted. Later I would find out that he chatted with each of them about their personal relationship with him, and how that could continue in their hearts. Then he told them he loved them, would miss them, and, in a last gesture of physical love, he hugged them and told them good-bye." Edith started crying. Me too.

"When he was done with the grandchildren, he called in each son-in-law separately, then each daughter. When it was Barbara's turn, the session became markedly longer. He spent another twenty minutes with Charlotte. Both had come out of the room sobbing. Rudy knew his death was imminent. We all did.

"Finally, as if I knew it was my turn, I went into our room and shut the door behind me, asking the kids not to disturb us. He asked for some morphine and I obliged. The hospital bed, which seemed so cold and sterile before, was inviting now. I climbed into bed with him for the first time in weeks. I gently put my arm under his neck and pulled his head to the top of my breast. I rested my chin on his forehead. My hand rubbed his face. I wanted my whole body to be touching his…even my feet were rubbing his legs.

"I was crying so hard I could barely mouth the words, I love you. He was crying too. 'I hope I haven't been too much trouble,' he muttered with a chuckle.

"'Thank-you, Edith…for our wonderful…life together,' he told me. 'I really hate to leave you…I have loved you so much…' Saying these words was a physical struggle but I knew he truly wanted to say them. After that, we tearfully held each other. No more words needed to be spoken. A peace came over the room. Dawn was beginning to break. Birds chirped in the distance. Finally he fell asleep. I closed my eyes to rest a while, but I guess I fell asleep also.

"When I awoke, he was dead.

"I held him tightly one last time and thanked him. Then, in almost business-like fashion, I got up, washed his face, arranged his covers, put his hands over his chest, and left to tell the family."

As Edith relayed this story to me, tears fell steadily down my cheeks. How beautiful, I thought.

What a touching love story. "Thank you Edith for sharing such an intimate time with me. I feel privileged."

"And thank you for listening. It helped me to share it with you. Come here Claire—give me a hug."

It was dark when I drove home from the rehab center, initially thinking how depressing it was that Ross and I wouldn't have an ending like that. I was actually jealous. But those thoughts were fleeting because once again Edith had activated memories of my own mother, whose last day had similarities to Rudy's. Grandchildren present, stories told, laughing, crying, all of us knowing that death was lurking, ready to steal away *my* mother. With my memories vivid, I started grieving for her, and after pulling my car safely off the road, I started sobbing.

13

The night before Ross's surgery, I chauffeured all out-of-town kids home from the airport. Peter, tired from his twenty-four-hour marathon from China, stayed in his old room, as did Kate in hers. The next morning we would meet at the hospital for the long wait.

Ross and I had had lunch the day before, prior to starting his NPO (nothing per oral) order in preparation for anesthesia. He felt compelled to tell me where the will was, even though Rossy had been named executor. He also wanted me to know that I would be taken care of should a catastrophic event happen during surgery. For the first minutes, our lunch conversation had a business-like formality.

Then, as if out of nowhere, he blurted, "I am so sorry that we separated. I wish I had tried harder. I really miss you."

I was stunned by his unexpected words. My eyes opened wide as I looked away, with my hand automatically drawing over my mouth.

After a pause, "It has been hard on me also. Starting over at sixty years old is not how I envisioned it."

"Would you consider reconciling?" Then, as if

catching himself, "What a desperate thought. Here I am going in for cancer surgery so this is not exactly the most romantic time to ask for another chance."

"Ross, I'm planning on being with you and the kids through this ordeal. We have too much history to abandon each other now. But I think it is premature to talk about getting back together." Though I wanted to be truthful with him, I did not tell him about Scott. Given the circumstances, I felt it unnecessarily cruel.

Interestingly, just a few months ago, I would probably have jumped at this reconciliatory chance. Before school, therapy, a job, and Scott, I might have considered, out of loneliness, rebounding back into his arms.

"The affair with Amanda was a stupid, frivolous fling. I was lusting after lust…and lust has no staying power. I am sorry I hurt you—really, truly sorry." His eyes were wet.

"Apology accepted, but please don't blame it all on yourself." I grabbed his hand, "I also take responsibility. We were in a rut that neither of us knew how to get out of. I did not take advantage of my life's opportunities after the kids left. Without intention, your affair jolted me out of complacency. Perhaps I should thank you."

"Yes, but instead of working on our marriage, like you wanted, I started looking for a fantasy, one with trouble written all over it. The day after you left, I knew it was wrong to let you go…the biggest fucking mistake of my life."

Seems that a cancer diagnosis motivates one to cut through the bullshit. I appreciated his candor and his expression of regret. Yet, while I was emerging healthier from our depressing separation, I hadn't a clue how he had felt. I felt sad…sad for him, for the kids, and even for me. And right under the surface— *Damn you!* thoughts were ready to explode, but I composed myself instead.

"Ross, we were two different people forty years ago, when we *had* to get married. Who knows if we would have gone through to the altar if I wasn't nine weeks pregnant. Yet we took the responsibility for our actions and raised a terrific family. You worked hard and I will never forget that. We both did what we thought we were supposed to do."

"We were young…so young."

"And naive! Let's not forget that neither of us had a clue."

"But we did love each other, didn't we?"

"Of course I loved you. And with talks like this, I realize I still do. Even though we are almost divorced, our lives are forever intertwined with the three beautiful lives we brought into this world. And it goes without saying that I want the best for you in your life."

"Claire, you are an amazing person. Why did I let you slip away?" With a tear slowly descending down his cheek, "Do you really mean it when you say you still love me?"

My hand reached across the table again, this time rubbing his. "Yes, I do. And we've both got a lot of living to do yet. Let's get through this operation."

We ate in silence for a while, then he said, "There is one more matter I would like to discuss. Our divorce is not final yet. I have talked to my lawyer and he informed me that if I die and we are not divorced, as my widow you will receive my pensions, which will take the place of your alimony."

"Ross--"

"No, I am not saying that we have to get back together. But legally, my widow gets these benefits. I suggest we hold off on the final divorce until we see what my prognosis is. Look, this is something I can do for you. If something happens to me, it will guarantee you are set for the rest of your life. You don't have to live with me or anything. Also, I have already made sure that my rather hefty life insurance policy keeps you as a beneficiary."

"This is getting complicated. Do we have to discuss this now?"

"Claire, yes, it is important. I want you to have this. And it is not charity, rather what is fair and right, considering the time we spent together."

"But our final divorce papers won't be signed until after we have been separated a year. That's three months from now. By then, you will know a lot more about this cancer."

"Claire, think about it. This is your ticket to financial freedom until you die or....er...get married again."

"Oh...Do you know something that I don't know?" For an instant I worried he already knew about Scott.

"Not really. Just trying to fix things the best way I know how."

"I'll think about it. Now let's end this gloomy discussion.

***

I walked into the surgical family waiting room, and my three children, the most important people in my life, came over to hug me. I had told the agency and my professors that I would be skipping work and classes. Imogene, Marion, and Marilyn, of course, empathized. Stevens coldly could have cared less, "As long as you don't go over your allotted absences."

A nurse came out to ask if I had arrived. Ross demanded to see me before he was wheeled into the operating room. "Thanks for everything," he whispered in an already groggy state while tightly squeezing my hand.

"This is not your funeral, you know. In a couple of hours, you will wake up to a new day. I expect you to fight. No whining. It ain't your time yet. I love you."

"I love you too, a lot."

Waiting was the normal excruciating experience. In between worrisome projections, the kids and I managed small talk. I was interested in Peter's latest reports from China about his job, wife Jennifer, and the adoption they had talked about. Then there were Kate's graduate studies and Rossy's wedding plans. Often there was silence as we each dissected the enormity of this situation. I wrote in my journal:

Silence—that arduous interval between knowing and not knowing. The silence that depicts an uncertain future. The silence when no words can describe what is happening.

I anxiously rubbed my sweating palms. My thoughts drifted from a controlled panic to a strange calm. For a few minutes I felt claustrophobic in the windowless waiting room. I took deep breaths. Later I excused myself for a short walk outside.

The kids chatted but my listening was sporadic, "Mom, did you hear what I said?"

Three hours passed when Ross's surgeon, still in

O.R. garb, a surgical mask hanging on his chest, came to apprise us of our future. "Ross did well in surgery. He is in the recovery room resting quietly. The tumor spread but I think we were able to remove it all, and chemotherapy can hopefully extinguish what we didn't see." His words were carefully chosen.

"You mean he will be cured?" Peter said with excitement.

"No, I cannot say that. We have to wait for pathology reports and get him started on chemo right away. It will be weeks before we know anything more definitive but I am cautiously encouraged. And, I might add, the next few weeks will not be easy. He will need a lot of help."

"When can we see him?" I said.

"His breathing tube has been removed but he is still groggy from the anesthesia. Since there are no surgical complications, he will not need to go to the ICU—he can go straight up to a bed on the surgical recovery floor, probably in about two hours. One of you can go back now for a few minutes, just to say hello. He'll be happy to see a familiar face."

The kids all looked at me, as if I should be given the right of first refusal. "Why don't one of you go?" Within a second, Kate jumped up and followed the doctor back.

"Oh Mom, maybe he has beat this despicable disease," Peter said while hugging me tightly, showing he needed his mother.

"Let's hope so, honey," my outstretched hands rubbing his back and head.

"I haven't eaten yet today and I'm starving," I finally said. "Why don't we get a late lunch after Kate returns? We'll be back by the time he gets to his room."

The boys gratefully accepted and within minutes of Kate's initial progress report, we were in my car. There was another long period of silence, this time with an initial sense of relief that one hurdle has been passed. Kate broke the quiet, "I think I need to drop out of college to help take care of him."

"You don't have to make that decision just yet," I said to her with no return argument.

"I can take a few weeks leave of absence from work to help out," Peter volunteered.

"And what about your wife in China?" said Rossy. "Besides, you guys, Mom and I are in the area. And Jennifer said that she would help. Remember, she is also a nurse."

"Hey brother, have you set a wedding date yet?" said Peter.

"We thought we'd wait till you got back in the spring. By the way, little brother, will you be my best man?"

While they chitchatted, my thoughts focused on their inclusion of me in the recuperation plans. How deeply did I want to get involved? I had another life now, and I couldn't let this detour throw me completely off track.

Later our whole family gathered around Ross's bedside. In his narcotic-induced haze, he repeatedly relayed his gratitude that we were all there for him. The kids started joking, using humor to relieve the built-up tensions. "Hey Dad, this is no way to spend a vacation." "Dad, want me to press the morphine button again? Might as well enjoy these drugs while you can." Ross smiled with his eyes closed and drifted off to sleep. Finally we left.

I arrived home late, knowing my children would talk until the wee hours seeking solace with each other, perhaps with hopeful anticipation that this crisis would reunite their parents. After talking briefly with Cedric and Scott (both of whom had made me promise to phone), I tried studying for another psychology test. I fell asleep with a book opened and my clothes on.

14

Paying the price for late nights, early mornings, and inefficient multi-tasking, I could hardly drag myself out of bed the next couple of days. I couldn't stay focused even in Marilyn's class. I felt I did poorly on a tricky Stevens' test. That era where I could burn the candle at both ends was over; my aging body had rebelled.

After classes, I rushed to my job at the agency, hoping it would be a quiet day. No such luck. The phone rang repeatedly and several people waited outside my triage office, some with heart wrenching requests for assistance. One woman was being evicted with no other place to live except her car. She suffered from untreated obsessive-compulsive disorder and presented with extreme hoarding. Her apartment across the street, which I had seen after a previous appointment some weeks ago, was so jammed with stuff that it had finally been pronounced a hazard by the fire chief, which is why she subsequently rushed to my office to forestall the eviction.

"Mrs. Jones, we have got to do some major cleaning," I had said at the time, while brushing off the many fleas that were jumping on my legs. "Let me start by getting some of these newspapers to the dump. And let's get some flea medication for your cat."

Immediately she had stopped me in the most threatening tone, "I'll do it myself. Don't touch my things!"

I was out of my league, not capable of understanding this mental illness and how to help her. The agency's seasoned social workers were also throwing up their hands in frustration after obtaining medications that she refused to take or getting her into therapy only to find she failed to keep appointments. Calls to her son met with, "I don't want her. She has been like this all of her life." If truth be known, I couldn't blame him. So on this day, I referred this highly dysfunctional woman off to Sylvia, who couldn't see her till the afternoon.

I referred another woman, recently widowed, who came in with an electricity cut-off notice, a shoe box of other bills, and not a clue how to deal with them. She had never written a check in her life, yet her checking account contained over $27,000.

A distraught family had recently called the police when their grandmother, still in her pajamas, got lost trying to retrieve her children from their school bus, children that were now in their fifties. Unable to afford a nursing home, they applied for the dementia daycare unit, which unfortunately had a waiting list. Two other seniors were too poor to afford their medications.

Later that afternoon, I attended a two-hour seminar for grandparents raising their grandchildren. The stories of their children's drug and alcohol addictions were painful, leaving in their wake innocent third-generation kids. Grandparents, some in their 70s and 80s were again raising teenagers, already emotionally unstable and acting out, some on the verge of their own addictions.

I was discovering that many problems had no simple solutions and did not disappear after waving a referral wand or pointing them to a program. Given the complexity of many lives, how unsophisticated to think I could resolve things in neat simple packages. "We don't change the world," Imogene kept telling me. "We try to make dreadful situations better. Don't take failure personally, and don't forget to take care of yourself. Burn-out has caused many a good, kind person to quit because the case load is unbearably sad. Keep focusing on how many people you have really helped." She was right. There were lots of resolved problems. I had managed to make some people smile.

Before I left for the day, I talked to Ross, knowing I would not see him till tomorrow. Then I straightened my desk to see if I had any loose ends. "Well, hello there," I heard a smug voice from my doorway. My heart skipped as I looked up to see Earl Jr. Fuck! It's late, and I am alone with Mr. Arsenic.

Without invitation, he brazenly sat in a chair in front of my desk, and crossed his legs and arms. "They had nothing to arrest me for, just like I told them, so they had to let me go. Why did you put mother up to this?"

"I am glad your parents are going to be alright. Please understand, arsenic poisoning is a serious matter and this circumstance mandated investigation of everybody close to your parents," I said after laying my shaking hands flat on the desk.

His voice raised in a threatening tone. "Yeah, well, I was the only one they went after….because of you!"

"Mr. Behnke, why are you here? Can I help you with anything?"

He raised his voice, "You have just about fucked up my life and your do-gooder attitude is bullshit! Who do you think you are, coming into people's lives when it is none of your goddamned business?"

My heart was racing, and I felt the flush of my face. "Your parents were sick and, quite frankly, dying! I will not be harassed by you. You need to leave this office immediately!" My shaky voice was also loudly pitched, so much so that it was overheard by Sylvia next door, who I hadn't realized was still there. She called 911 before bolting to my office.

In the meantime, Earl, Jr. was unmoved and not moving, leaning back in his chair, just staring at me, fingers in prayer position tapping each other, apparently relishing in my discomfort.

"Sir, you may not threaten my employees!" These strong words and intimidating tone came forth from 5-foot-two-inch Sylvia, who now stood right over the sitting Earl Jr. glaring down into his eyes. "If you do not leave, I will press charges of verbal assault and threatening behavior! These are serious charges with enormous consequences."

He stood up and soon towered over my brave, lovely Sylvia. "Oh yeah? This woman accuses me of attempted murder and I am supposed to be nice to her? Now I could lose my farm, my inheritance…all because she got an idea up her ass and ruined my life. She's the one who did the harassing, not me!"

I picked up the phone to call the police, not

knowing Sylvia had already done that. He looked fiercely at me with hostile eyes and reached to grab the receiver, but somehow changed his mind, instead ordering, "I'm not finished yet. Put it down!" Very scared, I complied. Sylvia was now visibly nervous, which heightened my own fears substantially.

"Sir, let's all cool down," Sylvia said in a firm, calm way. "This has been traumatic for all of us. I know your parents. And they love you. According to them, you will get one-half of the proceeds from the farm. That is a lot of money and both of your parents want you to have it. However, if you insist on insulting my people, you will be spending lots of that money on lawyers to defend your actions here today."

Those were the words he needed to hear. I could see him calculate the costs, not to mention the slippery slope he was building towards an eight by ten cell block. He was guilty as hell and stupidly pressing his luck. How dumb could this guy be?

"Fuck you both!" He stormed out of the office. My head was throbbing. Sylvia was visibly shaken as she grabbed the chair's arm and sat down. Both of us were silent, needing a few seconds to collect ourselves. "I am so glad you were here, but I am sorry I got you into this," I finally said with tears in my eyes. "Thanks Sylvia." Within minutes, two police officers arrived. Lieutenant Savage followed a minute later.

While the officers searched the building and grounds, Savage insisted we press charges. "If you don't, this guy will be back. We have got to stop this behavior. You can always drop the charges later, but right now, he needs to know the seriousness of harassment. This is for your own safety. I will also get a court order forbidding him from coming near this building or either of you."

Later, as Sylvia and I walked to our cars with elbows locked and me looking around for hints of Earl Jr. stalking in the bushes, she simply said, "I'm glad not all days are like this."

***

Scott was sitting on a bench outside my condo when I arrived home a half hour late for our date. "I have really got a good excuse," I said while hugging him. "I am going to make you a key. I tried calling you at home, but you must have already left. You didn't answer your cell."

"I was hoping you hadn't forgotten me. I have really missed you. Are you okay?"

"Not really," I said with a kiss to his cheek before we went inside and I launched into the Earl Jr. experience. What a great listener he was. Just talking about it helped me feel better, and he concurred with Lieutenant Savage about pressing charges.

"The creep was already gone when the police arrived, so they will have to find him first. By now he has probably moved into his parent's house."

"And how are his parents?" he said while pouring water into a teapot.

"Both are out of the woods from the arsenic poisoning. Apparently they caught it before the damage was permanent. They are now living in an assisted living facility, but Mr. Behnke is not doing well. He has been weakened by this and wasn't in good health to begin with. He still can't accurately comprehend what has happened. But Mrs. Behnke wonders why she didn't move years ago. She has enjoyed the other residents, as well as eating nicely prepared meals in a sunlit dining hall with fresh flowers on the table. It is no surprise that Earl Jr. has yet to visit them."

"Is the farm for sale?"

"It will go on the market shortly and the developers are already lined up. The Behnke's will go from poor to rich in a matter of weeks, just with a down payment. But, under the circumstances, I am not sure that happiness will follow. This whole incident has left them deeply saddened, and I doubt if they will use their newfound wealth to cruise around the world."

"However," I added, "Mr. Behnke is getting much-needed physical therapy and Mrs. Behnke finally feels safe. Priceless!"

"And how's Ross?"

"Much better. He walked today and his pain is tolerable with medication. He should be out of the hospital in a couple of days. No test results back yet."

"And," I asked, changing the subject, "How did your doctor's appointment go today?"

"Thanks for remembering. Good news, I am not forever impotent. I will, however, have to make some minor adjustments."

"As Cedric would say, 'Details….'"

"The blood pressure pills are definitely a factor, so he has changed the medication, but there is no guarantee this problem will not continue. He did give me a prescription for an enhancer but he wants us to try some techniques without it."

"You're going to a doctor who feels comfortable talking about sexual techniques?"

"Tim and I actually went to college together, so I

have known him for forty-five years. Besides being a friend, he is the best damned doctor I have ever known."

"I'm all ears on the techniques."

"Well, I must admit, it is related to performance anxiety. Except for masturbation, I haven't had sex in two years, well, actually longer because Kate was too weak to have sex the last few months of her life. For me, this is coupled with a man's natural change in sexual dynamics throughout life. Erections that used to be a '10' for the younger man, now become a '6' or '7' for him as a senior. In other words, the gold standard of sex for a twenty-something is not the same standard for a sixty-five-year-old. I can say goodbye to that era."

The teapot was now whistling and while talking, he busied himself making tea for us as I leaned against the kitchen counter. I found myself quite comfortable discussing this sensitive topic, and considering his level of sharing, he felt the same.

"I *was* putting too much pressure on myself. Trying to please you. Wanting our sex to be fulfilling, exciting," he continued, "plus the added stress of a new partner, the first one in decades. Tim told me to relax, stop even thinking about intercourse. 'Enjoy the journey,' he said. 'Have full body sex.'"

"What's that...full body sex?"

"Actually full body intimacy, sensual sex. Kissing, hugging, touching from head to toe....all kinds of stimulation, massage."

"This sounds like something I could really be into. Besides, we have already done a lot of that, which is why I have enjoyed making love with you so much."

"He even told me to waste some of my erections. I mean, like get hard, then let that go. Don't immediately think I have to hurry up and have intercourse before I lose the erection. That just increases the anxiety."

"I am very comfortable with that." At times, I couldn't believe I was sixty-years-old and having such an honest conversation about sex for the first time in my life. Who'd have thought?

"Thanks Claire. You know this is a very hard conversation to have with a new lover; actually I suppose many men could not have it with anybody, even their wives. Anyway, Tim also said that intercourse is entirely possible with only a partial erection. For this part, we will have to experiment with positions."

"Scott, I can see how two seniors can put a lot of pressure on themselves. We still maintain that image of younger people making love with orgasm their goal, maybe even their only goal. I'm eager to learn to love the process…it's a new experience for me also." I winked at him, "Can't wait to try."

"How about some dinner first? I'm starving!"

Over salad and spaghetti, we talked more, elevating our trust, both of us seemingly comfortable with the level of emotional honesty. He passed on a glass of wine, having learned that alcohol can lead to further difficulty in erectile function. That night we experimented with full body sex. We let his first erection go while he satisfied me. His second erection, while not full, sustained vaginal thrusting and he ejaculated. I suspected he was more relaxed now; that his self-induced pressure to perform had already subsided somewhat.

The next morning we both slept in since I had no classes and didn't have to work until noon. Sleep, wonderful sleep. I was still sitting in bed reading when he laid my coffee down on my night table. At my eye level I could see his already hugely erect, rock-hard, red-as-a-beet penis literally tearing loose from his boxers. "Dear God, do I turn you on that much?"

"Shut-up and make love to me before it wilts."

"Gladly."

Both of us rolled playfully. I immediately knew this morning's sex would be different, starting with extra lubricant. We both worked up a good sweat.

"Guess this stuff works," he finally said with a big smile on his face.

"Enhancer? Whoa...I guess so."

"I think I can cut the dose," he said while looking down at his still partially erect and reddened penis. "Unless, of course, you are ready to go again?"

"Can I drink some coffee first?"

"By the way," I added. "We don't have to do this every time. Last night was equally satisfying---actually, even more so."

"I agree, and thanks, I mean really thanks for saying that. If you didn't have to go to work, I'd pull out a bottle of Champagne and we could toast to senior loving."

Holding up my coffee, "I'll drink to that!"

168

15

Ross began experiencing nausea and a predictably lessened appetite shortly after chemotherapy treatments started. His hair started falling out in clumps and he had tingling in his feet and hands, all accompanied by overwhelming exhaustion.

"I feel like I have got a brutal case of the flu," he told me while shivering on the sofa. "This treatment is more dreadful than having cancer! Now I know what some people mean when they say dying can actually be worse than death."

I hadn't thought about it that way—dying being worse than death—but I guess it made sense. With death, it is over, no more pain and suffering. But treatments to prevent dying and death? Well, a toxic treatment to hopefully kill a poisonous invasion—that really does suck. Ross's doctor said they had to almost kill Ross to—hopefully—cure him.

I wrapped him in a blanket. "Ross, I don't think you can say you are dying, even if these treatments make you feel like shit. Chemo has never been advertised as a vacation. You have got ten weeks of this, actually eight left."

"Yeah, no pain, no gain," he said with a forced

smile.

Rossy and Jennifer came in, bringing flowers and some unwanted food. The aroma reactivated the nausea. "Sorry," said Ross beginning to retch, "but could you get that away from me. I'm dieting!" Rossy complied.

"Hey dad, I brought some old John Wayne movies and your all time favorite, *The Graduate*. I hoped they might help you pass the time."

"Thanks, son," Ross said shuffling through the stack. "Wow, *True Grit*. I haven't seen this one in years."

Everybody seemed at a loss for words. We all wanted to help but just didn't know exactly how. Finally I did what any dedicated ex-wife would do...I started cleaning the kitchen. Later I went upstairs to change his sheets. He would need a fresh bed. While I worked, a worried looking Rossy came into the bedroom and announced that Ross's ex-lover Amanda had arrived.

"How nice that you rushed to spare me, but I am not going to spend the afternoon up here waiting for her to leave," I said while fluffing the pillow with rather hard blows.

"Dad told me that his relationship with her was long over, so I am not quite sure what she is doing here."

"I need to get home," I said abruptly.

"No, Mom, please stay. Please. I'll get rid of her."

Rossy and I walked downstairs together. When Amanda saw me, she was visibly nervous. I loved watching her squirm.

"I, er, just came by with some flowers," she said.

"I am not staying. See, I haven't even taken my coat off." After hasty good-byes, she left.

"You never know who will show up when you are sick," Ross said, looking at me. "It has been months since we saw each other last. Claire, I am sorry she came when you were here. She didn't call first or anything."

"It's okay, Ross."

By now Jennifer was making her nursing self busy, getting him comfortable, rubbing his back, administering an antiemetic and a pain pill. We gathered around Ross and talked for a while until, visibly drained, he drifted off to sleep. Retreating to the kitchen, Rossy and Jen started updating me on wedding plans. It would now be substantially smaller, in April, with a hundred people at a country club. Ross's cancer had not only subdued their jubilation, but, feeling time might not be on their side, they decided to marry earlier than the original June date. Rossy was determined that his father would be at his wedding.

That afternoon, I took my leave to study for Stevens's exam the next day.

"Do you have to go?" Ross said almost incoherently.

"I'll be back soon."

***

The next couple of weeks I took him to some of his chemo treatments at the hospital and helped where I could. He always wanted to talk, not necessarily about his future, which he wasn't sure about anyway, but about the family and, eventually us. While we were together he repeatedly wanted me to call Peter, now back in China, or Kate in Boston, as if to show them I was hanging out more at 'home.'

"Will you spend Thanksgiving with us?" He asked while we sat at the kitchen table.

"I will drop by in the morning and spend a couple of hours with you and the kids."

"Ross," I continued hesitantly. "I'm, ah, seeing someone."

"You mean as in dating? Is it serious?"

I hated that question. "His wife died two years ago. We met a few weeks ago and have enjoyed each other's company. I am not rushing into anything. I have school and a job. He is going to Arizona for the winter."

"You are avoiding my question. Or shouldn't I ask?"

"I really care about him."

"Sorry to hear that. Oh, Claire, I am sorry about so much. This cancer has really made me put my life into perspective. Maybe I should have gotten it about two years ago."

"Ross, stop it! I wish you had never gotten this."

"Well, sometimes it takes being hit by a ton of bricks to see the light."

"I was talking to somebody at the agency," I said changing the subject. "There is a support group for cancer survivors. You might be interested."

"I haven't survived this yet."

"Oh, but you are surviving and can continue to survive. Why don't you give it a try? If you don't like it, you don't have to go back."

"I am not interested in becoming a cancer groupie sitting around commiserating about our common pitiful plight."

"I don't think promoting pity is their goal.

Anyway, here is their card. It is a national organization called the Wellness Community. They have a chapter near here."

"Not interested now, but I will keep this card. Thanks. Now tell me about this guy in your life."

He's retired, named Scott."

"Scott? I know a couple of Scott's."

"Scott Dison."

"Dison? Dison! I know him—not well, but he used to run the Community Foundation and got our company to give thousands for charity. Wow, small world! He was hard to say 'no' to. A very persuasive man. I liked him. You have good taste."

"If I beat this thing, you had better tell your Scott to watch out! I'll be back."

"Please don't go there, Ross."

"Why not, I can try a 'Hail Mary,' can't I? Besides, I'm better looking," he said forcing a smile, before becoming very quiet and visibly sad. I knew he wanted to ask me more.

I had just added another complication to our already convoluted relationship. At that moment, I was feeling very unsure of myself…and strangely drawn to this man I lived with for forty years. The cancer had precipitated an honesty neither of us had known while together. We were spending long hours reminiscing, even about our college days. He remembered I had been an excellent student and told me he was proud of my current work and academic efforts.

"Forgive one another or perish," said Morrie in the book, *Tuesdays with Morrie*. Forgiveness?—lots of lonely, mental work--it is almost easier to be angry at him. Forgiveness gets messy—one has to redefine a relationship. Later I wrote in my journal:

I don't know if I am ready for another serious relationship. I haven't yet resolved my old one. A part of me wants to move on—let the past fade into memory, including our bitter finale. Another part of me wants to somehow mend it. No, not a reconciliation mend—don't think I want that. Rather, a transition to platonic, civil, friendly.

Is a gold-mend possible? Right now it's tenuous, fraught with fragility, like inching our way across thin ice. Who knows where this is going? Would I be able to call him to share mutual excitement when a grandchild is born? Or, converse on less exhilarating news about the kids? Would we be on the same page? Wanting the same thing? The routine and rut of long-term marriage was easier than this.

16

Cedric had talked for weeks about his upcoming trip to San Francisco for some designer's convention. Several of his friends had immigrated there and reunions were being impeccably planned. He planned to splurge on a posh downtown hotel overlooking Fisherman's Wharf and Alcatraz.

"Wardrobe planning is such a bitch. Sweaters will overflow in my suitcase. I suppose I should take my Brooks Brothers trench coat."

"Dear God, Cedric, you are worse than my daughter when she was a teenager."

"Look Ms. Aging Hippie College Student--image is everything."

"Actually I am excited for you. I have never been there and my old college roommate, Gloria, lives in the area with her family."

"And when was the last time you saw her?"

"Oh about thirty years ago, although we have kept in touch at Christmas and with occasional phone calls. She and I were once close, but too many kids, family obligations, and distance impeded both of us from sustaining an active relationship. I regret that we didn't work harder to maintain our friendship. We were dear buddies."

"Like it's too late? Are you copping that pathetic attitude about how life-has-passed-you-by?"

"Staring at him over the rims of my glasses, "Do you need a ride to the airport?"

"Thanks, what a nice offer. Tell you what—I'll take you up on it---with one condition…"

"And that would be…?"

"Bring a suitcase packed with your party clothes and join me."

"Yea, right!" my whole face frowning. "I have got to study, and—"

"What? No guts!" he said, interrupting my laundry list of excuses. "No sense of adventure? Claire, just screw your scheduled life and embrace the spontaneity that life can offer."

I smiled as I shook my head. "It's just not practical right now."

"Look," he continued. "You can stay with me in my four star room—two beds--with terry cloth bathrobes and chocolate mints on your pillow."

"And what about your privacy…should you want to entertain?"

"Well, you bunk with Gloria for one night, can't you?"

"I don't even know if she is available, or even wants to see me."

"One way to find out," he said handing me the phone. "I dare you."

Gloria answered the phone and we briefly caught up with the news of my separation, Ross's cancer, our kids, her career in nursing, and her marriage with Ron, her college love. They had separated once a few years ago (something she hadn't divulged in her

Christmas cards) but they managed to work it out. Cedric had left my apartment soon after our initial hellos, as if he realized we were going to blabber on.

"Oh Claire, I would absolutely love to see you. Too many years have separated us and it's time. As a matter of fact, Ron is leaving Saturday to visit his dad, who lives upstate in a nursing home. He stays with his brother and comes home Sunday evening. "Claire, do it! Just say yes!"

My very organized life never had much room for frivolity but now, here I was, going to the airport with Cedric, with Scott driving us! A very considerate Marion allowed me to switch days with her—days I would pay back when she went on vacation. This jaunt was luckily scheduled so I didn't miss any classes. To avoid excess guilt, I packed my books.

Long lines met us at the airport. Weather problems in various parts of the country delayed many flights. A young man behind us was anxious to get home to reunite with his two-week-old infant son. He enthusiastically showed us photos of the delivery and gave Cedric a cigar. Suddenly the man in front of us, who just found out his flight to New Orleans was postponed eight hours due to equipment failure, started shouting: "You bastards! You don't know how to run an airline! I have to get there. You asshole. Fucking get me on another flight!"

Cedric and I backed up. "What's with the major adult temper tantrum?" whispered Cedric. "This guy is an ulcer waiting to happen."

The agent, visibly shaken as he pressed hard on his computer's keyboard, was finally able to book him on another carrier. But unfortunately only first class tickets were available. "You had better fuckin' pay the difference, you goddamned moron!" People all around us stopped talking and stared. The now visibly overstressed agent, probably remembering the customer-is-always-right speech in orientation, was trying to smile through his gritted teeth. A supervisor summoned to the area firmly told the bastard to calm down or security would be alerted.

Reluctantly the man wrote a check for the difference, which he threw into the face of the agent and checked his suitcase saying, "only losers work for an airline like this." Then he stomped away.

Still recuperating from the verbal lashing, the agent snorted at me, the next customer in line, "Yes, lady, what can I do for you?"

Handing him my ticket, I said calmly, "You handled yourself well. I would have killed the jerk." He didn't answer but continued pounding on his keyboard to process my boarding pass.

I tried again, "Please, let me have the name of your supervisor so I can write a letter telling the airline how well you handled yourself under such pressure."

With that, he came out from behind the counter, climbing over the luggage scales and stood right in front of me with his face only inches from mine. Cedric got right next to me as if to protect if necessary. "Lady," he said softly. "That man might be going to New Orleans but I sent his fucking suitcase to Juneau, Alaska!"

"Eeee God!" said Cedric about ready to roll on the floor. With eyes wide, my hand covered my open mouth. "Shhhhh, don't say anything or I surely will get fired," said the agent. I couldn't. I was speechless. What a creative non-violent act of sabotage. Cedric and I laughed all the way to our gate, fantasizing if the 'jerk,' as we now called him, would ever find his lost luggage. For the first half of the flight we shared our own sabotage stories, none of which topped what we just witnessed. In the future, many of our conversations would start with, "Send any luggage to Juneau today?"

Cedric attended his conference while I walked the streets of San Francisco, tasted food in Chinatown, puffed up a steep Nob Hill, strolled Fisherman's Wharf, and booked a boat trip to Alcatraz. We both slept comfortably in the same room. He strolled around in his underwear but I used the hotel bathrobe.

One morning Cedric ordered an elegant room service table, complete with candles, flowers and fresh strawberries. "I could get used to this," I said while dipping my berries in fresh cream. "Thanks for this wonderful treat."

"You're welcome. I only do this for special friends," he replied while searching the closet for what to wear.

"I'm honored."

"Which shirt should I wear today—yellow or blue?"

"Cedric! Who cares?"

Late that afternoon, I read a chapter in my psychology textbook and took a nap, then joined Cedric and two of his old friends for a dinner where we enjoyed both serious conversation and laughter-filled stories. As the clock struck midnight, I was dancing in a gay nightclub with Fran, a beautiful young drag queen who called me grand-dame lady. He was Peter's age, a man by day teaching community college English, a woman most Saturday nights—gorgeous, happy, gracefully flicking his hair back with professionally-done nails, exuding pride in his effeminate demeanor. He was so delighted to be a woman, something I took for granted.

He was moving to the up-beat music in such sexy ways and I mimicked his every dance step, though not nearly with such bravado...or talent. We both worked up a sweat, even as Cedric watched, rolling his eyes, "You're dance-challenged, like my mother. Stop with the jerky 1960's moves! You look like you're milking a cow with your hands. Let yourself sway!"

With my inhibitions fading, Fran and I danced, breathing hard like one does after the end of a rigorous aerobics routine. Then, as if the disc jockey knew when to offer a break, a slow dance followed. He (she) grabbed me tightly, both hands around my waist. Hesitant at first, my arms dangled. Then with a 'what the hell' attitude, I put them around his neck and laid my head on his shoulder, his Adam's apple touching my nose.

He put my hand on his breast. Dear God, was this a come on! Was he interested in women? I didn't even know, but I told him his breasts felt nice and what did he use to make them feel so---so, well, voluptuous? "Mastectomy prostheses," Fran said matter of factly. "But finding the right bra was a bitch."

Later Cedric cut in almost as if to rescue me. "Dance with me Claire? Every once in a while I need to hold a woman to make sure I am still gay. And you don't have to touch my breasts."

"Cedric, I don't understand her wanting to dance

with me and touch his, I mean her, breasts. I'm confused."

"No, Claire, he wasn't putting the *make* on you. Besides, you're too old for him!"

"You know Cedric, with some practice, I could learn to dance like that."

"Haaaaa!" he gasped accompanied by a huge belly laugh. "You'll need lots of practice. We have got to suppress the matron in you."

"Matron? That's a low blow," I said laughing.

Sometime during the wee hours, I took my leave in anticipation of my upcoming day with Gloria. The atmosphere of this gay club had been liberating. I wasn't even worried about looking as if I were milking a cow. With nobody to impress or attract, I had fun with a friend. Cedric never did get back to the hotel.

***

On Saturday morning, Gloria picked me up at the hotel for the hour ride to her home in Palo Alto. It was as if we hadn't missed a beat—the two of us together again after thirty years. She was a hefty woman now, for which she made no excuses, wearing a plus-sized muu-muu and no make-up. Her home was modest, simply decorated, slightly messy, but very homey. The big chairs in her family room invited one to take off shoes and snuggle in, which we did with coffee in hand.

At one point we had a conversation divulging our life's most embarrassing moments, starting with high school menstrual periods and blood-stained skirts. Not all memories were funny—we both had some regretful embarrassments, including lying, cheating, spreading gossip that was really hurtful.

Once we shoplifted some silverware from a restaurant just for the fun of it. Both of us had our share of drunk stories.

Eventually our conversation turned to the naivety of our 1960s sexual coming of age. "I learned about sex from a romance novel," Gloria said laughing. "Remember those?--His pursed lips sucked her titillating erect nipples, while her groins, wet with anticipation, ached for the pleasure and caused her to groan, head back, with epileptic excitement." I pulled a throw pillow to my stomach to absorb the joyful ache of heavy laughter.

"Why is it that we couldn't talk about sex back then?" she continued.

"Well, we just didn't know how to tell him. I mean, what were we supposed to say: Pull back my labia--now massage--further to the left—harder—no Jesus, not that hard, your tongue feels like sandpaper—more lubrication please. Dear God, we were in such a hurry, we didn't have time to talk."

"Oh Claire, sex was a raucous synapsing of erectile tissue, a bee-line to the pubic hairs, which had nothing to do with that organ between our ears. Remember also, we were still in the age of good old Sig Freud, who had taught us that clitorises were bogus undeveloped penises and genuine orgasm for women was solely vaginal. No wonder our mothers were frigid! We were destined to fake it. What an actress I became."

"Oh yeah," I added, "Besides the big fake, I also learned all about penis envy. In fact, I admit, I had penis envy. I mean a penis was a credit card for power and prestige, as well as being able to pee without squatting or wiping, a remarkable feat that still makes me jealous, especially when I sit on a wet toilet seat. To make matters worse, when I finally discovered masturbatory orgasm, I simultaneously learned it was a sin, a disgusting one!"

"And don't forget the studs, Claire. Remember when Wilt Chamberlain bragged about having sex with a thousand-plus women. Lots of jocks on campus emulated him."

"Yeah, but did he know how to make love? Was he a lover, or a robot with a dick?

"Find them, feel'em, fuck'em, and forget'em."

"Oh Gloria, you're bad."

"Remember Kim?"

"How could I forget?"

At different times, Kim had been a roommate to each of us. A victim of an abusive home, her longing for love sadly translated into an attraction for exploitive relationships. Too bad she correlated having sex with being in love. She couldn't keep her legs together long enough to find herself. By Thanksgiving of her sophomore year, she had screwed almost the entire football team of a Division 1 university. Naturally her name got around. "Want some pussy? Call Kim. Quick Lay? Call Kim. God, I hate the word pussy."

"And don't forget the word cunt. Equally degrading. You know, Kim would have slept with Wilt in a heartbeat, then cashed in on her bragging rights."

"Gloria, that was so painful to witness."

"Yeah, especially since we were both barely beyond virginal Presbyterians from Smallsville, USA, who were still feeling guilty (well, somewhat) over not having *saved* ourselves for the right person."

"I'll never forget when she brought home that $400 in cash from that son-of-a-bitch jock, who split fast when the rabbit died. Let's see? Wasn't it 1967?"

"I have still never been so scared as I was taking her to that shopping center. I still can vividly see her getting into that dark-windowed sedan."

"Remember, she was blindfolded and told to lay down on the back seat floor?"

"I remember like it was yesterday. When she came back bleeding, I called my mother, who turned out was only twenty-two years more naive than myself. Then there was the second pregnancy with a different stud. I don't think I'll ever forgive myself for rejecting her when she had to get a second abortion. Like the horny, pompous jocks, I called her a whore."

"Sadly, me too."

"God, Gloria, weren't we judgmental when we ourselves had not one iota of insight? She was looking for love for all the wrong reasons, in the wrong places, spreading her legs to be touched and told some tender words—however grossly manipulative—loving words that she never heard in her childhood."

We both knew that eventually Kim dragged her tattered self into therapy, stopped the sadomasochistic screwing of both her body and head, and told her pitiful parents to go to Hell. Old beyond her years, she finally discovered, for the first time, the potential of internal worthiness and self-love without the narcissism.

"Ever hear from her?"

Shaking my head, "No, I hope she found happiness."

***

By afternoon, we had finished talking about our past and began disclosing our current lives---her son's bouts with severe depression, his attempted suicide, her slippery slope from heavy drinking to alcohol dependency; she was now a nurse in a drug rehab center. I shared my biggest regrets—not finishing college, getting knocked up, my descent into underachievement. I even told her how I felt abandoned when she got together with Ron.

"Claire, I never knew that. I was oblivious. How about an 'I'm-so-sorry' forty-years late? I can see now how my actions were hurtful. I've learned something since about abandonment."

"We can chalk a lot up to our immaturity at the time," I added. "Actually feels good being older and wiser. I would never, ever want to go back."

That night we made dinner together and took a jaw break to watch a DVD chick flick, *Mamma Mia!* We forced a midnight lights out so we could arise for an early morning walk on the coast in a nearby park.

"I have really enjoyed this time with you," I said as the ocean waves pounded in the background.

"I love you Claire," she replied grabbing my hand. "This visit has been very special. I feel renewed."

"Wow, Gloria, thanks. I love you also." I was a bit taken back because no one outside of family had ever said that to me. "Do we have to wait another thirty years to do this again?"

"Shit girl, I'll be dead in another thirty years. Perhaps we should not wait that long."

We walked the rest of the way holding hands, then arm in arm. By afternoon we were back in the car together to retrieve Cedric and return to the airport. Having not slept at all the night before, he started snoring while taxiing for take-off. I dozed on and off during the five hour flight, only awake enough to savor the events of the past three days.

Gloria had known me when I had pimples. She was a barometer to my life. We had experienced irreplaceable life events together, and now successfully made the transition from old friend to new one. In the past two days we safely made ourselves more vulnerable with each shared joy and pain, screw-up and proud moment. I told her things I'd never shared with anybody, including Ross; secrets, big and small, finally pulled from the depths of repression. In my journal I wrote:

Why did I not have her closer to me in these last decades? How could I not hold on to a female friend such as this? How could I not realize what she meant to me? Like so much in life, friendship takes work or it slowly diminishes into a memory. I grieved this huge void. I didn't know what I had missed until just now and I promise not to let it happen again.

I feel like I've repaired another crack in my life…oh yes, with gold.

17

School, work, Scott, and Ross all wanted a part of a very weary me. I had done mediocre (again) on a psychology test, only getting a "C." Okay, I said to myself, there goes *magna cum laude* down the drain.

A short visit to Ross turned into a long reminisce about double-dating with Gloria and Ron during our college days. I shared what I had journaled about friendships.

"I love you Claire," he said as I put my coat on.

"I love you too Ross."

With a second wind and friendship on my mind, I left Ross to visit Edith. Unfortunately my schedule only allowed for visits twice a week and I missed the spontaneous drop-ins we had initiated as neighbors. She had been such a support to me after I moved. Now I cringed at the way her daughter treated her. Barbara should relish these last years with her mother instead of regarding her as some moronic relic. At least she still had a mom!

How was it that Barbara and I saw Edith so differently? Perhaps there was a past that made Barbara bitter. I saw Edith as vibrant, loving and kind---traits obviously not inherited by this daughter.

Maybe there was something I didn't know, and frankly, I wasn't inclined to pry.

Edith had ditched the wheelchair, was walking to and fro with the aid of a walker, and was doing remarkably well in physical therapy. She could even climb stairs. "I could be out of here before week's end," she said proudly.

"And have you made a decision about where you will go?"

"Home! Barbara is not happy to say the least. I even had to call our family lawyer, whom I asked to visit me here, then I had a candid, back-off talk with Barbara. She made one threat too many. I am nowhere close to incompetent, mentally or physically, at least not yet! Claire, I fear this experience has put a permanent strain on our relationship."

"Edith, I'm sorry."

"Me too. It didn't have to be this way. If I was a *person* to her and not some five-year-old, it might have been different, but I have no room in my life for dictators. Getting old is hard enough without someone trying to govern your entire life. She has got some major issues, and an attitude problem of equal proportions."

"Maybe," she continued, "I will only be able to live alone for a while longer. But I deserve that opportunity. Maybe I will fall again, or get Alzheimer's, or lose my driver's license. God knows, maybe someday I really will need Barbara to help care for me. There are lots of 'maybes' in my life right now. I am not naive enough to think I can live alone forever. When I get home I will start visiting assisted living places for when that day comes. I do need to start preparing."

I loved Edith's determination, which I believed did not stem from unrealistic stubbornness. Perhaps I wouldn't have felt this way before I worked at the agency. My professional experience with seniors, short as it was, had definitely impacted me.

"Maybe Barbara will grow to understand," I said.

"Whatever, it's her life. Loving her as a child was easy, but when she grew up!--now that's been challenging with her Obsessive-Compulsive Disorder and all. Look here, we're just talking about me again. How was San Francisco? How's school? Ross? Cedric tells me you and Scott are becoming a real item. And Claire, Barbara is beside herself about my friendship with Cedric, and you're not exactly on her list of favorite people either."

The topics of our conversation flitted from one subject to another, as if to get in all we could before visiting hours ended. On the way home, I kept thinking about Edith's disclosure about Barbara's OCD. Of course things made more sense now; that missing puzzle piece explained a magnitude of behaviors.

***

The next day I visited Shirley for the first time in two weeks. Ross was on my mind.

"Do you think you're still in love with him?" she said.

"Love vs. *in* love? No, not *in* love."

"Do you feel sorry for him? What do you think it is that draws you so strongly to him now?"

"Absolutely I feel sorry for him. Cancer seems to have brought out the best in him. There is a hidden Ross emerging from his suffering, a really sensitive guy. The guy I wanted all along in my marriage. And he needs me now."

"He needs you? So what does that mean to you?"

"I know you are going to jump all over this Shirley, but I want to help. I'd love to rescue him."

"Can you *rescue* someone from cancer?"

"No, but I can help him get through it."

"How much are you willing to sacrifice your own needs to do this?"

"I know where you are going Shirley. I love my life now. But I want to have a good relationship with Ross. I want to finish our unfinished business. If he dies, I want to bury him knowing we spent forty years together and parted as friends."

"Do you think he maintains hope of winning you back? If so, is it fair for him to believe this? You told him you loved him. How could he interpret that?

"Stop with the hard questions, will you?"

"No way! You are paying too much money for me to sit here, hold your hand, and mother you. My *gentle* time with you has ended. You are far too intelligent, with tremendous potential and strengths, for me to waste my time comforting you. Go read a soothing self-help book if that's what you want." She said this all in her amazingly gentle voice.

"You're right. I know, I know."

"Soooooo?"

"Why couldn't he have done this before?"

"Claire, this is called grieving. First you grieved at the ending of your marriage. You wanted to get the marriage help. He refused. Instead he had an affair, which predictably ended and so he is contrite. Now, both of you are grieving that he has cancer. Only you have found another life. So I will ask again….Do you want to go back to him?"

"I don't know. I am so confused. Forty years with someone is such a long time. But Scott is so wonderful. I don't know. If only I had been there to make Ross get an earlier physical. He's a damned moron who shacked up with a fucking whore."

"Retaliatory anger? Is there a part of you who thinks he is getting what he deserves?"

"Ouch, Shirley." I grabbed my hands and bowed as if in prayer. This one hurt. The tissue box got passed.

I looked down at the floor, anywhere away from her intense eyes. Her words stung and she knew it. Yet it felt good knowing that she diagnosed my emotional well-being as strong enough for me to hear the truth. As usual, she did not beat around the bush, and she was right to ask the big questions. Could I really forgive him? Was I still in love with him?

Finally she said, "Look Claire, do you think it is an 'either/or' situation? Perhaps you can embrace your new life while also healing your old one? Perhaps you can find a way to mend the two lives together in a beautiful new pattern. Do you think you could love both Ross and Scott--in entirely different ways, of course?

I couldn't articulate an answer to any of those questions.

***

I spent Thanksgiving with Scott's family after visiting Ross and the kids, minus Peter and his wife, who wouldn't be home until right before Christmas. Kate and Rossy did not hold back their displeasure at my leaving, with Rossy personally admonishing me with, "This might be Dad's last Thanksgiving. Can't you stay at least for us?"

I felt an urge to slap him, but behaved nicely instead, "I understand that you are disappointed."

"I'm sorry Mom," he said realizing his offensive words. "It's just, well, I guess I'm a little stressed right now, and I miss you."

I should have expected the kids voicing their regrets. Besides, they were left to cook a fifteen-pounder and get the lumps out of the potatoes, while I dashed off to the family of my new boyfriend. They knew about Scott now, which further thwarted their hopes for reconciliation simultaneous with their father's precarious future. And, of course, I was conflicted as well. This would be my first Thanksgiving without my family. I loved my kids. It was painful to say good-bye.

"I am really sorry you cannot stay," said a weakened Ross, who took the opportunity to insert his own guilt trip. "Our Thanksgivings have always been so special. Remember how we used to get out the family photo albums and give thanks for our time together?"

That did it. I started crying. Damn him! The drive back to my apartment gave me time to center myself again.

***

Scott's kids and their intergenerational families were welcoming, as if they realized their dad had grieved sufficiently over their deceased mother, demonstrating that he would never get over her death even while he readied to move on. They were happy that he was happy, and so I was greeted with hugs and "so nice to finally meet you," and particularly touching, "so you are that special lady in Dad's life?"

I was immediately relaxed and enjoyed the day, which included watching Scott play with three of his grandkids.

At the table was an empty chair, in memory of those departed, a ritual the family had kept for many years. Perhaps to make me more comfortable, they gave a general toast to those departed without mentioning Kate's name.

"Scott has talked a lot about your Mom," I said as he squeezed my hand, "and Kate sounds like she was such a very special person. I am sure you miss her. This is a wonderful way to remember her. By the way, my daughter's name is Kate also."

Visibly relieved that mention of their mother would not be considered off limits, son Dan said, "Thank you for saying that." After a pause, his daughter, Julie, asked, "Do you want to acknowledge anyone?"

"Yes, my parents. They would have loved to be honored next to your mother."

***

That evening Scott and I talked more about his erectile dysfunction and premature ejaculation. He had obviously been doing his homework and had become well-versed.

"Did you know that a significant number of men over sixty have this condition?"

"I did not, but I have lately noticed an inordinate amount of enhancer commercials on the television. You know, before my mother died, my dad, a WWII marine, told me they hadn't had sex in five years because they 'couldn't.' That was as close as he could come to saying the word impotent. There was a whole generation that didn't talk about it, much less try to resolve it."

"Yeah, I'm fairly sure my parents ended sexual intimacy well before they died. I can't imagine. Even with many in *our* generation, talking about sex is still taboo."

"And I suppose having sexual enhancement drugs doesn't actually encourage more communication. It's the old adage; 'got a problem, take a pill, and no one will have to know.'"

"Yeah," said Scott. "The quick-fix phenomenon. Yet, it is nice to know it's available."

"You will get no arguments from me."

"I worry it will be a problem for us."

"A problem? Scott?"

"Here I have this wonderful new relationship. I am feeling complete happiness for the first time since Kate died. But you are younger, vibrant, taking the world to new heights, and I am retired, downsizing my life, and discovering I have this rather common senior citizen predicament."

"Is this about ego? Are you going to dump me?"

"Hell, no way! I'll binge on enhancers before I let *you* go."

"I'm sure that would *really* be healthy!"

"Scott," I continued, "we are due for this talk. I don't think it is premature. Where do you see us going?" I felt anxious and insecure as soon as I said those words.

"Here's how I see it. I want to continue my volunteer work by mentoring at the Community Foundation but I can choose how much I want to work. And, since I have financial freedom, I want to travel and spend time in Arizona. On the other hand, I see you in school for a couple more years and then in the workplace for a few more. Are we on the same page so far?"

"Yes, I won't quit college a second time and I find my job fulfilling. I missed that opportunity before; I don't want to miss it again."

"And I wouldn't expect you to drop everything and go off into the sunset with me. It would be most unfair to ask you to give up your ambitions again."

"You are just about the most understanding person I have ever met. So do you think we can both realize our goals?

"You mean, can we make it work as a couple?"

"Yes, I really hope we can. These last few weeks have been wonderful," I said grabbing his hand.

"I agree." Then pausing to take a deep breath, "Claire, I love you."

My heart fluttered. Then it somersaulted. "Oh, Wow!" I hugged him. "Those words are music to my ears." It sounded like a whole symphony to me as he held me. Okay, so it felt good to feel like a teenager every so often. "I feel the same way. I love *you*--and I am so thankful I found you."

"Wow, what a milestone in both our lives. By the way, thanks for asking me out. That took courage." We kissed and took a long pause, as if to relish the moment. Finally he said, "So let's see where that leaves us. We both love each other, but you are in school and have a job, plus a soon-to-be ex-husband with cancer, and Rossy's upcoming wedding. I am leaving before Christmas for three months in Arizona."

"Needless to say, I don't plan on dating while you are away," I added.

"Good, me neither, so we have resolved to be an

exclusive couple."

"Why don't I come to Arizona twice instead of once? Maybe we can also meet somewhere in the middle for a long weekend."

"Or if you can't get all that time off work, I could easily come home for a week. Also, I have been asked to do some Habitat for Humanity work and fundraising for them in New Orleans. Maybe we could hook up there for a few days?"

"Maybe I could get a class project out of it?"

"Even better! Okay, one more question. Enhancer? Yes or no for tonight? Remember, it takes about an hour to reach its effectiveness."

"No." I answered quickly, wanting my gentler lover this time.

He smiled.

I think our relaxed state helped make this night's love-making particularly satisfying. We had mutually taken our relationship to another level. It felt good. It felt right. He didn't maintain an erection and ejaculated in a short time, but neither of us was left wanting.

***

After Thanksgiving, I plunged into finishing off the semester. My only final was in early December for Stevens's class but I had a substantial paper due for Marilyn's. In addition, the court date for my assault charges against Earl Jr. was mid-December. Ross would be finished with chemo directly before Christmas, about the same time Scott would be leaving for Arizona.

A knock at the door startled me from my scheduling thoughts.

"Hello Honey!" said a jubilant Edith. "I'm

back!"

"Oh my God, just look at you. Wow, how'd you get here? I could have picked you up."

"I got discharged today and they brought me home in their van. Check out my new cane. Oh Claire, I can't tell you how nice it is to be home. Can you come over for coffee?"

"I have to be to work in a half hour. How about after I get home? Do you want to have dinner together?"

"Sure, although I'm still stuffed from Thanksgiving at Barbara's. They let me 'out' for the day but we'll save *that* conversation for another time."

"I'll have to study, but tell you what…I will make something simple, like a salad, and bring it over."

"I'll make that roast I have in the freezer. I'll also see what Cedric is doing. Oh, I am so happy! Thanks, Claire."

Work was fairly uneventful. The hoarding lady, on the threat of imminent eviction, was getting her apartment cleaned and had started taking her medication and seeing a therapist. Her son had finally visited and was helping her sort through years of accumulation without undue drama. He came to see me to say things were going well. "I told mom if she stops the medication or sessions with her therapist, that is a deal-breaker for our future together. She wants me in her life and she wants to see her grandchildren. I think she is finally motivated to get well, a real milestone. Yesterday I even went to therapy with her. This whole eviction threat really scared her, but is a blessing in disguise."

Cedric was happy to join us that evening and made a delicious pasta to accompany our pot luck dinner. Edith told us that she had met someone, a man, at the rehab center. "It's not going to be a steamy, hot romance because of his health, but he was just wonderful to me, motivating me in physical therapy every day."

"Oh, Edith, I see that sparkle in your eye. Might be premature to eliminate that *steamy* part just yet," quipped Cedric.

"Okay, Cedric, if you say so."

Later Edith poured herself a little wine in a crystal glass. "I get picked up three times a week for therapy, then I have these exercises in between, including short distance walks twice a day. Charlotte is flying in tomorrow to help out for a few days. I think I am going to beat this accident and have a full recuperation. My God, I'm grateful. Tonight I get to sleep in my own bed! Okay guys, I want further details on the San Francisco trip."

"Well, my dear, cute, little old lady, wow, it is soooo nice to have you back," said Cedric before going into specifics about our trip. Naturally he described in detail my rhythm challenge on the dance floor, and in typical Cedric fashion, robotically demonstrated my dance moves. "She was also feeling up the breasts of a drag queen!"

Edith choked on her wine laughing. "Look what you made me do. I am spilling my drink everywhere." Then holding up her glass, "Here, let's drink to better behavior!"

Laughing, she continued, "You danced with a drag queen, Claire? Please, Cedric, tell me you got a photo of that!"

"I wish. It would be perfect for blackmail later on."

After dinner, two of Edith's other friends from the complex came over offering their assistance. One offered to grocery shop the next day, "Just give me a list." The other would take Edith to the hairdresser's.

"Please Miss Edith, no blue hair," Cedric whispered in her ear.

Edith would do alright. She was beaming with happiness. She treasured life, fragile as it was.

***

I went home to study, but eventually pulled out my journal. I kept thinking about my sessions with Shirley and my feelings for Ross. It would help to write.

I love you like a brother/we have a history/not all of it happy/I feel deceived although I take my share of the blame/I love somebody else now, who makes our relationship seem primitive. He does not replace you/I don't need a replacement anymore/I am satisfied alone, I think.

The phone rang. It was Gloria. Her son had committed suicide. All of my little problems and business fell away in a moment.

'What ifs' and 'if onlys' dominated our conversation, even though his previous attempts curbed the magnitude of shock. At times she seemed to have a sense of relief. No, she didn't want me to fly out. I felt entirely helpless. She was in so much pain and I couldn't make it better. Listening was all I could do.

"At least his suffering is over," she cried.

I grieved with her at the unbearable loss of a child, every parent's nightmare. He had even dramatically jumped off the Bay Bridge, an infamous place for suicides. Fisherman had found the body already marred by sharks. Cameras from the bridge's surveillance equipment had been needed to identify him.

She read his suicide note:

"The constant pain it takes to stay is so much greater that the moment of pain it takes to leave. I need peace from this wretched depression, which has consumed my life. Please know that it was nobody's fault. I repeat: Nobody's fault! I love you all. I beg you to understand and I hope you will, in time, forgive me. Love, Brad."

In having Gloria back in my life, I realized that there would be shared joys as well as suffering. When we hung up, I promised to call her daily. Then, closing my textbooks for good that evening, I called Kate, Rossy and e-mailed Peter...telling them how proud of them I am and how much I loved them.

18

The end of the semester went off without a hitch. The final 'B' I got in Stevens's class was directly related to the study time needed to memorize and spit back answers on a multiple choice test, time I did not dedicate after my mid-semester 'A'. I actually didn't do that well on the final but nobody did, therefore he had to grade on a revised curve that pulled my final grade up. The students, he said, had failed to live up to his standards. "We" didn't study enough. "We" didn't analyze properly. "We—we—we." At age twenty, I might have accepted that at face value, but at sixty it sounded like the ultimate cop-out. His classroom was boring, his style seemed pretentious, accompanied by a sordid manner of treating co-eds, and his life experiences were sadly deficient. I wondered why some professors, with all their supposed brain power, were never taught how to teach.

I felt obliged to reflect this in his evaluation. I wrote that he treated us like we were in third grade and showed favoritism towards pretty, young women, something I found highly unprofessional, especially in a psychology department. My seat neighbor, Linda, had told me that only days before he had invited her to his office to "talk about a project she was doing." When she got there, he said he needed coffee and took her to a restaurant for dinner. She was too scared to say no. Later, she had asked me what to do, and I advised her never to go out with him again and to report the incident. She didn't. "I am sure he was only trying to be nice. I probably misinterpreted."

Since this type of harassment is such a gray area, and open to scrutiny, I wrote specific incidences on my evaluation---i.e. bending down in class to get three inches from the face of a co-ed who was unable to retreat from her desk-chair, rubbing the back of a girl as she tried to answer a question, calling people stupid in front of the class---knowing I could be called to defend my accusations. With a nervous hand, I even signed my name, something I would have never done just months ago. He needed to know what was being observed about him and by whom.

Next to Marilyn, he looked even worse. She motivated me to work, to study, to better myself. I would sign up for any class she taught, even if it was geography. With her, learning was fun and stimulating. My confidence soared under her tutelage. I worked harder than necessary on my final paper so as not to disappoint her. Doing my best work mattered more than any grade. I wrote all this on an evaluation form as well.

**

The department stores were playing carols and holiday decorating as Kate and I celebrated the end of our semesters and began our Christmas shopping. It felt nice having our 'girl' bonding time. I beamed with pride at my beautiful twenty-eight-year-old daughter, now close to finishing graduate school and preparing for the interview process for her first professional job. She was also in her sixth month of dating a guy from Boston.

"So tell me more about Sam. When do I get to meet him?"

"I have asked him to visit after Christmas. He is coming down on the twenty-sixth and staying through New Year's. Mom, he's special. I want to stay in Boston to be close to him while he finishes law school. We've talked about living together."

"Whoa, this does sound special! Is that something you want to do?"

"Oh yes, I really love him. I would have brought him home before, but with Dad's cancer—well—it just didn't seem like the right time. Mom, I think he is the one for me. No, scratch that--I am sure."

"Well then, I can't wait to meet him!"

"And, Mom, how about you? Who is this guy you're dating?"

"Gosh Kate, I feel kind of funny talking about my boyfriend."

"Come on Mom. It's me, Kate, your daughter."

"Yeah, but…"

"Look Mom, I know that you and Dad are over. And I admire you for sticking around to support Dad in this crisis. Sure, wouldn't it be nice if, like in fairytales, you and Dad got back together, but it would be selfish of me to expect that. Besides, I can see that you have changed since you left---for the better, I might add. You're in school, have a challenging job; you seem, well, so much more animated than before."

"Thanks Kate, for your vote of confidence. I

appreciate that."

"Soooo, who is this guy?"

I told her about Scott and my upcoming trip to Arizona. It turned out to be a wonderful conversation, girl to girl, rather than mother to daughter, although we spared each other the details of our sex lives. That evening she came to dinner at my home where she and Scott hit it off splendidly. Coincidently, Kate had worked one summer years ago with Scott's daughter at the Red Cross, which led to a lengthy conversation about the agency's continuing role in disaster relief.

"You have a wonderful daughter," Scott said after she left.

"Thanks, I know."

"By the way, I am leaving soon," he continued. "I want to spend as much time together as possible."

"Well, I am free from the clutches of school, so besides my work, I'm yours."

Scott had a keynote speech at a national conference in Philadelphia the next afternoon so he left early to finish his preparation and get some rest. We planned to go to Buck's County, Pennsylvania on Saturday night where he made reservations in an 1890's B&B with fireplaces in each room and a hot tub overlooking the Delaware River. There we would have our Christmas together.

I thought long and hard about what to get him for Christmas. He wasn't the kind of guy you buy 'stuff' for. In spite of his sizeable savings, he lived a rather simple life and had everything he wanted. Being retired, he didn't need many clothes. I finally decided to get him a good set of hiking poles, since he had told me he was using various sticks he picked up along the trails. It wasn't the most romantic gift, but at least it was a very usable one.

Ross had a good friend take him to his last chemotherapy treatment. After the holidays, he would have tests to determine its effectiveness. The chemo had taken its toll. His hair was gone. He laid around most of the time, battling extreme fatigue, only occasionally going into the office for two or three hour stints, constantly fighting the urge to sleep at his desk. He worried about a young, ambitious protégé who he suspected was angling to take over his position. Ross had seniority, but in his business world, the bottom line mattered more than any personal past accomplishments or, for that matter, any person. If he couldn't continue to produce, that could bring about an invitation to early retirement, something Ross was loathe to face.

He asked me to purchase specific presents for him to give at Christmas, mostly for the children. I was used to that request, having done much of the shopping over the years. I gave some of the list to Kate who wanted to shop for her brothers as well as Peter's wife, Linda, and Jennifer; I would buy for his close friends, Jeff and Frank. Like me, Kate enjoyed shopping only to a certain extent. We always used lists and rarely strayed from them, not wanting to get stressed during the holidays. But this year my list had expanded to include Cedric, Edith, and of course Scott. For Gloria, I had already framed a forty-year-old photo of us in our dorm room in our pajamas.

Edith, looking like her pre-accident jaunty self, was flying to Charlotte's home for Christmas. Cedric was going back to San Francisco until after the New Year. One of his professional colleagues, Greg, whom he had met years ago at New York's Parson's School of Design, and whom I had met at dinner and on the infamous dance floor, was rapidly becoming a steady romantic companion. Already he had come east to visit for a weekend. Cedric now talked with him daily, and they were planning a vacation in Europe. Like Cedric, his long-time partner had died, and he was very involved with AIDS philanthropy. The business savvy owner of a high-end furniture store, Greg was unlike Cedric in that he portrayed not a hint of his "gayness." In fact, I had noticed that Cedric was playing down his previous openly gay characteristics.

"You seem different since you met Greg," I had said to him.

"You noticed."

"Remember, we talked about this before over dinner…about why you want everybody to know that you are gay from the moment they meet you."

"Greg and I have actually had some serious conversations about it. I told him why I do it. He asked me why I still needed to. I thought about it long and hard. Does that sound screwed-up to you? He comes from a family that loves him. I was the rejected one. Guess I have been overcompensating. Don't worry though—I am not going to become some John Wayne macho football type who burps in public."

"So the toned-down version is the real you? I like it."

"What? You don't want me acting like an over-the-top fag?"

"My friend, I love you however you want to be."

"Thanks love. Not to change the subject, but are

you ready for your court date with Earl Jr. tomorrow?"

"I wish I would never have to see that dirt-ball again."

***

The next day I faced a soberly dressed Earl Jr., accompanied by his lawyer. Gone was his tacky goatee, and newly cut hair replaced his greased, slick-back look. His dated suit hung loosely over his shoulders calling attention to either a significant weight loss or a poor size choice. A thin tie gathered the oversized shirt at the neck. Outward appearances displayed a humble, unassuming man with the meek demeanor of a wrongly accused loving son. The agency's lawyer, Kara Pusey, accompanied me to our table. Directly behind us were Sylvia and Lt. Savage.

To make matters worse, Mrs. Behnke, manifesting her own fears, had reneged on pressing charges of elder abuse. "I need to spare Earl Sr. this stress," she had said. "I just cannot do this to his only child." Despite her not wanting to be involved in any sort of trial, she had been subpoenaed to testify on how Earl Jr. had treated me on the occasions when I was at the farm. A flu-like illness curtailed her personal appearance, so her previous statements to police were ruled admissible in court.

Kara warned us that the judge would not likely convict. In spite of Earl Jr.'s intimidating rant in my office on that day at the center, including his demand to put the phone down, he really hadn't openly threatened me. Kara had told us, "His lawyer will try to justify his anger, since he was allegedly falsely accused in the arsenic poisoning and there were no charges filed. Our main goal is to end up with a restraining order." Kara noted that his lawyer, rather conveniently, also represented a developer, one who in the last five years had tendered two offers on the Behnke property and was bidding again now that the property was officially for sale.

"How do you plead to the charges of harassment and verbal assault?" asked the judge.

"Not guilty!" replied a defiant Earl Jr.

"Counsel, how do you justify these charges?"

Kara got up to speak, "His mother, a frail elderly woman, saw the need to take a tiring bus ride from the country to tell my client that she felt her son was poisoning her husband and herself--"

"Objection!" said Earl Jr.'s attorney. "He was never charged with this and bringing this up has no relevance to this case."

"Overruled. The court knows that Mr. Behnke has not been charged with the attempted murder of his parents," said the judge looking directly at Earl, Jr., "at least not yet!" A meek- acting Earl Jr. covered his eyes with his hands, feigning tears.

"With the threat of attempted murder," continued Kara, "my client became an advocate for his stepmother. When the police were called and my client accompanied her to the farm, he called her a 'bitch,' and accused her of 'putting his Mom up to this.' Later he said, 'I'll get you for this.' He subsequently had to be handcuffed, in what is now a proven inebriated state---"

"Objection…not relevant. The client was at his home. There is nothing illegal about having too much to drink in the privacy of a residence."

"Your honor," chimed in Kara, "the police had a search warrant. One elderly person had confirmed arsenic poisoning. Later, we found out his father also had it. The police had a right to search the premises without harassment! My client had the right and legal responsibility to protect an elderly woman from further abuse."

"Objection overruled."

Linda was sweating now as if experiencing a hot flash. At forty-five(ish) she was not going to let this corporate attorney, dressed in a designer suit and carrying an expensive briefcase, get the best of her. Her dark navy plus-sized perma-press washable suit showed years of wear and tear, no doubt from countless pro bono projects. Her long frizzy hair cried for styling. These two attorneys represented opposite ends of the spectrum, as different as night and day.

She knew this attorney cared more about the estate than the parasite Earl Jr. Keeping him out of jail would expedite the sale and put his developers ahead of the pack. Defending a despicable son was necessary to cement the deal.

The judge turned to Kara. "The charges presented to this court today are for harassment and verbal abuse. Ms. Pusey, besides Mr. Behnke having called your client a bitch, what other accusations do you have?"

"Your honor, Mr. Behnke came to the agency late one evening accusing her of 'fucking up his life' and 'coming into his life when it was none of her business.' In addition, he demanded she put the phone back as she tried to call for help. My client and another social worker feared for their safety, so much so that Lieutenant Savage sought and received a temporary restraining order."

"Judge," said Earl Jr.'s attorney, "my client was under duress. He was falsely accused of a horrific crime. For God's sake, this son moved to the farm to be closer to his parents so he could care for them."

"Not true!" Kara interjected. "He had to move back to his parents' because he had lost his job, was behind on child support, had his wages garnished, was regularly unemployed, and couldn't drive after two DUI's. His parents bought the mobile home so he could live there when he had nowhere else to go. In addition, his mother has said that he was needlessly rough with both of them."

"Objection!" yelled back his attorney. "This is irrelevant. He has not been charged with elder abuse."

"Stop it, both of you!" said the judge, now obviously perturbed. "Ms. Pusey, did he threaten your client?"

"Yes, your Honor, both directly and indirectly. Directly at the farm when he said, 'I'll get you for this.' And indirectly at the agency by his threatening words and intimidating tone."

"Mr. Behnke, did you demand she put the phone down?"

"No, sir, I asked her nicely to put down the phone. It was not in a forceful way like she says. I just wanted to talk about it. I was upset. My life was in turmoil. She tried to set my parents against me. Yes, my parents were sick, but I didn't do anything to make them that way. I was scared for them too."

"Judge," interrupted Pusey. "I have a witness here, a social worker who will attest under oath that he forcibly demanded she put the phone down!"

The judge stayed silent for a few long seconds,

then addressed Earl, Jr. "Mr. Behnke, you stand on pretty shaky ground here. You have a criminal record, stand to inherit a great sum, and somehow your parents mysteriously contracted arsenic poisoning. Instead of cooperating with police, you start threatening people---

"Actually, your honor," Junior's attorney interrupted, "he never actually threatened."

"Counsel!" the judge's eyes glared. "First, do not interrupt me! Second, calling a professional worker a 'bitch' under these circumstances and demanding she put a phone down does qualify as threatening harassment. Now, Mr. Behnke, I am issuing a permanent restraining order, which means that if you even come close to the offices of the Area Agency on Aging again, or any of its employees, both at the agency or in their private lives, you go directly to jail. You will not contact them in person, or by any type of mail, or by phone. If you do, it will be considered in violation of this restraint and you will be imprisoned. Do I make myself absolutely, perfectly clear?"

"Yes, sir, your honor," Earl, Jr. said nervously. "I promise to obey your rules."

"You had better. If I see you in this court again, your life as you know it is ancient history. Court adjourned!"

I was relieved. It had happened just as Kara said it would. Earl Jr. left the courtroom with his lawyer, and neither of them even looked toward us. No doubt, an appreciative Earl Jr. would be told how he'd been saved from certain jail time. Kara surmised that his attorney's fees would be waived if he was able to convince his parents to sell to his attorney's developer client. Thankfully the senior Behnke's would get half of the selling price, enough so they could live out their lives with their needs met.

Even with a restraining order, I found myself looking over my shoulder more. That pariah had unnerved me, bringing forth my dormant paranoid tendencies. I was convinced this guy had tried to murder his parents, his plan thwarted by a frightened stepmom who took action, and an agency that stepped in. He was being defended solely because his power of attorney status would make some people richer. While the Behnke's were spared, justice was sacrificed. I finally understood why many frail and vulnerable elderly needed advocates.

19

The phone was already ringing as I entered my office. "I pray, ah, you can, ah, help," a trembling voice said while repeatedly clearing her throat.

"Tell me how I might help you?"

"My neighbor down the street, Edna Mae, is mentally retarded. She celebrated her sixtieth birthday right before her eighty-five-year-old father died about three months ago. Her mother has been dead for years. Her dad took good care of her and planned for her continuing care after his death by a supposed loving second-cousin. Only I think this cousin has abandoned her. She seems to have disappeared, perhaps along with the inheritance. This sweet woman cannot live alone or take care of herself properly."

"Have you been to the house?"

"Yes, I went this morning and yesterday, bringing her some food. She cannot cook and she has no money for food. A week's worth of mail, mostly bills, was in the mailbox. I'm worried. I haven't seen this cousin in two weeks. The place is in shambles. I called you because I have volunteered at your agency in the past. What should I do?"

I took down name and address information and told the woman, Sally Allen, I would follow-up with her by day's end. Sylvia and Imogene were at a meeting out of town, while two other social workers had clients scheduled all day. So I called Lieutenant Savage's office and he agreed to meet me there at noon. After being relieved by Marion, I drove to the home, fully aware of my complete sense of déjà vu. I once knew the neighborhood well, having had a childhood friend who had lived on the very same street. During middle school, we spent much time at each other's homes until she moved away.

Edna Mae lived in this area of modest, but mostly well-kept homes. Hers was a small white bungalow with dark shutters, one of which was on the ground leaning on the house. A malodorous garbage container overflowed on the front sidewalk, and leggy rose bushes, perhaps once stately, competed with tangled dry saw grass. I waited over fifteen minutes for Savage before impatiently deciding to go in.

I could hear a TV blaring as I knocked on the front door.

"Who's there?" Someone shouted. "Strangers not allowed."

"Edna Mae, is that you?"

"Are you a stranger?"

"Edna Mae, your neighbor, Sally, asked me to check on you. It is okay, I am not a stranger. I'm with the Area Agency on Aging. Sally told me all about you."

She opened the door. "Hi, want to play?"

"Sure," I said as I walked in. The house was filthy, reeked of rotten food, body odor and urine. Edna Mae had obviously been wearing the same dress for days. In front of me stood a woman looking much older that her sixty years. Her gray hair hung in knots below her eyes, which were slanted from Down's Syndrome. Her large-framed glasses were clouded and caked with splattered food. She was bent over as if she had arthritis or some other deformity.

"See my doll," she said with a huge smile on her face. Her halitosis was so bad I had to turn my head.

"Isn't she pretty. Come, let's play with her."

"Pat a cake, pat a cake, baker's man….." I started clapping the doll's hands. "Edna Mae, who is taking care of you?"

"My doll wants to eat. Here is her bottle. Do you want to feed her? Me hungry, too. Got any hamburgers?" She started to whimper. "Please feed me."

"Yes, I'll feed your doll and you will eat real soon," I said scooping up the doll and placing a small fake bottle in its mouth while looking around. The house was a disaster. Tightly drawn drapes furthered darkened the bleak living room.

"Edna Mae, look at me. Who is taking care of you? Who lives here with you?"

"Jesse be back soon."

"Jesse takes care of you?"

"Jesse be right back."

"Where is she? Edna Mae, I need to call her. Where is she?"

"You a nice lady. Doll Baby full now. Time for a nap."

We put Doll Baby to bed and I fetched my lunch from the car to give to a hungry Edna Mae. Almost inhaling my sandwich, barely chewing, mouth filled with many bites, she didn't notice at first when Savage appeared at the door.

"No strangers allowed," she finally shouted at Savage with food chunks flying from her mouth.

"He is a friend, a policeman. They help people," I said to her.

"So Claire, we meet again. What have we got here?"

"Right now it doesn't look like anybody is taking care of Edna Mae."

Before I could continue, Sally, who had seen the police car pull up, arrived. "Hi Miss Sally." Edna Mae greeted her. "These are not strangers. This lady helped me feed Doll Baby."

Sally, a neighbor for decades, told Savage what she knew. The cousin, Jesse, was Edna Mae's designated guardian and trustee of the disability pension and small estate. She was supposed to live with and care for Edna Mae until her death, after which she would inherit the home and what was left of the estate, which also included a car. For three months following the father's death Edna Mae seemed well cared for. Then with no explanation, the cousin disappeared with the car, leaving Edna Mae to fend for herself. No forwarding information was left.

Both Savage and I agreed that Edna Mae could not stay alone any longer, so I contacted a nursing home that partnered with our agency in emergency placement situations. Sally and I put Edna Mae in a bathtub of warm water. Remnants of past bowel movements were caked on her underwear. We washed under her arms and large breasts, then washed and combed her very knotted hair. "I am so sorry I didn't take care of her sooner," said Sally. "Actually, I didn't want to be alone in this house. That Jesse and her friends were scary characters." While Sally dried her hair with a hair dryer and calmed a now nervous Edna Mae, I searched for clean clothes. In the drawers I found used syringes and packs of white powder. Savage had called in more police units after his initial search found other evidence of drugs.

"Her parents were so loving and kind," said Sally. "They took such good care of Edna Mae. I can't believe this cousin duped them so. Edna Mae's dad, Chester, was relieved when Jesse volunteered to take custody. She seemed so loving toward Edna Mae but she was thrice divorced and if truth be known, I never trusted that lady. I bet she took all of the money with her. He kept lots of cash in the basement in a metal container."

"Did you see any activity here besides Jesse and Edna Mae coming and going?" asked Savage.

"Oh, yes, lots of cars, sometimes late at night. All the neighbors were talking. I am sorry I waited so long. I feel terrible."

"Doll Baby is awake!" interrupted a gleeful Edna Mae. "Time for her bottle." The small empty doll's bottle served again for the pretend feeding. Sally looked for toothpaste to brush Edna Mae's teeth. Not found, she brushed them with baking soda retrieved from the kitchen.

Sally offered to take her but Savage was mandated to temporarily place her in a licensed facility. "She will most likely become a ward of the state until we figure this out," he said, motioning to another officer to drive her to the nursing home. I knew that meant agency director, Imogene, would become her legal guardian.

"I don't know how she will do leaving her home to stay overnight in a strange place. She never has, except with her parents," said a concerned Sally.

As we took Edna Mae and Doll Baby to the police car, she started to panic. "No, noooooo! Stranger's car! No! Doll Baby scared!"

Sally hugged her. "Look Edna Mae, you and Doll Baby get to ride in a police car. Boy, are you lucky. Look, Doll Baby is saying, 'let's go for a ride in a police car.'"

"Sally, will you be so kind as to accompany the officer and help us get her to safety?" Savage asked.

"Certainly, this woman deserves better than this." She got into the back seat with Edna Mae who was crying again. "When I get back, my husband and I will take the garbage to the dump."

"No, don't do that, we will need to search for clues," Savage said talking to Sally through the car's backseat open window. "This is now considered a crime scene. We will also need you to come to police headquarters to answer some more questions. What kind of car did Jesse drive? What's her last name?"

"Jesse Marcus, same as Edna Mae's last name. Very thin woman, fifty-ish, with curly dyed platinum blond hair, usually piled on top of her head. The car's maybe an early 1990s Buick, dark red with a black vinyl top. I bet it is still registered to Chester. I will gladly help in any way. I know the name of the attorney who drew up the will. Maybe he can help. Oh, and her physician is Dr. Sloan. I know Edna Mae is being treated for hypertension and a heart condition. I bet she hasn't taken her medications in a while. I saw her prescription pill containers in the bathroom and they were all empty."

"Please tell them this at the nursing home so they can call the doctor."

"Stranger's car. Jesse home soon. Miss Sally, Daddy dead."

"Please tell me why people do stuff like this." I said to Savage as we watched the police car drive off with Edna Mae. He stared at me sadly without answering. "Will you need me anymore?" I asked.

"No. By the way Claire---For the record, you should not have entered this home until I got here. You could have jeopardized your safety."

"Sorry. Won't happen again."

"The world can be a cruel place. I have a mentally handicapped nephew. It makes me sick to see this." Then kicking into high gear, "Officer Busby, Jake, get the crime mobile out here and let's get an all points trace on this person and the car. Daniels, secure the scene, then help me search the house. Put on gloves."

By the time I got in my car, other neighbors had gathered on the lawn. "Hackett, start questioning these people one at a time," Savage commanded another officer. I drove to the end of Edna Mae's street, about six blocks. After turning left and going another few blocks, now about a half mile from the house, I noticed a parked older model dark red Buick with a black top and a curly blond-haired woman inside talking on a cell phone.

"Holy shit! That's the car and the cousin Sally described."

If this was Jesse, maybe she had noticed the police cars at the house. I continued driving past the car as unobtrusively as possible before dialing 911, since I didn't have Savage's cell number with me.

Parking a block down the street, I waited with the car in sight through my rear view mirror.

Suddenly, after making a U-turn, she started to drive away. No police were in sight. I quickly turned my car around and started following her. Savage's car, with sirens blasting, passed me going the opposite way. I called 911 again and stayed on the line giving them directions as to where we were.

"We just passed Franklin Street, heading north. She's turning left on Oakview."

Finally, what seemed an eternity, I heard sirens behind me. Savage passed me giving me a thumbs up as he saw the Buick some fifty yards in front of me. Upon seeing Savage pursue her, Jesse speeded up for a few seconds, but then, as if she changed her mind, slowed down and pulled over, as I did from a safe distance back. Savage had his gun out when he ordered the woman from the car.

I could hear her say, "What's wrong? What are you doing?"

"Face the car and put your hands on the hood. Now!"

She was immediately cuffed. "Is your name Jesse Marcus?"

"I am not saying anything to no cops until my lawyer is present."

I drove away shaking. Seeing a gun pointed at a suspect unnerved me. This wasn't TV.

***

"I don't understand how someone could do that," I said to Scott as we drove to Lambertville, New Jersey late that afternoon for our weekend away. "Edna Mae might never be able to go back home. Sometimes I yearn for my sheltered life, when my crises did not include chasing suspects or going to court to get restraining orders."

"I have learned in my long life that we can never go back."

"I suppose."

I remembered Lambertville from my childhood; a mostly blue collar town with a shabby roller rink, brick row houses with front porches so close you could talk to a neighbor four houses in either direction without raising your voice. But, times have changed. Today it was a bustling tourist destination connected to New Hope, Pennsylvania by a bridge. The row houses, long abandoned by original owners after the factories closed, were trimmed with designer colors and many sported well-groomed winter greenery arrangements in chic window boxes. Upscale stores had sprouted up in original stone buildings, some dating back to before the Revolutionary War. Crowds of people walked the tree-lined streets, decorated with Christmas lights. On one street corner, carolers in eighteenth century regalia sang to a small crowd. Lavishly decorated trees were everywhere, each one uniquely beautiful. I found out later that the area decorators competed for awards in an annual charity festival of trees.

After checking into our delightful B&B, Scott and I strolled hand in hand in a place that invited moseying. On this brisk but calm and sunny day, we peeked in several galleries, window shopped, and treated ourselves to cappuccino in a historic railroad station, now an elegant tearoom overlooking the river. The first snowstorm had already melted away from the sidewalks, leaving only a few snowplow-made drifts, and in front of one home stood the remnants of a once robust snowman.

Scott looked dignified in his scarf and Indiana Jones hat. I loved putting a hand in his pocket as we walked. "A town full of stuff," he said. "God knows, I don't need more stuff."

"But one must keep up with the latest in Christmas plates," I joked. "How can you live without Santa Claus trinkets and appropriate seasonal Wedgewood mugs for hot toddy? And check out this hand-painted wooden tray."

"Gaudy Santa-painted trays used only a few times a year? What do they charge for something like that?"

"A mere seventy-five dollars, cheap when you consider the status that comes with it."

"And look here, for eighty dollars we can get six drink glasses decorated with jingling bells on a leather strap. Oh, and it says the bells are removable for washing."

"How have you lived without it? Surely we will need two sets." After a couple seconds, I added, "You know, there was actually a time when I would have wanted this tray, and mugs, and glasses."

"And why was that, my lovely?"

"I was bored and liked being complimented on my good taste in stuff. Defined myself by what I owned. Started believing that I *was* what I *owned*. Shall I continue?"

"You? Of course, I was *never* that way," he said, eyes twinkling.

Being silly humored us. We laughed easily. It cut the pain of thinking about Edna Mae languishing in a nursing home with Doll Baby, abused by neglect and omission of life-sustaining drugs. It was nice to escape, if only temporarily, the seriousness of it all.

I used to call myself middle-aged, but I was past that now...past menopause, past marriage, past a lot of things. I was trying to relish the present; living in the moment, not for the moment. My mind flashed on how many more Christmases were left for me in my life. In Scott's? In Ross's? And instead of buying the mug, tray, or glasses, I asked a sweet looking couple to take our photo with us holding them. Both of us were smirking--how silly we must have looked, how unsophisticated. The flash went off, preserving the child within for our descendants, who probably wouldn't ever understand the context.

That evening we ate in a cozy restaurant. At times our conversation strayed into a more somber realm, but neither of us wanted to go there for long. When we returned to our room, Scott had arranged with the innkeeper to ready the fireplace, and have decaf lattes delivered. Sitting on the floor in front of a roaring fire, we exchanged presents. He loved the hiking poles and while adjusting them said, "I'll even let you borrow them when you come to Arizona."

He gave me a briefcase on wheels, one that could relieve the burden of carrying heavy books to class, a feat that had exacerbated my nagging backache. I appreciated the thoughtfulness, "I can organize unwieldy papers and also look oh-so-professional."

Both of us were impressed with the practicality of our gift giving. "It would have been embarrassing," he said while sipping his latte, "if, after our pontificating this afternoon, we had exchanged useless trinkets."

I ignored him and started kissing his slacks between his legs. "Let's do it on the floor."

"What? With my joints? I haven't done it on the

floor in decades."

"Want a pillow?"

"How about six? And an anti-inflammatory."

"I would pull the mattress down but these bedposts would prevent that."

"Are you forgetting that we are not 20 anymore, or 30 or 40."

"Dear God, where's the Viagra? I think I slipped it into my blood pressure vial, next to the cholesterol pill. It is all next to the Tylenol PM."

We laughed and kissed and laughed some more. It would not happen on the floor but the overstuffed chair had our name on it. "Care for a little chair coitus?" Later we finally got into bed, sipped the rest of our cooled lattes, and fell asleep. The next morning, after I restarted the fire from lingering hot ashes, we gave each other backrubs under the down quilt and made love without intercourse with our pajamas on.

"It is getting harder and harder for me to think about leaving you," Scott finally said after putting on another log.

"I know."

"I hadn't anticipated falling in love again. You have put a glorious quirk in my life's plans."

I began getting philosophical. "You know, when we were young, we loved and bred, worked and raised a family, all the while hoping we would be remembered for our legacies. I anticipated growing old with Ross, you with wife Kate. There is this wonderful spark about new love, only this time it is not hormonal. We are not wooing each other so we can build a nest for the young ones."

"Interesting point, my floor-foreplaying damsel.

By the way, do you want to grow old together?"

He could see my somewhat startled look, a look that said what are you asking? "I am not talking about marriage, as least not yet," he said. "But if I was, would it scare you?"

"I am not scared talking about it; I am not scared to talk with you about anything." He already knew about Ross's proposal to stall the divorce so if he died I would continue to get his pension.

"I detect a 'but' coming?"

"But I don't know how I feel about marriage at this stage in my life. How about you?"

"It's tempting right now. I am having one hell of a time with you. Yet, we are not at the same place in some ways, like professionally, and that would be an important criteria for any march to the altar. But…"

"Oh, you have a 'but' also?"

"But it sure is fun to think about!" he said with a big grin. "And I will really miss you when I am in warm Arizona."

We ordered coffee and a newspaper from the innkeeper, which we enjoyed fireside. After an eggs Benedict breakfast, we strolled down a path by the river and reveled in being mature seniors and newly in love. We both had learned from experience that life is precious, tomorrow is not promised, and today is a gift to be treasured.

***

Ross had his last round of chemotherapy in mid-December. There was celebration and cautious optimism. A CAT scan after Christmas would determine if the cancer was still present. A week after his treatments stopped he was feeling much better, enough to accompany me to the airport to pick up

Peter and Linda. To our amazement, wonder, and then tears, they got off the plane with an infant girl, Kim, their newly adopted child---our first grandchild.

"We knew right after Thanksgiving that this adoption would go through," said a jubilant Peter. "We wanted to surprise you. Kim, say hi to Grandmom and Grandpop."

Linda and Peter were exhausted after tending to a colicky baby during the twenty-four-hour flying marathon. When we arrived at Linda's parents' house, just several blocks away from Ross's house (Peter and Linda were childhood sweethearts), they could barely visit for an hour before passing out. While they slept, four doting grandparents took turns holding our little Chinese wonder, now sleeping soundly despite being passed around. After taking a tired Ross home, Linda's mom and I shopped for diapers, formula, baby blankets, and clothes. We even found a used crib. We were ecstatic.

Over the next days, Peter spent a lot of time, often well into the night, with his dad and Kate, now back again from Boston. He had been stunned at the way his dad looked…his hair gone, his body emaciated, his energy drained to a small fraction of his previously normal vigor. The sight had shaken him.

"Is Dad going to die?" he had asked me.

"I don't know," was my honest, but disquieting, answer. "I think we have reason to be hopeful. I am glad you are here and I know your dad is also."

"I can request an earlier transfer back to the states because of this. I'll see what I can do." I didn't try to convince him otherwise.

On the night before Scott left for Arizona, I had

all of my children over for dinner. Only Kate had met him before. For the first few minutes, you could have cut the awkwardness with a butter knife, but Scott, the ultimate gracious host, soon had everyone relaxing. He even talked about Ross and the difficulties of facing cancer. Rossy, particularly, seemed stunned by his openness; my boyfriend talking about my sort-of-ex-husband? He obliged Scott's queries by talking about his fear of losing his dad. As saddened as my children were over the separation, they seemed to be accepting of their new family situation, and to be genuinely happy that their mom had such a kind man in her life. Later, when Scott went into my bedroom to fetch a sweater, Rossy looked at me smiling as if to say, "I know you are sleeping together."

We all determined that our little Kim would grow up to be a genius, as she intently followed our faces and even smiled when we played peek-a-boo.

The evening ended directly after dessert when Ross called Peter on his cell phone to say he was feeling weak and dizzy. It must have been so hard for him to know his children were all together with their mom and her new lover. While nobody had told him this was going to happen, he was intuitive enough to figure it out.

The night exceeded my expectations. Scott was complimentary about each of my children, and ended the evening by giving me a special photo frame engraved with "Grandmom," that he purchased the day before. In it was our ridiculous photo at the store with the belled glasses and gaudy tray.

The next morning, we had brunch at his daughter's where he exchanged presents. By early afternoon we were headed to the airport. It was not a completely sad good-bye since I would see him in a week, but he said, "I love you" with such meaning that my smile lasted most of the drive home.

***

The very next night, Cedric cooked dinner for Edith and me. She relished telling us the details of her previous night's date with Don, but she was saddened that his health was deteriorating. "Oh, why can't I find me a healthy old man? I doubt this one will ever detach from his walker. Thankfully he hired a cab to and from dinner."

Regardless of the setbacks, she proclaimed it a great evening. "There is nothing wrong with his mind. And he has a daughter just like Barbara! Can you beat that? We laughed ourselves silly over the comparisons."

It helped that she could fully relate with someone about Barbara, who was behaving like a shit since Edith was discharged and Charlotte had gone back home. A paranoid Barbara could barely mutter a 'hello' when she saw me, as though I had corrupted her mother and was trying to squirm in for a piece of the inheritance. Once when I passed by the apartment door I could hear Barbara yelling at Edith, who was holding her own and yelling right back. "I will not have you treating me this way. Either respect my wishes or get out!" Later Edith told me Barbara had apologized.

After dinner, I inquired, "So Cedric, do I sense an imminent move in the air?"

"Oh God, stop with the pressure."

"Just asking."

"Ask me in a week when I get back. I don't want

228

to rush. It's a huge step for me. And I won't settle for just any job. But Greg is so wonderful and three-thousand miles is way too long-distance.

We exchanged presents.

Cedric gave me another pillow, intricately embroidered. Edith gave Cedric and me one each of twin hand-painted glass vases that her grandmother had given her. "I am not buying presents anymore. Instead, I am giving away what I don't need."

"Edith!" Cedric blurted. "No way am I taking this. Too valuable."

"Trust me Cedric," she retorted. "My daughters are into crispy, new, and tacky. They will have an auction when I die. On the other hand, I know both of you will appreciate these and remember our times together. It's been a wonderful year since I met you. Claire, yours has a crack in it…I dropped it when I was a teenager. Last week, I had an artist friend paint that crack in gold."

"Dear God Edith! I can't believe you did this! I am really touched. It's beautiful."

The next day, after they departed to their respective destinations, I sat on my couch with a novel in hand and enjoyed being alone without obligations for the first time in ages. Life was good.

20

Snow was falling as I rang my old doorbell on Christmas Eve. Last Christmas, Ross and I were on the verge of a separation, now I was going home again, to his uncertain future and our newly defined, strangely ambiguous relationship.

I was greeted by my three children and their assorted significant others. Ross, who hugged me tightly, was up and about, feeling better. With a glass of wine in hand, he seemed determined to enjoy this Christmas, as if he realized its possible significance. Frank Sinatra crooned in the background as the fireplace blazed with dog Zep next to it. The Christmas tree was lit with all-blue lights, a tradition I had brought from my childhood. The decorations on the tree were a collection of memorabilia--family events and souvenirs of trips past--several being the handmade ornaments of my once small children.

Little Kim was wearing a red outfit that said, "My First Christmas" on the front. The kids had begged me to make my Christmas cookies and jelled fruit salad, and I had dutifully complied. All of them would be spending the night. Due to Ross's illness, Linda's parents had deferred their daughter's presence at their home on Christmas Eve and morning.

Cancer trumps the usual obligatory family and in-law sharing of kids…and grandkid. So these significant celebrations were both at our (Ross's) home.

It took Rossy, Peter and me three trips to the car to retrieve all the presents and food. The snow had covered the ground and the trees glistened. Before I loaded my arms with the last casserole dish, I couldn't resist the sudden urge to throw snowballs at my sons. They responded in kind, and we relished our short regression to their simpler, carefree childhood times.

Later, as I looked around the room, I thought about the possibility of Ross's death and how it would affect each of our kids. We might be losing him---a huge personal loss for each of us. But then I looked at Ross and realized that he would be losing everything. Is there any comparison?

Ross spoke to each of the kids as if, perhaps, he knew something the rest of us didn't. "Peter, I am so proud of the life you have made…." "Rossy, you are the best lawyer in this whole area…." "Kate, my smart, wonderful girl…." The typically non-demonstrative Ross was on a mission of legacy, almost maudlin.

Sometimes, especially at the beginning of the evening, a forced laugh, a gallows laugh, emanated throughout the room. Rossy, assuming a more patriarchal role, tried to keep the conversation light and upbeat. At times, when our talking focused on the future, we went out of our way to include Ross. But there was no escaping a hairless, thirty pounds lighter Ross, who drifted from upbeat to quietly introspective. Sometimes I could see him surveying the scene, lost in his thoughts, and most assuredly his fears. Once, after Peter talked about Kim's future soccer playing potential, he left the room as unobtrusively as possible with eyes welled-up. Only Jennifer and I noticed this as our own eyes followed him and then locked on each other.

Linda, Jennifer, Kate, and I delighted in dinner preparation. I had always been at home in the kitchen, especially this particular kitchen. We concocted a superb ginger sauce for the leg of lamb and roasted our veggie medley until it was crisp and succulent. Occasionally I glanced out the window as the snow continued to fall; a white Christmas. Kate had set a beautiful table, just as I had taught her. Candles were everywhere.

After lingering at the dining table, we retreated back to the living room with our coffees and after-dinner drinks, quietly surveying presents strewn under the tree. Following tradition we would each open a present on Christmas Eve, one at a time. I gave Ross a leather-bound book for journaling, a process he had started at my suggestion.

Ross then decided he would present his significant gifts this night. To Kate, he gave his mother's diamond ring, to Peter his father's watch, and to Rossy, his father's cufflinks. Tears were shed all over, although Ross did not allow this to linger or take over the evening. A bit of sentimentality would be allowed, but only to a point.

"I might be giving some of my stuff away, but I am not burying myself yet, so cut the tears."

His gift to me was the climax. I nervously opened the small package, professionally wrapped, to see a wide banded elegant diamond and sapphire ring engraved inside with the words, "The Way We Were."

I felt overwhelmed with gratitude and sadness.

With tears in my eyes, I told him, "I will treasure this gift forever."

The emotion of the evening's end took its toll on Ross's energy level. He now faded rather quickly and I could tell it was time to take my leave. "Hey, Mom, did you see the snow piled up outside?"

I hadn't paid it any mind since fixing dinner. "Mom, it's about four inches now," said Rossy.

"I'll take it slow."

"Like Hell you will, I'll drive you home," said Peter.

"We'll both go," added Rossy.

"Look guys, there is no sense all of us going," I responded.

Then Kate chimed in, "Looks pretty dangerous to me."

"I don't want any of my family out in this mess," Ross said in a particularly authoritarian voice. "After such a wonderful evening, the last thing I need is for someone to be in an accident."

"Well," I finally said, "driving home tonight and back here tomorrow does not sound exciting." I awkwardly added, "Is the guest bedroom still empty since I took the furniture?"

"You can sleep with me," said Kate.

"Okay, I'll stay." I was nervous, but I'd be more so in a car skidding around. "Does anybody have any sweats I can borrow?"

"Sure thing," said Ross rising up from his chair. "Why don't you come upstairs and pick what you need." He knew I had loved wearing his sweats.

As we entered his bedroom, he sent me to the drawer where his warm-up suits were kept, the same drawer that had always housed this element of his clothing. While I was picking out what I needed, he laid on the bed obviously exhausted. "I'm glad you are staying," he said with his eyes closed. "I would have been worried with you driving in this."

I walked over to the king-sized bed to kiss him good night. "Please stay with me for a while. Don't worry, I am too tired to put the make on you. You're safe."

For a moment I was tempted to rest with him. "I am going to visit more with the kids. I'll be back later to see if you need anything."

The kids and I talked till midnight, then I called Scott, three time zones away, just home from an evening with his son and his family. Staring at my new ring, now on my finger, I talked with him for an hour. He knew I was stranded, spending the night, and was matter-of-factly relieved I wasn't driving. On the other hand, I failed to mention how nervous I was...or about the ring.

Ross's call for help ended our conversation. He had vomited and I helped him put on clean pajamas and got him back into bed. "Combining two glasses of wine with the lingering remnants of chemo is not a good idea," he said. "Guess I overdid it. Claire, please stay with me a while."

I got in the bed next to him and we hugged. Although he tried staying awake, he was physically unable, falling asleep soundly in a few minutes as I stared into his face. With window curtains opened I turned to gaze at the falling snow by the streetlight. I was in bed with my sort-of husband. Everything seemed so surreal.

***

The next morning I awoke to an empty

space beside me and the voice of tenor, Mario Lanza's "Oh Come All Ye Faithful" coming through the open bedroom door, a recording Ross's father and now Ross habitually played on Christmas morning. With the new dawn, I could see that everything outside my window was blanketed with snow. The white limbs of trees, beautifully weighted, made a stark contrast to the blue sky's background, now sporting the pink clouds of a morning sunrise. Even with the music, I knew the kids wouldn't arise at the crack of dawn, something they hadn't done since they stopped believing in Santa Claus.

The coffee was brewing as I walked into the kitchen. "Merry Christmas," Ross said as he hugged me.

"Merry Christmas."

"I am glad you stayed. There must be three or four inches out there."

"How are you feeling?"

"Much better…I got a good night's sleep. Claire, can we talk before the kids get up?"

Before I could answer, Linda came into the kitchen with a crying, hungry Kim. By the time we prepared formula, Peter had entered followed by Jennifer. Soon we were ensconced in a Christmas breakfast of lox and bagels, while Peter woke up the rest of the crew. By ten o'clock, we had all eaten and unwrapped the rest of our gifts. Since we had long ago given up wrapping paper in favor of environmentally friendly reusable bags, we easily reorganized the ribbons and bags back into their large plastic container.

While Kate would stay with her dad, Peter and Linda prepared to go over to her family for Christmas dinner and Rossy to Jennifer's. Since it was Christmas Day, the road clearing trucks were silent, the crews no doubt with their families. Thankfully the snow on the streets was already melting as the sun shone brightly.

Later, while Kate was having a lengthy conversation with her boyfriend, Ross picked up what he had stopped earlier. "I feel honored that, given our separation, you were here last night and today with me and the kids. Perhaps if I didn't have cancer, you'd be long gone. It was the biggest mistake of my life to consider an affair with Amanda and let you go. I will regret it to my dying day...which might not be that far off!"

"Ross, thank you and I am glad to be here, really I am. You know," I added laughing, "you did not have to get me such a nice ring because you feel guilty. Your affair with Amanda was just the straw that broke both our unhappy backs." I was nervous now, hoping this conversation would not lead to him asking for a reconciliation.

"Sometimes it is only after you lose something that you realize it meant the world to you. I took you for granted."

"I took this marriage for granted also."

"The grass seemed greener. But I quickly learned that it was growing over a cesspool. Once I got to know Amanda, I realized that she had more issues than I wanted to deal with. Underneath her sweet façade was a real oddball, not short on hostility. I am sorry. I was blinded by romance. I wonder how many men like me royally fucked up during their mid-life crisis, or in my case, my senior crisis. Finding new honey comes with stinging bees. Instead of working on our meaningful relationships, we seek the easy way out."

"I'm not hopeful that we will get back together, nor is that even my goal anymore," he continued. "I am happy for you and your new life, and I am happy that I get to share you a little bit. I regret that I was too much the narcissist to see your pain, too much in love with myself to see past myself."

"Ross, stop!"

"Hush, I am not done yet. I am attending that support group of cancer survivors--the one you gave me the information on—so this is healthy for me. Claire, after talks with my doctor, I will be very surprised if I have licked this cancer. I just flat out waited too long. Granted, we won't know for sure until next month. However, even if the news is bad, I could still have some quality time left, and I want to make the most of it. And that starts by being honest with myself and with you. I don't think I am being manipulative by asking for your forgiveness and friendship, even if I live a long time. And I am not going to wallow in my past. It's over."

Oh, why weren't we this honest with each other before the marriage died, I thought. I was moved by his words, and choked up.

"Claire, you and the kids are equal beneficiaries of my will, which now includes that substantial life insurance policy I got years ago. By the time everything is sold, like the house, you should live comfortably for the remainder of your life…if, of course, you budget accordingly and don't take too many around-the-world trips on the QEII." We both smiled. He knew how easily I got seasick.

"Additionally, my pension will take the place of

your alimony payments, assuming you thought about delaying our final divorce next month."

"Thank you, Ross. I told my attorney to hold off on the final divorce, but I hope this issue becomes a moot point. I want you to live a long and happy life. I feel so grateful that our separation has not been steeped in hate and animosity. I know the kids have enjoyed having us together today and I did too." I started crying. "I'm glad we did not throw away forty years as if it never happened." He started crying also, rushed forward and kissed me on the lips, after which we rocked back and forth holding tightly while "Drummer Boy" played in the background.

"By the way, the ring was not a guilt gift," he finally said with a mischievous smile.

"Ha! Yes it was!" I laughed. "But I'm keeping it anyhow. You always had good taste."

***

I wondered if Ross and I really could transition from husband and wife to friends. It helped that Amanda was no longer in the picture. Later, alone again in my apartment, I was overcome with questions and started writing:

Can my forgiveness be legitimate? Or is it superficial, shoddy forgiveness? Would this be happening if it wasn't for the cancer? How much do I now love this stranger I have known for forty years? What is the difference between my love for Scott and my love for Ross?

The snow, the cancer, the gifts, the apologies, Ross's transformation…where are they taking me?

***

On the day before I left for Arizona, I babysat for Kim while Peter and Linda looked at houses to live in when they returned. Kate brought her

239

boyfriend, Sam, over and we chatted the afternoon away. She had chosen a nice, easy-going man. They seemed very much in love. Later the entire family gathered at my apartment. This was a farewell dinner for Peter, who would go to the airport with me, and fly back to China a week ahead of Linda to begin his final stint before permanently returning to the states.

It was the first time Ross had been to my home and he insisted on a personal tour. Photos of Scott were tucked away for the evening. In spite of the joyous atmosphere, Ross never really got comfortable. I would catch him staring around, perhaps thinking how strange it was to be here among my familiar things, knowing I was soon off with another man.

"Your Grandmother's desk looks good against that wall." Small talk prevailed between us. I knew his visiting my home would be an exception to our friendship. I could not envision it happening often. Nonetheless, I was glad to be finally sharing this part of my life.

21

How nice it was to hug a tanned and healthy-looking Scott at the Tucson airport. We spent the early afternoon roaming the paths of the Desert Museum amidst saguaro cacti and brilliant desert flowers, stilled in a breezeless day except when visiting hummingbirds stirred them gently. The sun felt warm on our faces and we held hands as we walked.

Later we arrived at his comfortable apartment, nestled at the base of Madera Canyon just south of Tucson. As we talked on his patio, neighbors and friends from the large senior complex stopped by from their walks around the compound's many maintained paths. We grilled steaks, then slowly digested dinner while taking our own stroll.

With everyone in the complex being over fifty-five, it was my first exposure to a homogenous population of age contemporaries, all living in one place. While I was younger than most, as was Scott, I was fascinated, becoming an instant anthropology student soaking up this opportune experience. I had seen so many unhappy seniors in my work that I felt relieved to see such contentment all around me.

Most were healthy and active. Certainly some had had their hips replaced, their heart vessels stented, or assorted clogged arteries bypassed. When they were in bathing suits, I could see the bulging of pacemakers at their shoulders. Pharmacy delivery cars came through regularly with an assortment of medications aimed at healing, preventing, or helping them cope with an endless array of age-related disorders.

For a population that had in the past consumed their share of super-sized Big Macs and Whoppers, they now headed for the health food section of low sugar, reduced sodium, and cholesterol-free staples. They peeled the skin off chicken and used "light" mayonnaise in coleslaw. I saw a couple of motorized chairs, and a few shuffled in walkers, but most walked confidently, some in such good shape they easily outpaced me. They were dedicated to staying healthy-old for whatever years they had left. Most hoped to live well, then die quickly; no lingering if they could avoid it.

They were from all parts of the United States, especially the wintry cold parts. They had taken their gold retirement watches, hoped their college-educated kids could finally make it on their own, and headed for a new life in these Sun Cities and Leisure Worlds of Arizona. Some of their friends had chosen places in Florida or Texas, anywhere considerably south of Buffalo or Newark or Cincinnati.

Few were actually rich, but most had saved well, no doubt because they grew up in the Great Depression when everybody saved for a "rainy day." While on a budget, they were not wanting. They had put in their forty-five years (give or take) of paychecks into social security and were now more than ready to collect their share along with Medicare. Most had gladly simplified their lives, passing the family heirlooms to kids and selling the homestead, now way too big and too much work. Friendship and family took on a heightened importance, while material possessions took a back seat. Pricey gift shops, like the one Scott and I browsed in Lambertville, were used for window shopping or buying gifts as opposed to self-indulgence.

Once, on a beautiful, tree-lined path winding between with massive boulders that started in the mountains and descended into the desert, Scott and I smelled a strange, but familiar odor. "That's marijuana!" said Scott.

"Do you believe this?" I said. "I haven't smelled dope in years." We couldn't see anybody at first, then suddenly Scott spotted two men, perhaps in their seventies, sitting peacefully in the forest away from the path. A cocker spaniel and miniature poodle slept at their feet while they quietly smoked a joint. Already high, they seemed to not see us…or perhaps not to care about our presence.

"Ever smoke dope?" Scott asked.

"I grew up in the 1960's."

"Would that be a yes?"

"It would be. How about you?"

"Loved it when I was in my twenties before I switched to Johnny Walker. Haven't indulged since. Smelling it now sure brings back memories; makes me hungry. Guess some hippies never grow up."

Our philosophical talks continued. Over the days we noticed how new widows and widowers were supported in loss, because everybody knew their turn was coming. The complex seemed on guard for anticipatory grief. Some had started attending church again after years of hiatus, as if taking a crash course in God would somehow augment their ascent into Heaven, even if they still privately questioned mystical existences. It was as if they were covering their bases, just in case.

Many were prone to reflection, and sort of doing an inventory of the meaningfulness of their lives. Some, I suppose, came up short, having made way too many compromises. Retirement was a new beginning from a life of regrets. I am sure the question, "Is this all there is?" was commonly asked, some seeking more than superficial answers, others afraid to delve too deeply.

Some couples got closer and actually fell in love again. Grudges were replaced with 'forgive and forget.' Others, who probably should have divorced, continued their façade, becoming more roommates than lovers. I had found in the past that the ones who publicly smooched the most were often the most phony, going home to sleep separately, interest in sex, or each other, long ago faded. Some marriages became especially strained when neither was working anymore and they were together for way too many hours during the day.

Former workaholics regretted what they missed. Some held jobs that had been time-clock boring, causing them to live only for 'when they retire.' The name of their career game was to muster as many benefits and time off as possible. What they actually did on the job was secondary, a means to an end, any end but the daily grind. They had long ago stagnated, working in zombie-like states, while appearing busy and convincing themselves they were important.

While this was a largely white collar retiree complex, some had still hated their assembly-line quasi-management or 'Willy Loman' positions.

In some cases, it was possible to see the emergence of "dirty-old-men." Dead, dying, and limp penises somehow prompted sexual prowl, a last ditch effort to assert manhood. You could really tell those who were trying to act forty.

I also loved watching the women. One, always colorfully dressed, attempted to demonstrate a physical oxymoron by wearing two inch heels without backs while using a quad cane. She was one tumble away from frail, but I suppose she thought looking good was worth the gamble. Falls killed, or at least started that downward trajectory. Everybody knew it. Falls landed you in hospitals, made you prey to a surgeon's knife, brought on confusion-inducing anesthesia, new prosthetic hardware, and a stint in a physical therapy rehab facility, conveniently close by.

No one wanted to become a burden. It was everybody's fear.

With the Christmas season over and grandkids back in school, snowbirds were flocking in. The complex filled up more every day. For sale signs on some condos always produced much speculation as to what happened to the couples who wintered there in years past.

"Last year, Joe was having trouble breathing. I wonder if his congestive heart failure finally did him in?"

"Chester was in the hospital last year and he went home early."

"Candace died and Bill didn't come back. Their condo is for sale."

The clubhouse was a mecca for cards, book clubs, music, brochures for trip planning, and yoga. Outdoor tennis courts were always busy and no one seemed embarrassed that they shuffled to retrieve a bouncing ball. If they didn't get to it in time, so be it. No ball was worth a sprained ankle. Doubles surpassed singles and golf surpassed everything. Golf carts were everywhere, sometimes, unfortunately, ending up beneath somebody's car. Driving reflexes suffered with age. Sometimes the parking lots seemed like one big bumper car arena.

Mornings were reserved for serious lap swimming and guided water aerobics, but in the heat of the afternoon, the swimming pool filled up for more casual 'social' cooling off. Groups of people covered in sunscreen talked the day away while standing in four feet of water, occasionally splashing their shoulders and faces, or dunking their bodies under water for a few seconds.

I often overheard conversations about teenage grandchildren who these seniors yearned to know better. Kids back home were continually too busy for afternoons with grandparents. How sad, I thought, that they would never know what they were missing. Wouldn't it be nice to ask grandparents about their first dates, or what it was like to live through the Great Depression. For some grandchildren, by the time they became interested, it would be too late.

People aged like they lived. The risk takers continued risking, albeit in more age-friendly degrees. The couch potatoes brought their La-Z-Boys and watched *Wheel of Fortune*. Busy bees volunteered at the area's state parks, hospitals, and non-profits. The complex had every type of personality, with one important thing in common…this was not a heaven's waiting room, or, at least they didn't look at it that way.

When you have so many seniors in one specific area, certain things remind them of that Bette Davis proclamation, "Aging ain't for sissies." Ambulances were all too common at the large complex. Sometimes they'd pick up the non-life-threatening fall from the bathtub without sirens or fanfare, and nondescriptly exit to the nearest X-Ray equipment. The serious heart attack, however, warranted the full high-decibel entrance, breaking up a quiet afternoon, refocusing all thoughts on whether "Joe" would make it. It was disconcerting when Scott and I watched a full cardiac arrest in progress, medics pounding his chest and catapulting his body skyward with defibrillating voltage before rushing this critical soul to the hospital with his terrified spouse following. People stood around, "Who is it? Oh, no, not John." The next day John was flown home in a body bag.

Moments of silence were held at the monthly condo meetings to remember the deceased or the never-returning tenants whose families beckoned them back for end-of-life vigils. These people knew that life can change in an instant. "Live today. We don't know about tomorrow." Death of contemporaries is difficult; death of friends inevitably painful; our death always creeping closer to center stage. I thought about what Edith had said going to the funeral of her childhood friend, Maria, "Death does not get easier with practice." At this senior complex, like thousands across the United States, there was plenty of practice.

One night Scott and I attended an educational

program in the recreation center on late life depression, a disease affecting, to no one's surprise, upwards to twenty percent of all seniors, and commonly triggered by cumulative loss. We had to stand in the back until more chairs were brought in. The week before, a once socially vibrant elderly widow, who became progressively arthritic and secluded in her apartment, finally called it quits and succumbed after swallowing a whole bottle of pain pills. I learned that white men over eighty-five have a significantly increased incidence of suicide. The one-hour program, led by a family doctor, lasted well into the evening as he patiently answered numerous questions, some talking to him privately after the event. Afterwards, I told Scott about Edith's bout with depression.

Once, at a party, a widow, desperately looking to replace her husband, latched onto Scott. Unless he was actually married, she considered him available. Another divorcee repeatedly invited him for dinner. She actually strutted around the complex in flimsy see-though tops, and wore dangling platinum blond hairpieces from the drug store mixed in with her own dye job. She was looking for that one final marriage to cap the four she already had. When Scott proved unavailable, she nonchalantly moved on to the next guy. Women outnumbered men three to one and she would not, thank-you, find herself passively in the back of a long 'eligible' line. She was an upfront and center kind of lady.

Many of the women had traded their former wasp-like waists for more flowing tops. Chic polyester was in. Nobody wanted to iron, save this one lady who always had a perfect crease from the top to the bottom of her slacks. She always looked, well, so starched. Truth was some of these women, including myself, had grown up ironing sheets and underwear along with blouses and everything else. Many of us had long ago rebelled against ironing's hot, laborious toil by rarely ironing again. Besides, modern materials finally unwrinkled us for good.

Scott had made some significant friends over the years, including one special couple, retired university professors, who were in their early seventies. Together we drove up to the Grand Canyon where Carol and I hopped on mules and rode to Phantom Ranch at the bottom of the canyon while the guys hiked down on foot. The next day, Scott, me, and my sore butt hiked back up, no easy feat, even with his new hiking poles. During the eight-hour exhilarating and spectacular trek, we passed only a few our age or older and were grateful that our bodies still cooperated with our ambitions.

The four of us often talked about our own aging and what we wanted to do in the time left. Phil, a burly, peacenik ex-philosophy professor, often talked in esoteric terms, dissecting the difference between anxiety loneliness and existential aloneness, the former being afraid of being by oneself and seeking company even if superficial, the other relishing opportunities for introspection and contemplation. I asked a lot of questions, but he seemed patient with me, loving that I was a student and he could once again reignite his teaching capabilities. Unlike Carol, he hated having to retire.

Scott and I inevitably talked about our own goals of aging and what we wanted to do, health permitting, in our advancing senior years. Scott had decided he wasn't quite ready for full-time senior complex living. "I have a few more years of intensive volunteering. I need to give something more back to society that has given me so much and has such considerable needs." The question was how he would leave his volunteer mark and which organizations would benefit from his last productive years.

The time in Arizona went quickly. It was invigorating to be active and hike picturesque trails with babbling brooks and the boulder remains of spewing volcanoes. I enjoyed meeting his friends, most of whom joined us on various trails. Some days we hiked fast, keeping up with the 'wanna-be-forty-again' types, still focusing on speed and endurance. Other days we sauntered with the arthritic or knee-replacement crew, who stopped frequently to 'smell the roses' and rest.

I enjoyed living with Scott, short as it was. The day to day stuff was easy, no arguing, an easily resolved disagreement, doing things together or sometimes giving each other a bit of space. We sometimes napped in the afternoon, often after having sex. We read and played Scrabble.

Our perfect vacation was dampened by Ross's pessimistic CAT scan, which showed significant metastasis to the liver. The kids were devastated. Ross would not make it to live in a retirement complex such as this. He would not enjoy an old age. On several days, he and I had lengthy conversations, while Scott gave us privacy by going to another room. Once, when I cried at the significance of losing Ross, Scott silently held me. Sometimes he noticed me drifting into an introspective place and he did not interrupt.

Sometimes after making love with Scott, I would think back on my marriage with Ross. Almost like apples and oranges, there was no similarity in our lovemaking. Ross and I had screwed our way into three kids and a huge rut. Our sexual bonding was like being in grade school when I juxtaposed it with the almost spiritual bonding that I felt with Scott. Talking about sex with Ross had been such a touchy issue. We never brought up our needs for more excitement or position updates. One did not want to step on any ego-sensitive toes, which regrettably included mine as well.

Sometimes when having sex with Ross, I was also thinking about my grocery list and other 'to do' lists. We never talked, just did it, at night, when we both were tired, in a 'hurry-up' mode so we could get some sleep. But even though our sex was predictable, we had forty years of intimacy and family. On some levels he knew me better than anyone else ever would.

Journal: *Why the hell didn't Ross want to go to counseling when I suggested it? Yes, we needed to jump-start our apathetic mental and orgasmic batteries. But it wasn't the end of the world! We did not have to separate and seek divorce. Thousands of couples make it past mid-life. In fact, many discover a renewed closeness with each other. Storms occur in every marriage, and even if it might look like it, the grass is rarely greener elsewhere.*

Marriage is flat out work and we didn't do it. Laziness killed us. Our fairy-tale ending crashed and burned due to neglect. The small steps of detachment, like a child's daily growth, remained unnoticed. Our young and immature love never really grew up, and somewhere along the way we even stopped dating. We didn't look to each other for the necessary spark; he looked elsewhere while I gave up and embraced motherhood, justifiably important but not my only option. For all these years I had resented him without even knowing it. I was the quintessential desperate housewife, a hamburger helper, only I wasn't screwing the plumber, just myself.

We could have saved it, nurtured it. Dead gardens can be restored to blooming splendor. Weeds can be removed. Sometimes I got so angry at him, at me, at us. Now he is dying and I had to ring the fucking front door bell to get into my own fucking house.

I guess I still have some anger issues.

Now, after all this time, we are finally being honest with each other. It took one of us at death's door to jolt us out of our complacency. God dammit! Fools we are! We created our own Arthur Miller tragedy and if we had been watching, we would have pronounced ourselves idiotic.

Why didn't we shake each other up? Why didn't one of us grab the other and shout, "Let's wise up! We are blowing it big-time! We might regret this!" Why weren't we cheerleaders for each other...and our partnership? We kept chasing the elusive romance when it was the communication we needed to enhance. In the end, we had even stopped being nice to each other, a fatal flaw. Divorce court beckoned us like some psychotic whispering voice, "Come, I will fix it. Take care of yourself. Find someone else to make you happy."

Once, when I was lost in thought, journal open, Scott came up to me and asked, "Penny for your thoughts?"

I shared them, warts and all. He appreciated my candor. There was no sense hiding it. I was sick of psychological games; sick of secrets. My husband, a man I had lived with for four decades, was dying. Let's face it...I had unresolved issues. Scott deserved to be fully apprised.

I certainly was a good person. Shirley helped me

see that, but I was also confused, far from self-actualized, and heretofore had never realized my full potential. I wanted to make sure now that I wasn't replacing Ross for a newer, improved model, desperate to curb my own anxious loneliness and hike into the sunset.

In Arizona, I had seen women trying to hook up with men, and vice versa, to curtail their loneliness and isolation. They wanted to replace bodies who had died or departed. They hated being alone. It depressed them. Better to be lonely at a party talking about trivia than lonely at home talking to yourself. Could I be a modified version of that shameless, sexily dressed Arizona gold-digger, only with a bit more class?

Scott was patient with my musings. He knew I had to work through it. Besides, he wanted someone with stable mental health, not widespread uncertainty. The only thing I was sure of was that I loved spending time with him. I couldn't envision cutting Ross out of my life, but I couldn't imagine my future without Scott. I did love him…A lot.

Toward the end of my stay, Scott and I talked seriously about meeting in New Orleans during my spring break, Ross's condition permitting, while he helped in a Habitat for Humanity project. I wanted to take every opportunity to be with him.

22

After three weeks of fostering my wonderfully promising relationship, I reluctantly shifted from a serene Arizona schedule into high New Jersey gear. My first week back included working full time to repay my counterpart, Marion, for covering for me. Edith and Cedric were eager to reunite for our regular dinners. Ross was anxious to talk more and Jennifer wanted to shop for my mother-of-the-groom dress. Classes would begin shortly.

The Behnke farm had sold after three developers engaged in a bidding war, but a rapidly fading Mr. Behnke might not enjoy its fruits. Earl Jr. and his Gucci attorney tried to declare his father and stepmother incompetent in a last ditch effort to gain further control of the estate, including who would get to buy it, but agency lawyer Kara Pusey thwarted these efforts. She had represented many clients whose relatives attempted to bypass a senior's rights in favor of their money-grabbing desires. Nobody believed Earl, Jr. when he pleaded, "I'll use the money to take care of them!" For him, greed prevailed--having one-half of a lucrative estate sale was not enough. Thankfully he had lost, leaving his parents with enough money for long-term care.

Edna Mae had become a ward of the state with Imogene appointed guardian. During the time I was away, Imogene had transferred Edna Mae to a reputable staffed group home for mentally disabled citizens and with Sally's help, she was adjusting well. The cousin, Jesse, had been charged with drug possession with intent to distribute and reckless abandonment of an elderly disabled citizen, and faced a lengthy jail sentence. She pleaded innocent to the drug charge, proclaiming she didn't know the drugs were in her house—her boyfriend, whose whereabouts she didn't know, must have put them there. She also stated that the demands of caring for Edna Mae proved too much for her, causing her extreme mental distress. To the charge of reckless abandonment she pleaded insanity.

Unfortunately Edna Mae's trust fund had been squandered to a few hundred dollars after only three months under Jesse's supervision. The agency's attorneys were able to confiscate the house and would use the profits from its sale to fund Edna Mae's care. Its run-down condition forced a reduced asking price, but thankfully Edna Mae qualified for supplemental disability welfare assistance.

Edith and control-freak daughter Barbara had called a truce after a clinical psychologist specializing in aging guided the two of them into a constructive resolution. With further fighting stopped, Edith could enjoy the time with her grandchildren. Her week at Christmas with Charlotte and the other grandchildren was savored. She had come back carrying her cane rather than using it.

Cedric spent three weeks over Christmas with his new lover. He came back to announce he would move to San Francisco in the spring to be with Greg. Already, he had two job offers. At first, they planned to find a new place instead of him moving in with Greg. However, the condo unit directly next door to Greg's had gone on the market. They would be able to buy it, break open a couple of walls and join the two apartments into one. "It's a decorator's dream," he said. "Our place—not his or mine. And, since the kitchens share an adjoining wall, we can make one big dream kitchen."

I was happy for Cedric but I knew I would miss him. He had been such an important part of the first year of my new life. Edith was saddened also. "You cured me of my homophobia, once and for all. Guess it's true that if you know someone who is gay, your attitude changes."

"Well, I am not moving tomorrow," Cedric said. "We can rack up some nice quality time together between now and then. And, my darling Edith, how is your sex life?"

"I'm afraid there is no sex life, but it's actually okay. I have gotten to the point where it doesn't matter anymore. I might never make love again. I accept that. I had my time for lovemaking. Don has a heart condition, so enhancement drugs are out, and I don't want somebody dying on top of me. Truth is, he'd probably not be able to get on top of me."

"God, Cedric, how do you get me to talk about my sex life?"

"Why not," he retorted. "You are still so alive and vibrant!"

"Cedric and Claire, let me tell you something," she continued, "Late one night in the rehab center we got into bed with each other--not to have sex, just to hold each other. A nurse came in and we immediately thought, oh my God, we are in trouble. Instead, she excused herself and told us she'd give us privacy by closing the door behind her. What a dignified gesture. Don and I spent a lot of time together in rehab. We grew close fairly fast."

"How nice that the rehab center had such a progressive attitude," I said. "Not too long ago such behavior would have been labeled disgusting. At many nursing homes or rehab centers, two elderly lovers, even spouses, would have been pulled away from each other and separated, humiliated."

"Bad, bad, perverts!" sighed Cedric, as Edith laughed out loud.

"He holds my hand. That feels good. We talk a lot, especially about the spouses we buried. He was married sixty-two years. I enjoy talking about Rudy. Don doesn't get tired of it and he can talk about his wife, Pearl, just as much. Last week, we went through old photo albums at his place. We will continue this week at mine. He is a charming friend and I adore him. Hopefully we will have some time together, but he thinks he'll die soon. We are spending a lot of money on cab fares these days. I am still nervous about driving, especially at night, and my driving days are numbered. His are definitely over."

Just then I had a brilliant idea. "Why don't you sign up to go to the senior center? There are buses to take you to and fro, and you could meet Don a couple times a week."

"Claire, that's a wonderful idea. I'll call Don later and see what he thinks."

"I can arrange it for both of you. Let me know," I said feeling ever so good about using my professional skills to help my friends.

***

Ross and I talked on the phone for a couple of days before I went to visit, as if wanting to postpone the inevitable sad reunion. The kids had left, back to their own lives, but not before setting up a coordinated schedule of availability for their dad. Peter had been granted an early leave back to the states and would be returning in mid-February. He had worked hard for his company and it was nice to see them reciprocate with family-friendly empathy.

Ross was certainly moved by his children's show of love. Dying would be easier, more meaningful perhaps, if surrounded by them. Ross, the ever efficient manager, would make sure all of his business was concluded.

By late January, he began another round of chemo--to buy time, not cure. He might be dying, but he sure as hell would not give up or depart earlier than necessary. His company, however, was not quite as understanding as Peter's. He had extended his leave of absence in preparation for the upcoming chemo side effects, but his protégé had already taken over most of his job responsibilities—permanently. "If you can," said his CEO, "try to get to the office as much as possible to help in an orderly transfer of duties." In conversations with professional colleagues, only cursory inquiries were made into his physical status. Most did not really want details after asking, "How are you feeling?" Their lives were going forward and he had stepped off the financial express train. Plus, like so many others, they were uncomfortable and unsure what to say. Fortunately, the offer of a generous early retirement package made the cold stark reality easier for Ross to swallow.

"Their attitude has been a major disappointment," said Ross one day. "I was simply a pawn in the game. But fuck! Screw them, it is not important anymore."

"You are amazing," I said. "I don't believe I have ever seen you so wise and courageous."

"Yeah, too bad I didn't get this sooner," he said jokingly. "Seriously though, I have even surprised myself with how I've accepted that and looked to the future. I am going to fight for more time, and not spend a second of it thinking about my old job or my regrets."

"You and the kids have been so helpful...and so have Frank and Jeff," he continued. "They have been here religiously. God, I am so grateful to have friends like them in my life. I don't think I ever appreciated them so much. Jeff can talk to me about my future, or lack thereof, while Frank still has great difficulties. He can't even say the word 'cancer.' If I talk about my death, he will hear none of it. But what he can't say, he makes up for in actions. He calls daily and visits several times a week. Last week, he spent two hours just doing chores around the house. I had to finally tell him to get the hell home to his own family."

Frank, Jeff, and I had done our share of talking over the phone as we coordinated car pools to chemotherapy treatments. While our families had spent a significant time together, the three of them were buddies and had often male-bonded on the golf course or on fishing trips. In the later years, sons accompanied them. I was relieved that their friendship could survive this crisis. At first, Frank stayed away, scared he would say the wrong thing, and afraid of losing emotional control. His infamous words after first hearing the diagnosis were, "Call me if you need me."

I learned from Edith that cancer patients, along with widows, widowers, and the whole gamut of sick people, hate these shallow, meaningless words. "They are the ultimate cop-out," Edith had proclaimed. "They depict our discomfort, and are right up there with the overused cliché, 'God never gives you more than you can handle.' Even my minister thinks that that phrase's hidden meaning is 'let's keep the conversation light and irrelevant so as to avoid emotion.' To put it crude terms, it means shut up and stop whining. So much for honesty and sensitivity."

Frank, at one time or another, had said about every inappropriate thing there is to say. Once, right after Ross had finished vomiting due to the chemo, Frank said, "Don't you look good today."

"I look like shit," responded Ross, "and I feel like it also. Dammit, Frank, stop lying to me! Don't think your job is to cheer me up." Frank got the point after that, and curtailed his indiscreet remarks, sometimes by not saying anything, which was ultimately better. One time Ross blurted out "Cancer sucks!" and Frank instantly shouted, "Yes, it does…Fucking sucks!" From then on he was more relaxed around Ross.

***

I thought long and hard about dropping one of my two classes before the semester started. Due to my work schedule, one of my courses was in the early evening. What if Ross needed more care? Could I handle it? Of course, I was taking another Marilyn

261

class called Social Work and Aging, but I was also taking a Death, Dying, and Bereavement psychology course taught by a well-respected professor. Besides helping me professionally, it would also help me cope with Ross's loss.

For now I decided to take them both. I could always drop Death and Dying later, but I just might learn something before I had to do that. I had become like a sponge in my educational quest. My new philosophy: so much to learn, so little time! Sure enough, the first classes were impressive---lots of work with exciting teachers and timely subject matter.

I got cracking that very night by going to the library, away from any phone interruptions, including a cell phone. For Christmas, Rossy had given me another cell phone to replace my broken one, but it was still boxed until he could fulfill his promise of "personalized and patient" instruction, which I told him would absolutely NOT include text-messaging. The last time I felt this intimidated was when I learned about computers and e-mail. At first, I was incredibly uptight, until I finally hired a tutor to walk me through each step, starting with how to turn it on. Many hours later, after no small dent in the checking account, I graduated from electronic illiteracy.

Sometimes you really can teach an 'old dog new tricks.' But being chained to a cell phone bothered me. It was comic on campus. As soon as a thousand students got out of class, a thousand Blackberries or cell phones were activated. They walked around campus twittering or chatting away like robots with their hands to ears:

"Hi, what you up to? I just left class."
"Oh really."

"When do you want to eat?"

"Oh really."

"No."

"Yes."

"Maybe."

"Oh really?"

"Talk to you later."

Why did they all need to talk to each other so urgently about nothing?

The first month of the new semester went smoothly, as did work, and my long-distance relationship with Scott. I looked forward to Peter's return from China and my spring break in New Orleans. Marilyn had approved my project on elderly relocation after disaster. I would also be working with Scott on helping New Orleans non-profits get more funding. Marilyn loved the fact that we were dating.

Ross's second round of chemo proved more grueling than the first. I started going 'home' twice a week to help. He rarely ate even when I cooked his favorites. A second CAT scan revealed a new metastasis in the lung, after which Ross stopped further treatments.

"It's not worth it. This poison is making me sicker and for no positive results. Time to face it. Let's just go for quality time. The pain so far is not that bad."

"Fuck!" I blurted out sobbing.

"Yeah, fuck is right." We sat crying silently for a long time, holding each other tight. Later I accompanied him to bed and we continued hugging until he fell asleep. There would be no sexual intercourse between us. It wasn't physically possible for him and I was relieved. Having sex with my technically ex-husband, even if only for old time's sake, would have complicated things. Besides, I was a monogamous gal and I wasn't about to cheat on Scott, not even emotionally. I loved Ross in a very unique way, not romantically anymore, but I truly loved him. And yes, I had forgiven him.

"Claire, I have an idea," he said upon awakening a short time later. "I want to do some videotaping. It's sort of, well, my ethical will; something for the kids and grandkids to remember me by. Actually I also want to do the eulogy for my own funeral. Will you help me?"

"Certainly. I'd be honored."

"Don't tell anybody we are doing this. Here's my credit card. Will you buy a new video camera, the small kind? Our old one is toast."

The next day, I purchased the camera, attached it to a tripod, turned it on, and he began talking. At first both of us were uncomfortable, but over the ensuing days we forgot the camera was there. Sometimes when I wasn't around, he would talk alone to the camera. Often he erased and started again, as if wanting to get it exactly right. Sometimes we had intense philosophical discussions. One time I asked him what it felt like to be dying. "I'm scared. It sucks. I feel cheated. I want to see my granddaughter grow up." His candor was right out front.

Slowly as the chemo side effects faded, he began feeling better. One night I arrived to find him in a cheap wig and a Hawaiian shirt with another matching one for me to put on. With camera rolling, he took me bowling while he pretended to be Stanley in *A Street Car Named Desire*. "Stellll-la!" he yelled as I rolled a gutter ball. "Hey guys," he spoke into the camera, "as you go through life remember it is not the end score that counts...stay away from gutters and get a ball that fits your hands." This statement, he later admitted, didn't make much sense, but he liked it anyhow.

We were together now out of mutual respect, to honor an almost lifetime of commitment, and, yes, because of the kids. If truth be known, being with him validated my decision to separate. Sometimes we seemed on such different planets. Once we argued and I almost left in frustration. Instead we both apologized.

"So how much are they paying you at that take-care-of-old-people agency?" he had said.

"Ross, it is not totally about the money. I derive tremendous satisfaction in what I am doing."

"Oh yeah, right."

"Ross, what are you saying, and in that tone of voice?"

"Guess I never had the luxury of a job for just the satisfaction. Had a family to raise."

"You SOB," I shouted, but caught myself *before* saying, "And I am not screwing one of my colleagues!"

"Ross, sorry I said that. Let's not do this. It is not worth it."

"I agree, I'm sorry—Guess I just feel pissed about how my company treated me at the end. Maybe I'm jealous. I might have made the money but...at least you work with compassionate people."

As in other parts of my life, I wanted to do better with Ross this second time around, at least get some things right. Both of us wanted to treat each other with respect. The time for pettiness was over.

Cancer had brought us back together before death would inevitably separate us again.

One time Frank stayed for dinner. Captured on camera, we laughed about old times. Ross loved a sentimental atmosphere. I could see the look of appreciation on his face when Frank choked up. Even though he toughly said, "Come on guys! No wimpy emotions now," I could see he treasured them. Having friends display their grief authenticated his life and gave him peace. "Thanks, Frank. Better to tell me while I'm still able to hear your words," Ross had said, "than to say it at my funeral."

Peter and family arrived back home and decided to live with Ross until they found a home. While they had searched, nothing seemed to suit them and I rather suspected Peter wanted to be close to his dad and become the primary caregiver. Peter had taken Ross's terminal status the hardest, at least outwardly. He'd always emulated his dad and with Linda's support, wanted to pay him back. Their taping ran for hours as Ross lovingly played with a four-month-old Kim, often napping with his granddaughter on his chest.

Life went on even during inevitable endings.

23

With Peter home caring for Ross, I was comfortable traveling to New Orleans over spring break to meet Scott, whom I missed terribly. While it had only been six weeks since I'd seen him, regular phone conversations and e-mail could no longer supplant our desire for face-to-face contact. Although we had tried to schedule a rendezvous in between, it just didn't work. In an affectionate gesture, he had taxied to the New Orleans airport with fresh daisies in tow, surprising me at luggage claim.

Our time together was no relaxing vacation this time. By week's end I was nursing blisters and popping drug store pain relievers. With a squad of people, we made major headway towards finishing a 1600-square-foot ranch home. The locals among our work team were the family who would live in the house. Other workers included a lovable muscular Boy Scout looking to earn another badge, and two permanent Habitat crew members. The rest of us were a hodgepodge of retirees living plane rides away from Katrina's tragic destruction and the pathetically slow rehabilitation of the once vibrant city.

We started working just after the crack of dawn

and quit at dusk. On two occasions, tired and sore, Scott and I fell into our hotel bed, without showering. One night at nine P.M. I ordered Chinese takeout. How very strange to be in the hometown of Emeril Lagasse eating in bed from plastic containers and unwrapping fortune cookies. Scott was too tired to get up and find the enhancer, let alone perform from its effects.

Our private conversations were about Ross, my courses, Scott's volunteer schedule, and our now serious relationship. "I was doing okay with being a widower until you came into my life," he told me. "Now I have sort of regressed. I don't like it when we are apart for such long periods. I miss you."

Once, while on the job, another Habitat volunteer asked if we were married. "No, but we are in a significant relationship," I answered comfortably in earshot of Scott.

That night he wanted to talk about marriage. "Do you ever see us married?"

"Is this a proposal?"

"Actually no, but I am testing the waters to see if I should practice getting on my knees. You know, many a single senior woman would seize this opportunity to jump again into the marital sack," he said laughing. "But I suspect you are an exception and we are going to have to come up with an alternative."

"Do you want to get married?"

"I want to do some long-range planning, form a consensus. I could see us blissfully happy, dancing in the sunset, even married. Even if Ross's pension ceases if you marry again, your life style wouldn't change. I have saved wisely. We don't need your money, although I know that's important to you."

"I agree with the blissfully happy part," I responded. "I just don't know about the rings and making a new will. What will your kids think about me messing with their inheritance?"

"Oh, yes, the kids. Well…"

I interrupted. "I will tell you this…I feel so honored to be by your side. I do want to dance with you into the sunset. I love you a lot. I'm in love with you. But right now I don't trust myself that I would marry you for the right reasons. Naturally that is an issue for me. My life is in transition. I'm really vulnerable. 'Jumping into the marital sack' might not be what I need to do. And it wouldn't be fair to you unless I was sure."

"I'm glad we are talking about it," he said. "This conversation needs to be ongoing. But do trust in me that I will not be pressuring you to the altar. I can go either way. At sixty-five, I do not need a license to love you. Truth is, though, six weeks is too long apart."

"Sometimes I think I don't deserve you. I have never had this type of open communication. Where did you come from?"

***

Feeling increasingly comfortable, I told Scott about my newly defined relationship with Ross. "Do you still love him?" he asked.

"Cancer has provided us the opportunity to cut through the bullshit, and our marriage was a lot of bullshit. It's a gift really. I have appreciated our time to reflect, rise to a new level of emotional intimacy. Forty years is a lot of time to live with someone."

"So, are you still in love with him?"

269

"Yes, I love him…in a way that defines siblings. We hugged in bed about two weeks ago but never made love," I said without hesitation.

He was silent.

"Are you disappointed?" I asked, now with hesitation.

"Yes, Claire, I must admit, I am." His words struck like a hot iron on my chest. Why did I tell him that piece of information?

"What you just said puts quite a new dimension on things. I guess I could understand you wanting to be with him as a caregiver…and even wanting to make peace with your past. But, getting into bed with him? What are your boundaries? I am beginning to wonder if you are more conflicted than you let on."

"Trust me Scott. My newly defined relationship with Ross has uncompromising boundaries."

"I do want to trust you Claire, but this is new territory for us both. I love you but you are spending a lot of time with an ex and now hopping in the sack with him. Granted he is dying, but I guess I just discovered some limits to my tolerance."

"I'm sorry, Scott. Please trust me," I continued almost desperately and still in shock at his reaction. "My love for Ross is hugely different than my love for you."

"Claire, I just talked about marriage, and you proceed to tell me you are sleeping with your ex-husband. How am I supposed to process that? These last months I have also had to line up behind your school work, your job, and now this. Maybe we *are* on vastly different pages."

My heart was racing. OMG! This was not some little spat. "I am conflicted, Scott, but not about you.

Ross's cancer has been an opportunity to mend a broken 40-year-old relationship. Yes, it is tough to define our new turf. But I assure you, I am not cheating on you. I was hugging a dying man. Please don't take that personally. It is not about you."

"And if he weren't dying, then what?"

"We're trying to become friends, not get back together." I said crying, with my voice raised. Then as if catching myself, I quietly said, "And I guess I am failing miserably. I don't know how to do this. In another few weeks or months, he'll be dead and I don't want to pass up our opportunity to actually *live* our forgiveness." My tears turned to sobs. "I am so sorry I hurt you."

He broke a long silence, "Claire, we shouldn't be having this conversation when both of us are so exhausted. Let me go out and get some fresh decaf. I'll be back in a little while."

Dear God, what was happening? Why did I stupidly tell him about hugging Ross in bed? How could I think that I could deal with Ross's death and have a serious relationship with Scott at the same time? Feeling entirely inadequate, I wanted to scream!

"I'm sorry," he said upon coming back.

"No, I'm sorry. Really Scott, you don't deserve this mess I've made."

"No love, it's not a total mess. It's a bump, maybe a big one—Also I'm tired and drained--- emotionally and physically."

We sat in bed with our coffees but he fell asleep almost immediately. The next day we slept late and rushed to the job. Both of us felt unbalanced, interacting in a forced rather than spontaneous way, dreading the looming conversation that had to happen. That night, the Habitat team gathered for dinner. We got home late, and went straight to bed. I wanted to sustain our hug, but he pulled away.

***

Thankfully, after four days both of us moved on from the physical labor of house building to other projects, me to interview some of the elders in nursing homes, Scott to do a seminar and consulting work for a number of needy non-profits. We were each pulled in a myriad of directions, none of which included being together for more than a few minutes, and too tired to talk at night.

Many of the elderly I talked with in the nursing home suffered from depression and Post Traumatic Stress Disorder. They had lost their houses and ended up institutionalized prematurely. Whatever spark of life they once had seemed to be flickering towards extinction. Too many sat in fixed, almost catatonic, positions in recliner chairs staring into space, unresponsive, often talking to themselves in gibberish, seemingly unaware of the surrounding environment or blaring TV. A bored-looking exercise therapist came one day with a plastic beach ball and instructed a circle of seniors to throw it to one another. Half-heartedly they complied as the ball aimlessly bounced within but mostly out of the circle, forcing the therapist, now rolling her eyes, to continually retrieve it.

Here, I did feel like I was in Heaven's waiting room. The living dead. Everything done except the burial. All dignity had been sucked out with the receding waters of Katrina, and with few, if any family members returning to uplift them. There was nobody with whom to talk about the past or start a sentence,

"Do you remember when...?" Visitors were rare--many, the nurses told me, had simply moved away or struggled with their own survival. Long-term goals centered on making it through the day.

A give-up attitude was etched on many wrinkled, vacant faces. One woman, hair matted, clutched a book called, *God's Calling,* as if advertising her readiness. Several talked openly about death, one even asking if I would help her end her life. "Please! Just get me a bottle of pills. I can't stand one more day." That same woman had a monitor around her ankle that triggered an alarm at the front door if she tried to escape one more time. Once I found her strapped in her chair.

In between observing and talking with the staff and patients, I ached for a talk with Scott. I felt we were on the edge of a cliff, our supposed strong union ready to fall apart. I was easily distracted. Oh, the unfinished business we had to deal with, and in a couple of days we would part again, me to New Jersey and he to Arizona. I couldn't envision settling this on the phone. Sometimes I could feel my heart palpating as if signifying my emotional distress.

For a while I watched a visitor making rounds with her pet dog. Some residents instantly perked up, a sudden awakening spurred by touching a furry head and having their face licked--a momentary reprieve from boredom and purgatory. Then, because there were so many patients to visit, the dog was gone, not to return until next week—168 hours to the next stroke of a wet muzzle, possibly the closest they would come to unconditional love and acceptance.

I was saddened by the lives discarded, like a leper colony of the old. I suspected that New Orleans presented an acute version of our ostensibly warehoused treatment of the elderly. Perhaps it could have been anywhere.

I became captivated by one voiceless lady, wondering who she had been once-upon-a-time--that unseen person whose vigor was long sucked away, now touch deprived, aching, diapered, lifeless, waiting to check out. What had she looked like thirty or forty or sixty years ago? What kind of parent was she? Who was her lover? What color was her hair? Who would remember her? Like the uninformed nephew at Edith's friend's memorial service, there were hidden segments of lifetimes behind each despairing face.

The three-day experience would haunt me. I wasn't in some third-world location, or was I? During my time at the nursing home, I had barely seen Scott. He worked late into the night, mostly on location with representatives of the non-profits he was trying to help.

At the airport, Scott and I sat at breakfast before saying good-by at our respective concourses and beginning another month's separation. We had gotten up early so we would have time to talk. Neither of us wanted to separate with such unresolved issues.

"I didn't realize this trip was going to be such a marathon."

"It was worth it," I replied. "But I regret we never finished our talk. What have you been thinking about us over the last couple of days?"

"It is going to be harder than I imagined. But you know what---I am not throwing-in-the-towel just yet. Maybe it is unrealistic to think we can make this work.

But Claire, I do love you. Quite frankly, I was jealous—jealous of everybody having a piece of you and me waiting in line. At first, it seemed simple until we entangled reality in the romance---I don't think either of us were seeing clearly, the proverbial rose-colored-glasses, but…but, maybe we both need some time to sort it all out," he added.

"Do you want to break up?"

"Right now, all I want to do is get some sleep. We need to keep talking, and we need to see if our life's priorities fit into this relationship."

"Scott, I meant it when I said that I love Ross in a very different way."

"Let's face it Claire, when he dies you will be his widow, not his divorced spouse. Along with that comes a sustained grief. Right now, I feel like we are having an affair, not a legitimate romance. Then you have school and a new career—I never realized how complicated this was getting."

"Do you want to work it out?"

"Is it possible?"

I looked at my watch, tears again in my eyes like so many times before in the last days. My flight would be boarding and I had to move with haste. "Scott, I do love you very much. I am not going to let you go so easily."

We hugged, stroking each other's backs. "I love you too Claire. Good-bye."

Good-bye? Shit, what did that mean? There seemed a finality to those words.

***

Not long after I returned, Gloria flew out for a visit. She looked fantastic, having lost twenty pounds through diet and exercise. "I never knew how

275

depressed I had become taking care of my depressed son," she said. "I have felt so guilty about my relief that I went into therapy, *again*, and joined a suicide support group. I'm doing better now. It's been almost three months."

"How did you feel relief over Brad's death?"

"God, Claire, I was his caretaker. This kid had been depressed since he was sixteen! Doctor's appointments, therapy, medications. He self-medicated with drugs and alcohol. Then I self-medicated with the same things. He went into rehab, finally got a job, couldn't finish college, got job after job, sometimes he'd lie in bed for a week. In bouts of tough love, I kicked him out of the house, refused to enable him, watched him slide into the gutter."

Oh, I thought, how emotional that would have been for any mother.

"Then," she continued, "he got the right medication, at the right moment, with the right talk therapist, and it all seemed to come together for a while, a couple of years. I thought, dear God Almighty, we are out of the woods, sober, drug free, and he's got a supportive family he can participate in. Fucking false! It was only a reprieve from the next descent into Hell, this time worse than last. However, this time I was sober."

"I'm sorry, Gloria. It had to be so hard to watch."

Her need to talk continued over the weekend. He had stolen money from her; trust was compromised. When the police came to the house to give the tragic news of his death, both her and Ron's first thoughts were, "our ordeal is over." She couldn't even cry until hours later when she thought about the waste of it all; what could have been.

Her shifting emotions ranged from "what if…" to acceptance, from grief to anger. One despicable woman at the funeral had asked, "Couldn't you have prevented this?" Gloria had been incensed, "God-damned bitch! I wanted to wring her fucking neck!" The suicide support group had helped her deal with people's insensitivities and attitudes, as well as her own sense of guilt.

"How is Ron doing?"

"He grieves very differently than me, almost a textbook model for male/female differences. He works hard, always has to have something to do, can't sit still and just hang out, doesn't want anything to do with a support group and rarely initiates conversations about Brad anymore. He grieves silently, but I know he is grieving. I've seen him cry when he thought I wasn't around. He never shows his emotions in public, yet we are slowly reinventing our relationship…for the better."

Our talks over the weekend were intermixed with fun. One day we went back to the campus of our youth, only a couple of hours away. It was a wonderful trip full of nostalgia—light years back to a time of innocence before we complicated our lives, or life complicated us. We even visited our dormitory and saw the room where we were roommates forty-plus years ago.

On the drive home, I shared what was happening between Scott and me. As any good friend would do, she helped me articulate my feelings. "Maybe it's good to have some space between you now," she said. "However, I don't think it was a mistake to tell him the truth about you and Ross."

Later, over lunch, we talked about ways to memorialize Brad. The mental health center where Gloria worked was expanding and there were all sorts of programs or building sections which could be named in his honor. I pledged my financial support to a fund she had initiated. Our friendship was back to stay and I cherished it.

***

As the new leaves of spring appeared, Cedric made final preparations for his move to San Francisco. He was a bundle of nervous energy, buzzing around daily with an updated 'to do' list. In acts of generosity, he gave away 'stuff' to friends or charity thrift shops. I inherited more pillows, now a tradition, plus an unused set of place mats, and an angora scarf, the reminder of a short-lived lover. He gave Edith his state-of-the-art toaster oven, an excellent choice for someone cooking for herself. However, it had so many dials, I doubted she'd ever master it. "Please just tell me how to toast a bagel and how to get it to 350 degrees. That's all I want to know."

Cedric had spent his last week attending an assortment of farewell parties with colleagues, clients, and friends. He loathed any gifts as another thing to move but I could tell he loved the gestures, as if measuring his impact in the area and the profession, a final report card. "Get a load of this wine decanter," he said looking at an ornately gaudy crystal carafe. "Tacky! Like I am actually going to pour a good bottle of wine into this."

He reserved his last night in town for Edith and me, an honor we appreciated. We had formed a friendship family, equally as important as blood because of the depth of sharing. He had taught me a lot, including how to laugh again. I knew I would miss him--his move was a loss for me, something I didn't take lightly.

"You know guys," said Cedric, "our friendship has been analogous to being on a river raft. At times we enjoyed the shared calm and beauty surrounding us, while at other times we negotiated the rocks and white-water rapids together, reaching our hands out if one of us fell out of the boat. I will treasure that."

"Great analogy. Oh, how I sometimes hate change," I said to him, "especially the type of change that spells l-o-s-s. Another significant emotional event."

"Hey, Miss Sentimental," he cracked. "I am only a phone call away. And our pricey new condo will include a guest bedroom."

"Don't expect me to get on a plane," quipped Edith. "I am now a true little-old-lady, complete with a cane. Besides, I would need a motorized wheel chair to traverse the hills of San Fran."

"Well, there is a power chair rental just down the street," Cedric shot back.

"I hope you have a good life, Cedric," said Edith with a crack in her voice. "Really I do. I wish you the best."

"What the hell?" I said to Edith. "Wow, that is a serious goodbye."

"Come on, Claire. If I see Cedric again, that will be my pleasure, but I am covering my bases. This might be goodbye. And if we do see each other again, we won't repeat what we have had this year. In the future, a dinner here, or luncheon there cannot ever bring us to this place again. We three musketeers have had spontaneity and the privilege of interacting in our daily lives. That is over, but I treasure what it meant."

There was a long silence as the wise words of an elder slowly sank in. How often I had said to people, "Let's get together soon," only to get ensconced in daily life, always putting reunions on the back burner as the years flittered past. Then there were those occasional disappointing reunions starkly confirming that it wasn't the same. I had recaptured it with Gloria, but that was perhaps an exception.

His move was like a mini-death—the death of what we had. It had happened to each of us numerous times, that instant that some part of your life makes the transition from reality to memory.

We each needed each other at a very special time in our lives—my separation, Edith's accident, Cedric's transition—and we clicked, just like that. Cedric allowed Edith to grapple with a long-held, guilt-laden homophobia and came out on top. Cedric, being disowned by his blood relatives, needed family and the security it brings. "Miss Edith," he had said. "I wish you had been my mother." In fact, we all needed surrogate family and during this vulnerable period, we had come together and been nurtured.

"I don't mean to throw a damper on this party," continued Edith, "but there was such security in our proximity to each other...and the relationship that developed from that. I hate to let it go, but we must move on. I have said it a million times before. Some moving on is painfully hard, like after I buried Rudy. This particular 'move-on' is also hard for me. Cedric is leaving, and I am so excited for him; and you Claire, well your life is busy now. Even though you are not leaving physically, you are pulled in many directions."

Cedric was tearful, as I was. "Well Edith, I give you a toaster oven and you tell me to have a good life. There must be a lesson here?" We all laughed. Then Cedric joined Edith and me on the sofa, plopping his tight ass right in between us, pulling both our hands to his knees as our heads rested on his shoulders. "I am going to miss you both…and thank you for not giving me another wine carafe. By the way, do either of you want this one?"

"NO!" we shouted in tandem.

"Oh, the present!" said Edith. "I forgot my present. Claire, can you get the bag with the handles?"

In it was a throw blanket that Edith had knitted herself, a dark gray cashmere, with intricate square patterns demonstrating numerous work hours. "They tell me San Francisco nights are chilly. This is for curling up with a good book."

Cedric was touched. "I will treasure this forever."

"Don't baby it. By the time you are old, I want it tattered and worn."

"Trust me, it will be."

I gave Cedric a photo of the three of us that we had taken in a booth at a mall, both Edith and me on his lap, all of us making faces. I had framed it to join his collection of people photos that graced his home. Cedric loved displaying his photos of times and friends, past and current. He had taught me that photo albums were secondary to actual displaying. He was right. Every time I passed a displayed photo in my own home, that time and place put a smile on my face.

"A special time with special friends," said Cedric. "I think this deserves a prominent place in my new home."

"How about the guest bathroom?" I suggested deadpan.

"Don't think that is so silly. You will want that place of honor when you see the bathroom I have planned."

The next afternoon Cedric pulled out of the parking lot for the last time, with a bag of Edith's freshly baked cookies and my care basket of fruit and cheeses. He would meet Greg at the Philadelphia airport, overnight with friends in the City of Brotherly Love, then leisurely drive across the country checking off some of their bucket lists. Since his furniture would be placed in storage until the renovations were completed, they had no strict timetable.

"I already miss him," said Edith when I came home from work.

"Me too. We were all good for each other."

"You know, I should have taken that carafe. I could have given it to Barbara."

24

Scott and I carried on our relationship via phone and e-mail.

"We should have never started that conversation in New Orleans with both of us being so tired," he said over and over. "I was feeling sorry for myself, fantasizing about us being together every day, knowing after New Orleans that we were going our separate ways for a month."

"Scott, I am not sorry we got this out in the open, even though I have been really stressed. We can't have a relationship if I can't be honest and upfront. You have got to trust me about my feelings for Ross...and that you are a separate entity, not part of an either/or decision. I might have to juggle my time, but I am not juggling my feelings, not anymore. It is not a "Y" in the road where I have to choose, unless you want to make it that."

"Maybe if we had met after his death...."

"But we didn't. Look, he is a big part of my life and has been for decades. He's the father of my children. For me, this is a significant life opportunity. You have got to believe that I am not keeping you at bay until he expires, then replacing him with you. I love you too much to play those stupid games."

Being assertive and honest was almost exhilarating. My confidence soared.

"And," I continued, "I am not going to beg you to understand. I would never forgive myself if I abandoned Ross and didn't finish our work. Scott, doing that could cause a permanent resentment between us."

"And school and your job?"

"Flip Wilson used to play a character named Geraldine, who frequently said, 'What you see is what you get.' I don't mean this in a pejorative, flippant way, to demean you, but this is what we are dealing with. I *am* my work and school and dying ex-husband. It is all teaching me something about life and I am better for it. If I let this go, my life turns banal again. I would rather take the risk of losing you than, than......"

"Claire, I have been less than understanding, thinking of myself. You're right, you know. Maybe subconsciously I was hoping you would drop everything and be with me full time. Even with all of my work, I am still a lonely old man. That is selfish and negating your feelings. Truth be told, these conversations have made me realize how much I do love you, just the way you are. I know what it is like to start over and I should have remembered what an important time it was for me. And, I can actually identify with your situation right down to a dying mate. It has caught me by surprise to feel threatened, and act childish."

"Oh Scott, I have been on pins and needles. I don't want us to fail."

"We're not!"

What we didn't say verbally, we wrote in long

internet letters. Finally, everything out, warts and all---and done with no sarcasm, shouting, or belittling---just the hard talk. In the end, we had more than just survived. I was so drawn to him.

***

Jennifer looked stunning as she marched down the chapel's candlelit aisle, practically holding up her own dad, who was visibly shaking. She wore her mother's wedding gown, only slightly altered, each bodice pearl painstakingly sewn in place by the loving hands of her grandmother, who, at eighty-five, was beaming that her labor-of-love masterpiece was once again center stage. Ross and I sat next to each other holding hands as we watched the smiling faces of our sons, groom and best man, and daughter, a bridesmaid, waiting up front for the approaching bride.

I was glad the wedding date had been pushed up. Ross, while failing, still had enough energy to don a tuxedo. He would not be denied his firstborn's wedding. Before we walked into the church, he swallowed a narcotic level pain pill. His hair was growing back again but cancer was written all over his body; thin, frail-looking, sunken eyes, a yellowish tint to his skin, bruises on his hands.

Rossy had graciously invited Scott, now back from Arizona, who in turn graciously declined. "It is for your family," he simply said to me. "My presence would complicate things. We can watch the videos together later." He was right.

The ceremony had some personal touches; Rossy thanked both Ross and me for our parenting as Jennifer did hers. It fell just short of sentimental, but, hell, we didn't care. Mushy was fine. We appreciated the public expression of feelings.

Ross held me tight as we danced at the reception, as much out of love as for balance. On the brink of tears, he gave a long and touching toast to his son and new daughter-in-law. Wedding guest greetings ranged from kind to ridiculously inappropriate. "I am sorry Ross that this is happening to you." "Claire, what a beautiful family you have." "My Ross, you look great!" "Call us if you need us." "What a handsome couple you make." "This is God's way of saying you should be together." "Claire, I heard you are dating someone." "Hey Ross, what a way to get out of working."

By nine P.M., too tired to continue, Ross called it an evening. Rossy had arranged a special limo in anticipation, and his friends Frank and Jeff would be going with him. I stayed, dancing with all the kids, including Kate who whooped it up with me to the beat of "Celebrate Your Love, Come on!" Sam, now her live-in partner, joined us midway through the fifteen-minute marathon version of the song. Wet hairs from my once beautifully coiffed hair were now pasted to my cheeks. It felt good to get the exercise and blow off a bit of the day's tension. I felt gorgeous in my sleek new calf-length, size twelve, low V-necked, navy blue knit dress, which Jennifer had spotted on our joint shopping trip. After the first dance, the partially beaded matching jacket was assigned to a chair's back. I had lost one whole dress size in the last year and my sixty-one-year-old body was in good shape.

That night, about as tired as I could possibly be, I laid awake in my bed. I had another married son, and Kate had told me she would announce to dad in the morning that she and Sam were getting married. Sam, knowing time was not on his side, was spending a lot of time with Ross. I was glad they would get to know each other.

The next day the front door opening and closing woke me from a deep sleep. It was already ten A.M. Scott was armed with roses, the newspaper, and coffee. "Tell me about it," he said as he took off his sneakers and jumped into bed. We spent the day relaxing.

Ross had much difficulty recuperating from the long day, hardly getting his tux off before falling into bed. He slept intermittently throughout the whole Sunday, and Kate called me in the afternoon full of worry. He could barely muster excitement about her engagement or respond when his granddaughter grabbed his feet. The reality of his demise was sinking in, staring her in the face.

Blessed Peter. He accepted the primary burden of care-giving for his father and never once complained. Many mornings he showered his dad in the oversized stall, helping Ross to his shower chair and making sure he was thoroughly cleaned. At first Ross had balked, but soon felt comfortable with this most intimate father-son bonding experience. Unfortunately, these encounters became increasingly sporadic as Ross's body deteriorated and weakness prevailed. On days when showering proved too strenuous, Peter simply bathed him in bed.

Sometimes when Peter's work schedule conflicted, I took over. It seemed the natural thing to do; I was comfortable and so was Ross. He had gradually lost his modesty as his infirmity increased and drugs clouded his mind. He always felt better after being cleaned up, changing to fresh clothes and getting his teeth brushed. I even figured out how to wash his hair in bed and massage his head in the process. I learned to give a soothing back rub, gently, over his protruding bones. He was always appreciative.

One day, with his arms around the shoulders of both Rossy and Peter, he came downstairs so he could get a change of scenery. He laid on the sofa for much of the day until he was helped back up. He liked it so much that for a few days, until his strength took another downward trajectory, this became routine.

***

Scott had been home for three weeks and we had settled into a routine as well; a couple of nights at my place, a couple of nights at his, a couple apart. This schedule would suit us for a while. Our respective bathrooms contained the other's toothbrush. We gave each other some closet space and an extra drawer. I bought make-up to leave at his place. He had an extra blood pressure prescription at mine.

One afternoon we went to his wife's grave on the third anniversary of her death. I was glad to be included in the experience and talked to her grave, saying she would never be replaced, and I would surely help keep her name and legacy alive. "I don't know if I would have invited you here a while back," Scott whispered. "But the present should meld with the past, bringing us to who we are."

"Like creating a gestalt of experiences."

"Wise words."

"I just learned that last semester."

When I studied, Scott would read a book or

288

prepare for another of the many lectures he gave. Often we congregated at a dining room table, papers strewn around, alternately working and conversing on some topic that intrigued us. He had become somewhat of an icon for non-profit fund raising, a guru in high demand as the economy sagged. On one occasion, I accompanied him to a seminar in New York City. Somehow he managed to find theater tickets and an Ethiopian restaurant, something not found in our area. I wore my mother-in-law-of-the-bride dress again.

I enjoyed hearing his speeches, given with a confidence that captivated an already motivated audience. He offered hope about raising money for their cause, whether an animal shelter, an autism foundation, or an inpatient hospice. Most left encouraged. In the current recession, the non-profits were suffering and bake sales and yard sales could not sustain budget demands. Many wrestled for every dollar just to keep their heads above water. With pride swallowed, most would beg without remorse, becoming evangelists for their cause. I was proud to be by his side and learned a lot listening to him.

As a former successful businessman turned social service worker, Scott gave them ideas on how to go for big dollar donations. He did not sugar-coat the work involved. My very own agency on aging, housed in a 1920s former Tuberculosis sanatorium that qualified as a disgraceful eyesore, was always searching for dollars. The original furnace regularly broke down and continuously leaked---a pan filled with kitty litter was stationed to catch the regular drips of fuel oil. Behind walls and ceilings, some pipes were still insulated with asbestos. Decades-old paint, three or four layers underneath recent paint jobs, was lead-based. I was cramped in an office that had once been a linen closet, although thankfully it had a window. The floor creaked beneath approaching footsteps. Everything was old, from the furniture to the bathrooms to the ill-fated people who needed our services. If this building presented a symbol of how we felt about aging, it reeked of rejection, a building relegated for castaways, not unnoticed by the visiting aged. A major campaign would soon be underway to build a new facility, and already Imogene and Scott had had several meetings to plan strategy for acquiring the nine million plus dollars needed.

***

One evening at dinner, Scott told me that Ross had called him. "Oh?" I inquired. "What was that about?"

"He was very kind, invited me over for coffee, even though he couldn't drink it. It just happened that I was available right then."

"And you went?" I said, not in a confrontational way, just amazed, eyes open wide.

"Sure, I wanted to tell him I would take good care of you, although you are quite capable of taking good care of yourself."

"You went to my house?" I was still stunned, frowning, but had a smile on my face.

"Yep, are you okay with that?"

"Yes, really, but...but I'm surprised, shocked at Ross's invitation."

"Ross has a mission before his death. He wants the whole family, the kids, and yes, you, in good hands. He told me he couldn't leave this world without a face-to-face meeting with me."

"Did he talk about our marriage?"

"Not much—no more than you have already told me—his regrets. He said in the end he simply wanted to meet me before his long journey beyond. There was no heavy agenda."

There was a chill in my body, a sudden thickness in my throat from this hit of reality, "What did you tell him?"

"That you talked about him a lot and felt grateful that his illness had given you both a chance to reconcile. He also told me not to forget your birthday because that was special for you."

"Scott, you are amazing. Sometimes I wonder if I deserve you." And although I didn't articulate it at the time, I was profoundly touched by Ross's gesture.

"I felt privileged that he wanted to meet me. We also talked a lot about our kids. After an hour or so, he was pretty tired so I left. I am really glad I got to meet him. What you said before about loving him like a sibling…I can see that now. It was as if he were your big brother and wanted to know who his sister was dating---A very pure form of love."

"You think it is that simple?"

"No, nothing is ever that simple, but he was trying. He truly had your best interest at heart. For that I give him credit."

25

"I can't stand this!" cried Kate as she walked downstairs into the living room where her siblings waited.

"I know it's hard, but, dear God, just think how Dad must feel," Peter responded not meaning any sarcasm.

Journal entry: *The dying process can bring a family closer, or tear them apart. It is life changing. I was proud of my kids for sticking it out, not avoiding it, unafraid to touch a dying man who wasn't very touchable. There was something about cancer that had permeated the entire house—the sights and the somber mood. You could see it, feel it, and smell it.*

At one point Ross had projectile vomiting and the kids wanted to call for an ambulance. Ross firmly said no; that he would not be going back to the hospital. We called our hospice nurse and the narcotics she brought were a welcomed respite from pain. Peter and I learned how to administer them intramuscularly since Ross could barely keep anything down. I inserted antiemetics into his rectum.

Morphine's side effects caused Ross to drift in and out of sleep, but he managed to stay alert some of the time. He wanted to visit with the kids, and me, every minute he could. "It is interesting knowing when you will die," he said to me. "Thanks for sticking around for the 'in sickness and till death do us part.' Wish we could have done the 'in health' part better."

Kate had dropped out of school for the semester and moved back home for the duration. Sam, who had also lost a dad to cancer, was supportive and visited often. I dropped my Death and Dying course, having secured permission from the professor to attend lectures without having to do the assignments. She was most accommodating, allowing me to audit the course, which would count in the future when I chose to repeat.

We all made arrangements so we could participate in the death vigil. Every day we grieved a bit more, as if in preparation for our lives without Ross. In witnessing his downward spiral, I became less scared of terminal illness. I had always said I wanted to die in an airplane crash, but cancer had its positive outcomes. Surely terminal illness sucked, but cancer gives you a chance to say good-bye, and make important amends. Besides, figuring I was not going to have a choice in how I died anyway, I accepted cancer as an okay alternative.

Many nights I ate with the kids. After a while we started planning the funeral. Of course, Ross had directed me in what he wanted, which included the video we had made. The taping was finished and Ross had had a documentary filmmaker edit it, complete with music. We watched it together only once. It was wrenching. "Okay," said Ross. "Take it away. I don't want to see it again." After telling the kids what we had done, of course they wanted to view it. So late one night when Ross was sleeping soundly, we plugged it in.

Predictably, we all became highly emotional. At different times, everyone sobbed. Peter was particularly uncontrolled. Rossy walked out of the room once to compose himself. Kate planted her face in a pillow. Not being able to rescue them from their pain, I cried just watching them suffer. Over the next few days, we watched the tape over and over, collectively and alone.

Emotion aside, the video wasn't actually maudlin. There were parts that made you laugh. On my third viewing, when Ross started talking about his golf game, I thought I'd bust a gut. I guess we were not used to thinking about a deceased person talking at their funeral. Eventually, as we played the tape more, all of us got used to it, de-sensitized if you will. It also prompted fun conversations with Ross. "Dear God, Dad, you are going to freak people out with your pitiful golf lessons." "You buried the golf ball where?"

I guess death is always a roller coaster of emotions, I said in my journal---*laugh, cry, maybe time for being pissed off. Did I say all I needed to say, do all I needed to do? Jesus, this is a disaster! Can you give me the number of the Life Crisis Center? Why me? Poor me! This is as bad as it gets. Life can change in an instant. Where's the gin? Stir in some Prozac, please. There is a part of me that is dying with you. You fucking bastard, why didn't you go to the doctor sooner? No, I don't want another god-damned sandwich! Why didn't we work on this marriage more? I will not even have the honor of being a real widow. All I will be allowed to be is the surviving semi-ex-wife. You bastard! I am as disenfranchised in your death as I was in your life. I love you so much!*

***

Scott was consoling and sympathetic. He understood my moods, even anticipated them. Never once did he hint that I wasn't spending enough time with him. He took his turn in line, behind Ross, the kids, school, work…waiting patiently in the periphery, familiar with the mourning process, and now comfortable with our relationship, unique as it was.

"Older people who come together bring their histories," he said one night when there was just the two of us. "This is the time for me to support you, not get in your way or demand a bigger share of your time"

"Oh, you wise old man."

"Got to have something to show for all of these wrinkles and wilting penis."

"You're not going to have a relapse into young-penis envy, are you?"

"I still get hard with a little help from my friend," he sang to the Beatles infamous tune.

"Oh, pluh-ease!" Being silly was a welcomed antidote. Once again, laughing helped the pain.

Later that night when Scott and I were sleeping soundly, the phone rang. "Come now Mom," Peter whispered.

Scott drove me to the house but didn't stay. The lights were on. Rossy drove up behind us. Without saying a word, we went upstairs. Ross was breathing sporadically, a labored wheezing, only a few respirations each minute. I called his name but he was barely responsive. I could tell he was in pain as the rasps continued. I gave him another shot of morphine to help calm his rasping, knowing it would hasten his death.

Rossy, Peter, Kate, and I surrounded him, all of

us on the bed. Linda had taken a fussy Kim out of the room. We each rubbed a part of his body. I massaged his head, crying almost uncontrollably. "We are all here, Ross. We love you."

"Thanks Dad."

"Hey Dad, have fun at the big golf course in the sky. Keep your eye on the ball."

"Don't forget to keep in touch, just a postcard will do."

"Love you Dad."

"Thanks my dear, wonderful friend."

As the last minutes of his life passed, we all fell silent. By now, Ross seemed relaxed, the labored breathing calmed, a look of peaceful relief on his face. The period between breaths drew longer. Yet, every time we thought it was over, he breathed once again. Then, finally, that next breath didn't come.

It was 2:05 A.M.

***

For a while we all just sat there, sometimes sniffles interrupting soundless tears, other times releasing full-blown sobs. We continued stroking him. Kate lay on his shoulder in an almost fetal position. Then, as if instructed by his father, Rossy left the room and returned with a bottle of Champagne and crystal glasses. After pouring, he toasted his father, "Here's to a great life and the legacy you left!" Reminiscing started.

"The thing I regret most is that Kim will never know him," cried Peter.

"Yes, she will. She will hear all the tales and see the tape," I replied.

"But she'll miss so much."

"I know. Guess there's never a good time to die.

Always something to live for…first steps, graduations, weddings, births, always something."

"Who's going to give me away at my wedding?" sobbed Kate.

"I will," said Rossy. "Me too," Peter added. "Dad will be there in spirit."

Conversation continued, stories were told, some of which I didn't know about. "You and your father did what?!"

After a while, Kate finally said, "What do we do now?"

"Nothing just yet. This is our last time to be together; our viewing before your dad is cremated. We can call the funeral home in the morning." It was already four A.M. We had been talking for almost two hours. I left the room to call Frank and Jeff, and make some coffee. When Jennifer arrived, she, Kate, and I started bathing Ross, continuing the ritual of history--- women bathing their dead, the ultimate privilege of women's work, only this time my sons helped.

Before the funeral home hearse arrived, each child spent some time alone with Ross, as did I. "Thank you again, my beloved friend. I love you."

***

Sitting in the front row of the funeral home made it hard to see the faces of the attendees when the video came on and Ross said with humor, "Welcome to my funeral. Sorry I couldn't be here in person." I could hear the chuckling gasps of surprise, as if hands went over their mouths to catch themselves. A couple of brave souls laughed out loud. One yelled out, "Go Ross!" Even my children now laughed. We had had eight months to prepare for this somber day and we had used our time wisely. All that needed to be said had been said.

The grieving process began long ago, and while it was far from over, the funeral truly was a celebration of life. At the seventh hole of the golf course, the one Ross triple-bogeyed most often, we watched as he sat on the green, legs stretched out, smoking a cigar in a enormous leather easy chair. The club was at first hesitant to allow this until Ross told them he was dying, then matter-of-factly reminded them of the tens of thousands of dollars he contributed to the club over the past thirty years.

The moving van had plopped the chair on the green at six A.M., while it was still dark, and left for one hour while Ross talked to the camera. When they came back, they hauled the chair back to the van, video still rolling, with Ross still in it!, saying, "I really don't want to leave yet!" Ironically the moving van was called Cloud '9.'

With video recorder in my hand, Ross had talked to me about his nemesis, that hole. "I worried about this hole too damned much, so much that I bogeyed it more because of anxiety than lack of talent. Hey, golf buddies of mine, I buried one of my golf balls right here by the green. Birdie for me, okay? Excuse me, will someone bring me a mint julep?" after which I handed him one. The audience roared with laughter. I smirked as I remembered shoveling dirt and a slab of grass over that golf ball, perfectly hidden so as never to be discovered by the groundskeepers. We had felt like teenagers doing some mischievous stunt, giggling, looking around so as not to get caught. I would later tell Jeff and Frank exactly where we buried the ball, and they ritualistically spoke to it every time they passed by. In fact, on Ross's birthday, they brought mint juleps to the hole.

In another scene, Ross sat in a lounge chair by the Delaware River bank, looking particularly ragged after losing his hair to another round of chemotherapy. "You might think that I have had better days. Trust me, I have. Cancer is a drag and if you are over fifty and haven't had a colonoscopy, do it now. Also, go hug your kids. And, if you are a workaholic, stop. You can't take it with you. Don't sell your soul to the company."

Ross never lost his sense of humor as the videotaping progressed along with his cancer. The last segment was taped in the living room beside a blazing fire, even as the warm air of spring came through the open windows. I was not present for this taping, where he talked lovingly about the kids…and me. "As Bob Hope used to say, 'Thanks for the memories.' I am going to miss you all. Come see me sometime, but don't be in a hurry. Bye now." The tape immediately went dark and a slide show of his life, put together by the kids, played to the Beatles songs, "A Little Help from My Friends" and "All You Need is Love."

After the slide show, people burst into applause before becoming silent. Then each of the children-- Rossy, Peter, and Kate—spoke; then Jeff (Frank just couldn't), and finally me. When I stood up at the funeral home's podium, I saw the large crowd for the first time, some with heads bowed, others, as if trying to prevent dams from bursting, were too emotional to make eye contact, while still others were smiling at me through their tears. In the back, Scott and Edith sat together, my friends from a different life. A new life.

Like all of the eulogies before mine, I was more uplifting than grim. I talked about the laughter we had together in making the video, how we had healed our differences, regressed to silliness on a golf course, and rekindled our loving friendship and mutual respect. I had to stop twice to take deep breaths and compose myself---my final act as a wife.

We had a reception back at the house, complete with a catered dinner. Frank and Jeff stayed well into the night. When they finally left, I gave each of our kids a personal letter that Ross had written to them along with a wrapped package that I knew contained a personal brass framed photo of each of them with their dad. "Dad asked that you read these letters from him when you are alone. Look, there is also one for me, which he did not tell me about."

"Are you surprised Mom?" asked Rossy.

I said no but later, as I sat with my letter and a black and white restored photo of Ross and me coming into the station after a roller coaster ride, I surprised myself with the depth of my love. It was a photo I had always wanted to frame but had never gotten around to, a photo I hadn't thought about in years. My head was back, his arms still up, and we were open-mouthed laughing from the thrill. I was glad I had shared a significant portion of my life with this dear man.

26

After dressing for work one sunny spring morning, I went out onto my balcony to determine if I needed a coat. The meadow was in full bloom with spring flowers including abundant, scattered daffodils, once a part of an original estate gardens, somehow spared uprooting by bulldozers of progress. I touched the soft almost fully sprouted leaves on the oak tree adjacent to my balcony. All bundled up in the early chill, Edith was sitting by the swimming pool with its winter cover still in place.

"I just love the morning sun on my face," she called out as I approached.

I was struck by her beauty as the early light shone upon her. Her lips quirked up slightly as she faced the sky, eyes closed. Her hair blew lightly over her forehead in the soothing breeze. Her wrinkles were kind, gentle, wise, the traces of a life well-lived. The vessels on her hands were like vines as her arms draped comfortably over the wrought iron furniture.

"A bathing suit might never again grace this well-aged body," she continued with eyes still closed. "You know, once I had a really nice figure, although we never wore bikinis in those days. We had to cover it all up…keep'em guessing."

"I bet you did."

"I always did love the sun on my face," she said again, her voice cracking.

"What's wrong Edith?"

"Oh, Don had to go back to the hospital and is not doing well. Trouble with living so long is that you outlive all of your friends. Thankfully Claire, you are younger and are one friend I will not outlive."

"Hopefully true, but, please, neither of us for a while yet."

"I don't know. The attrition rate of my friends is speeding-up. I'm an involuntary member of the funeral-of-the-week club. Shit…sure is tough to be old. I feel I am in a perpetual state of mourning, bereavement overload. I barely get over the last death when someone else dies. I hate to look in the newspaper anymore for fear I will know another name in the obituaries. You know the death of someone like Don, or any elder, is like the burning of a library. So, this morning is a time I choose to feel sorry for myself."

"Where is Don?"

"In the coronary care unit at the hospital. His youngest daughter called me. Really nice woman, not the one like Barbara. She didn't freak out when she found out her father was dating someone."

"Need a ride?"

"Family only. Plus I want to remember him as only half sick, not extremely ill with IV's and monitors and a 'Do Not Resuscitate' order. We had a great time for a few weeks, a few laughs. We shared our life stories…it was a fulfilling friendship, nice."

"Maybe Barbara is right," she continued.

"About what?"

"I am not really prepared for an acute event like another fall or heart attack or stroke. God, I hope I don't get a stroke. I prefer heart attack, even cancer is better than a stroke. And what if I get a stroke and have to live with Barbara? Now, that would be Hell on Earth!"

"So what are you thinking?"

"Claire, this is what I love about you. You are not gushing with, 'Oh Edith, don't talk like that...you-are-going-to-live-forever garbage.' I'm almost eighty-two. Maybe I will live another few years, hopefully healthy. Right now, I have choices. If I get sick, I won't have choices. I will be at the mercy of others, including one very controlling daughter."

"There is a multifaceted senior complex about an hour from here," she continued, "which, besides apartments, has an assisted living section and a nursing home. I can transfer to sections most suited for me at any given time. First I get an apartment, then, as I need more help, I move to assisted living. Hopefully, I die or commit suicide before I need to move to the nursing home."

"Suicide?"

"Oh, Claire, who wants to go out wearing diapers and drooling? We treat our animals better. We'll see if it has to come to that."

"Do you, er, have a plan? How long have you been thinking about this?"

"The sun feels so great on my face."

"Okay, if you are not going to answer my question, can I drive you to see this place?"

"No, you have too much on your plate. Actually I have an old acquaintance now living there who I haven't seen in years. I've already talked to her by phone. She has invited me for a personal tour then lunch with some of her friends there. I want to get a sense of the place before I officially involve Barbara, who will want me to move in the next day."

I nodded, then hastily added, "Hey Edith, I would love to take a road trip with you. It would give us a chance to visit. I finished the semester yesterday when I handed in my term paper to Marilyn. Besides, I haven't really seen you much since Ross's funeral."

"How are you and the kids doing, my dear friend?"

"It's bumpy. Each of the kids is grieving differently but they are resilient and have a good support system. Rossy is now pouring into his work, but Jennifer is keeping him grounded. Peter goes to the cemetery regularly, dealing I suspect with abandonment issues. He is attending a bereavement support group at hospice. And Kate, well, she seems to be looking to the future with Sam. Since she is in Boston, I can't really witness her coping skills first hand."

"I thought Ross wanted his ashes spread?"

"Most of them will be, but Peter wanted a place he could take daughter Kim. Ross consented, "No more than half!" he had demanded. Edith and I both smiled.

"And how about you?"

"Every day is different. Yesterday, I was browsing in a store that Ross and I had been in many times. All of a sudden, like a surge, I was overcome. I mean, Edith, the emotions came out of nowhere. One second I am fine, the next I am sobbing and had to run out of the store to compose myself."

"I had those after Rudy died. Still do sometimes.

Used to scare me, but not anymore. They are cleansing, if you know what I mean."

"I agree."

"How's Scott?"

"The Rock of Gibraltar in my life. Patient, kind, thoughtful, an empathetic listener, shall I continue?"

"Do you see a goal?"

"Like marriage?"

"Or living together?"

"Right now, I am enjoying the process, my in-the-moment existence. I am finally enjoying the freedom I gave up so many years ago. Scott and I are each defining how we want to live out the rest of our lives. We are having wonderful discussions. I don't want to live with him or marry for the wrong reasons."

"Like…?"

"Loneliness. Needing a man to cling to. Been there, done that."

"Lonely ain't easy. Take it from an old lady who knows lonely firsthand. Be careful you don't cut off your nose to spite your face."

"Think I should marry him?"

"Not for just a warm body next to you at night. Lonely is actually better than a compromise." She paused for a moment, finally opening her eyes to look at me, "Now, just listen to me with all my advice. Nothing worse than a know-it-all, especially an old one! Besides, as I said, I am feeling sorry for myself right now. Not wanting Don to die. Not wanting to die myself. Wanting to die peacefully. Not wanting to move, but being realistic. Scared to make new friends, then lose them too. That's why the sun is the only thing that feels right, for now."

"So we will see this new place together?" I said.

She grabbed my hand, "Sounds like a plan."

We sat silently for many minutes still holding hands, both turned towards the sun, before I had to leave for work.

"Oh…, Claire?" she called as I walked away. "I am not suicidal…..just keeping my options open."

"I know."

***

Shirley and I had extended our sessions to get me through the end of Ross's life, although I was not seeing her regularly anymore. Now both of us knew the time had come to part, but still, it was hard to cut the cord. She had literally been my lifeline to mental health. I came to look forward to our talks, even those about daunting issues.

With each bit of painful self-discovery, came relief. Sure some things remained sad, hard to digest, but I also felt unburdened. Somewhere along the way I stopped the self-pity and anger, and began to realize my strengths. I stopped feeling guilty about the time I had wasted and started feeling good about the time I had left. I also realized that my past was a part of who I was today, contributing to my present motivations and talents.

It was not "if" conflicts and stress would rear their ugly heads in my life, but "when." And I'd best be prepared to resolve them effectively, while working to curb conflicts when I could, a concept Shirley called 'preventative conflict.'

We spent many hours on forgiveness. Since I had a propensity for holding onto grudges, this was difficult. Foremost I had to forgive myself…for getting pregnant, quitting my education, and for building a decades-old rut for myself.

Shirley once told me mental health is subtractive rather than additive. It is what one stops doing that proves most beneficial to psyche stability. And stop I did....stopped berating myself, stopped the woe-is-me, stopped obsessing over Ross's affair, and stopped the I-am-worthless bullshit. Mental health is renewed empathy for our lives; a vitality...which is quite the opposite of depression. All easier said than done, but I worked hard. Once she kiddingly called me her "A" student. Actually I already knew it.

"You are more than ready to tackle this world all by yourself," she said with a smile.

"What if I screw up?"

"Pick yourself up, dust yourself off, and try again. Crises are not insurmountable. Mistakes can be corrected."

"I know, I know, failure is not trying, or as Ted Rosenthal said in *How Can I Not Be Among You?*, 'Life may be grim, but it is not necessarily serious.'"

"Claire, you are so animated, so alive. I am going to miss you! It has been my pleasure to work with you."

I flashed on when daughter Kate said I was more animated after the divorce. It was true.

"Can I call you if I really flounder?"

"Sure, but think about things first for a few days before you pick up the phone. I think you might be surprised at your own problem-solving abilities."

"I want to thank you for retrieving my lost confidence...actually, for discovering the confidence I didn't know I had."

"Remember, I did not give you your confidence. I was just a catalyst. You are the one who did the work, explored your mind, slayed your own dysfunction. You rose to the occasion and tackled your demons."

"You are so right. I feel, however, like I am regressing all over the place. I can't seem to pick myself up and get out of this room."

"Now you wouldn't want to be chained to your therapist, would you?" she said with a huge smile.

"You mean you won't be on-call for me?"

"Right now these sessions are actually holding you back. Go spread your wings. A year and a half is enough. Take your gold-mended life and get out of here."

We hugged goodbye and I mourned her loss in my life. She had been comforting, wise, trustworthy. No one else in my life knew more about me than she. Scott was learning, but our relationship was powerful in a very different way, rightfully so.

I felt strangely confident as I drove away from her office, my refuge, for the last time. At home I had journals full of writing, some passages scary descents into neurotic behaviors, rationalizations, and compensating mannerisms. They had explored the richness of introversion, discovering in myself what had previously been unacknowledged. Words had at long last formed a pattern and become my enlightenment. Finally, I had been intimate and vulnerable with my own innermost self so I could become better than my former self. This task, lifelong, would never be complete; no happily-ever-afters of the mind, just reprieves before the next storm and, thankfully, better mental equipment to weather it.

Shirley had gone from a gentle mothering attitude while I was in crisis, and progressed to a very ungentle push toward wellness. She never rescued me, but did hold me under her wing, or so I thought. Actually she knew I needed time to grieve the loss of my marriage, Ross's death, and my insecurity. Once I could stand, she forced me to fledge and spread my wings. It didn't matter that I was already an old bird.

Not until I acknowledged my limitations could I eliminate them and regain vitality and vigor. "You can go over, under, or around your mental deficiencies," said Shirley, "but, only in going through them can you release their grip on you." She had said something similar about grief after Ross's death, "Ignore your grief and pain and it swallows you alive. Learn to be your own best grief counselor. Find the gifts in his death. A death not learned from is a wasted death."

I remembered another thing she said, "You will never 'get-over' Ross's death. You will move on and love him differently, in separation. We live in a get-over-it culture. Well, you get over the flu, not someone's death."

In the end, Ross had given me many gifts, not the least of which was financial freedom. But only his dying allowed 'us' to heal. We both knew that; a cruel reality. His courage rekindled my love for him, and brought me to forgiveness. It was a rare opportunity. He pushed me, unknowingly, towards self-actualization. Finally grateful, I would not allow his death to be in vain. As I drove home I thought about his final letter to me:

Dear Claire, I love you. I am grateful for all our years together, and most especially these last few months. Thanks for forgiving me. May you live to a ripe old age. Enjoy our beautiful children as well as present and future grandchildren.

Life really is short. Create fond and meaningful memories and be at peace, Ross

    PS And, for God's sake, don't forget to change the oil and rotate your tires!

27

A few weeks after Don's funeral, which Edith did not attend, she began packing for her move to a cozy garden apartment in the senior living complex. Although she had already eliminated much furniture in her prior move from the large family homestead, Charlotte and Barbara were there to help divvy up heirlooms, as only the most sentimental or essential things would go with Edith this time--her bedroom furniture, favorite chair and lamp, a small table for dining, her mother's oriental rug. Without moaning, she signed her car over to a grandson for a dollar.

Edith refused to be sullen. "This is the way it is, and I like the people where I am moving. It's a good option for me," she said. "I have no regrets. My life has been good. Claire, I cannot be your neighbor anymore, but I am less than an hour away. Please don't forget me."

"I promise I will never forget you. Remember we have an ongoing date—the second Saturday of each month for dinner."

"Once a month will have to do, I guess. Here, my friend, I knitted you an Afghan just like Cedric's only in different colors." I started to cry. "I love you Edith. I am so glad our paths crossed in life. But please don't tell me, like you told Cedric, to have a good life."

"Oh, honey, I won't, because this is not goodbye, not yet. I love you, too, Claire. You occupy a very special place in my heart. I wouldn't have gotten through these last months without you."

***

The next day at work, I found out that Mr. Behnke had died. The farm sale had been finalized and Earl Jr. had become a rich man by his standards. He had quietly left town, returning briefly for the funeral. With a new lease on life, Mrs. Behnke had negotiated her husband's burial next to his first wife in the family plot on the farm, now surrounded by a white picket fence, to be tended for perpetuity along with the common grounds of thirty soon-to-be-built houses. The house and barns had already been leveled.

***

During the first part of the summer I worked full time at the agency while Marion visited family in another state. Eventually Imogene asked me to work full time, anticipating Marion's retirement, but I turned her down. I wanted to finish school (still at least a year away) and have time for Scott and my kids, and, most importantly, myself.

Peter enjoyed living at his childhood home, but unable to afford the estate's estimated purchase price, would move perhaps in the next year when the will had to be settled and the home sold. For now, so close to Linda's parents, it was perfect for him even though they rejected moving into the master bedroom. I babysat for Kim about once a week. Jennifer became pregnant. Kate, also pregnant,

314

married Sam in a small wedding at the house, her two brothers 'giving her away.'

One early summer morning while the town slept, the children, Frank and Jeff, and myself piled into Frank's pontoon boat and moseyed up the Delaware River. As the sun came up we spread the rest of Ross's ashes, as per his wishes, near the banks of his childhood swimming place, where from a tree's rope he had swung thousands of times into the water.

***

Scott and I spent the first week of a two week vacation trekking around Nova Scotia. The cooler weather was a welcomed respite from the summer dog days of New Jersey. One day we found a very isolated camp ground at the end of an eight mile dirt road. The cliffs close to our tent dove straight 1000 feet to the bay, which was filled with feeding pilot whales, serenading us with expulsions of air and water from the spouts.

No fence separated us from a fall to the water, making it nerve wracking to approach the edge. That night from the safety of our campsite, we sipped coffee and gazed at a million stars.

"I love you, Claire," he said.

"Thanks Scott. I have finally met the love of my life, and you're it."

We had decided not to live together just yet. I wanted to have more time on my own in my own place. And we would not marry due to complications of wills, insurance policies, and my pensions from Ross. While we spent most of our time together, I still had a couple of nights alone to read, write, and reflect. Some Saturdays I picked up Edith for an overnight at my place, complete with a movie, some popcorn and a phone call to Cedric. We'd ride, top down, in my new, used convertible. We loved it!

Scott and I delight in each other's presence, existence, bodies, successes, causes, welfare, loyalty, and trust. We are weaving our lives together, incorporating the other, rejoicing in each other, merging our realities, concerns, and cares, *but not* merging our identities. I have reached out for new relationships and raised the old ones to new levels. Since I turned sixty-two, my life has become inordinately better. Instead of living my dreams, I am living my life. I am the most fulfilled I have ever been. I have no desire to be younger. I feel wise(r), a work still in progress, with a lot of productive living yet to do for whatever time I have left. I'm a baby boomer, senior bloomer—mended with gold.

Suggested Discussion Questions

1. Early in the book, Edith makes the statement, "Death does not get easier with practice," in essence meaning that the last person we buried in our life is equally as difficult, if not more difficult, than the first person we buried. Do you agree or disagree with her statement and why?
2. How do you feel about the mending of broken objects with gold, making them stronger and more beautiful than before they were broken, as a metaphor for life?
3. How did Cedric stimulate change in both Edith and Claire?
4. Many in our society have had difficulty envisioning older adults making passionate love. How do you see that changing?
5. How do you see Claire as an example of older adults finding new life, personally and professionally?
6. Claire struggled with forgiving Ross and even herself for a mediocre marriage. How do you feel about how they finally healed their relationship?
7. What are your thoughts about how Claire and Scott resolved the conflicts regarding their different stages in life and Claire's relationship with Ross?
8. What did you think of Ross's unique video and giving his own eulogy at his funeral?
9. In therapy, Shirley and Clair discuss the following concept: "the more you give, the more you get, but the more it hurts when it is over. If you don't want to grieve, then don't love." What did you think about this conversation?
10. How do you see love and also friendship as work?

Suggested Readings

Albom, Mitch, *Tuesdays with Morrie*

Attig, Thomas, *The Heart of Grief*

Castleman, Michael, *Great Sex: A Man's Guide to the Secret Principles of Total Body Sex*

Colgrove, Melba, Harold Bloomfield and Peter McWilliams, *How to Survive the Loss of a Love*

Comfort, Alex, *The Joy of Sex*

DeSpelder, Lynne Ann and Albert Lee Strickland, *The Last Dance: Encountering Death and Dying*

Didion, Joan, *The Year of Magical Thinking*

Fine, Carla, *No Time to Say Goodbye: Surviving the Suicide of a Loved One*

Fromm, Erich, *To Have or To Be* and *The Art of Loving*

Horney, Karen, *The Neurotic Personality of Our Time*

Jacobs, Barry, *The Emotional Survival Guide for Caregivers—Looking After Yourself and Your Family While Helping an Aging Parent*

Klein, Marty, *Beyond Orgasm: Dare To Be Honest About the Sex You Really Want*

Lerner, Harriet, *The Dance of Anger*

Martz, Sandra (editor), *When I am an Old Woman I Shall Wear Purple*

May, Rollo, *Love and Will*

Miller, Alice, *The Drama of the Gifted Child*

Miller, William, *When Going to Pieces Holds You Together*

Peck, M. Scott, *The Road Less Traveled*

Pipher, Mary, *Another Country: Navigating the Emotional Terrain of our Elders*

Rambo, Therese, *Treatment of Complicated Mourning*

Rich, Adrienne, *Of Woman Born: Motherhood as Experience and Institution*

Rosenthal, Ted, *How Could I Not Be Among You?*

Rubin, Lillian, *Intimate Strangers*

Sexual Information and Education Counsel of the United States (SIECUS)

Sinclair Institute—Films on Human Sexuality

Solomon, Andrew, *The Noonday Demon: An Atlas of Depression*

Spring, Janis, *How Can I Forgive You?*

Yalom, Irving, *Staring at the Sun: Overcoming the Terror of Death*

For four decades, Dr. Carolyn Stegman taught psychology courses at the university level in aging, death and dying, women, and human sexuality. In her encore career, she is dedicated to serving older adults. Born in 1946, she is proud to be among the earliest of the baby boomers. She lives in Maryland with her husband. She is the author of *Women of Achievement in Maryland History*. This is her first novel.

Made in the USA
Charleston, SC
12 September 2013